T0007445

ANDREA
HOFFMAN
GOES ALL IN

ANDREA HOFFMAN GOES ALL IN

A Novel

Diane Cohen Schneider

SHE WRITES PRESS

Copyright © 2022, Diane Cohen Schneider

All rights reserved. No part of this publication may be reproduced,
distributed, or transmitted in any form or by any means, including
photocopying, recording, digital scanning, or other electronic or
mechanical methods, without the prior written permission of the publisher,
except in the case of brief quotations embodied in critical reviews and
certain other noncommercial uses permitted by copyright law. For
permission requests, please address She Writes Press.

Published 2022
Printed in the United States of America
Print ISBN: 978-1-64742-099-4
E-ISBN: 978-1-64742-222-6
Library of Congress Control Number: 2022907552

For information, address:
She Writes Press
1569 Solano Ave #546
Berkeley, CA 94707

Interior design by Tabitha Lahr

She Writes Press is a division of SparkPoint Studio, LLC.

All company and/or product names may be trade names, logos, trademarks,
and/or registered trademarks and are the property of their respective
owners.

Names and identifying characteristics have been changed to protect the
privacy of certain individuals.

For my parents
Donald and Helen Cohen

PART ONE

Chapter 1

MARCH 1, 1982

I thought I'd enjoy a mindless job after four intense years at college. I was wrong. I'm stupefied by the sameness of every day: open the store, dust the cases, check in a new shipment, hang up clothes, straighten the racks. And the customers, wealthy women who can afford this expensive boutique, are so disappointing. They leave wrinkled, makeup stained clothes on the floor of the dressing room. They shoplift. They buy things, wear them, and then try to return them. Even the ladies who look like they've stepped off the pages of *Town and Country* act like your average suburban fourteen-year-old girl. I know. I was one.

The small brass bell on the door rings and a blast of unusually frigid March air blows in a silver haired North Shore matron in a camel coat, well-tailored grey suit and expensive low-heeled boots. She loosens her cashmere scarf and strides straight for the rack of jewel colored satin blouses without a glance in my direction.

"May I help you?"

This Duchess of Lake Forest drops the ruby colored sleeve she's fingering, tilts her head, and trains her icy blue eyes on my way overdue for a cut hair, the careless dash of mascara, my high school-era rayon sweater and pleated plaid skirt. She checks out my scuffed loafers, her nose wrinkling with the little sniff I've come to expect. Her opinion of the twenty-four year old with a bachelor of arts selling overpriced women's designer clothing at Mariana's Select for two years, nine months, three weeks and a day? *Not one of us.* "I'll let you know, dear," she says.

I turn away from her as the bell rings again and a tall, striking woman in a blond mink jacket enters the store laughing. A studly dude follows, holding her bags, fawning. He's young enough to be her son, but I have three brothers and I know for certain they have never looked at Mom like that. Her huge diamond ring blinds me, but I still notice that her face is quite a bit older than her leather pants might lead you to believe.

"Mrs. Robinson" quickly rifles through the racks and then heads into the dressing room with an armful of cocktail dresses. Junior takes the opportunity to put down her packages, open his bomber jacket, and admire himself in the three-way mirror. Clearly, he spends a lot of productive time at the gym. He glances at his watch, the dressing room door, then back at his watch. He looks at the nearby racks and then spots me standing by the register.

"Got any guy stuff in here?" he says.

Before I can answer, Ms. Mink has opened her door a crack. "We'll shop for you next, sweetie. If you're bored, you can come in here and help me with this zipper."

"Sweetie" dives into the dressing room like Superman into a phone booth. They immediately start to giggle and coo. Do they think the flimsy dressing rooms are soundproof? I keep telling Mariana that we need to cut a couple inches off the tops and bottoms of the doors so I can see what's going on in there. Taking out the comfortable little settee would also be an excellent idea. Mariana disagrees with me: "We're going for a certain shopping *experience* here, Andrea. This isn't JCPenney."

Yes. A shopping experience. That explains the Muzak as well. I like totally hate the Muzak. And the tissue paper. Mariana insists we wrap all purchases in tissue paper before we bag them like they're a gift we're giving to our customers. I wait a minute and then walk to the back of the store and knock on the dressing room door.

"Can I get you anything?" I ask. I hear more giggling, and then the woman, a breathy "We're fine."

Back in the front of the store, I turn the radio up louder in case they start making inappropriate noises.

The bell over the door jingles again and I turn. Busy morning.

It's all but automatic. "May I help you?"

Surprise, it's a man. A young man shivering in jeans, a navy-blue sweatshirt under a jean jacket, and red and white Adidas is frozen in the doorway. He stares at me for a second or two and then surveys the rest of the store. Clearly, he's lost. But then he yanks his hand out of his pocket, comes up with a big shiny handgun.

"On the floor. All of you." The words tumble out. Just the trace of an accent. He points toward the floor, jabbing with the barrel of the gun. My eyes flick from the gun to the brightly inked parrot tattoo on his hand and back to the gun. I drop and stretch out face down on the polished cherry floor next to the Duchess still clutching the shiny blouse she's been considering. I hear the door lock clunk. Footsteps into the store.

I flash on my couple in the dressing room. Did they even hear the guy with the gun? Are they grinding in there, oblivious? My heart's pounding and my stomach's churning but the cool floor feels good on my flushed face.

A small ding alerts me that he's managed to get the register open. Out of the corner of my eye, I can see him taking bills out of the drawer. Putting them in his back pocket. Looking under the tray. Pulling out the checks and letting them drop to the floor. I think about how close he is to my purse in the bottom drawer under the register. There's twenty-four dollars in my wallet. Twenty-four dollars I need to hold on to. All the money I have until my next paycheck. The guy with the gun looks belligerent and plenty mean but his eyes are focused. He's not drunk or drugged or insane, so good.

He marches over, squats down, puts the gun on my neck. The metal's warm but I shiver as if it's ice cold.

"Where's the rest of it?" His lips are close to my ear. "Where's all the goddamn money? Is there a safe? Talk to me, Chica."

I'm weirdly calm. "No, there's no safe or anything. Most people use credit cards. But there's jewelry," I say. "Fourteen-karat gold. In the glass display case."

He pulls the gun off my neck, stands up and stomps over to have a look, raises his gun, the parrot flying, and smashes the butt on the top of the case, sending glass everywhere.

The Duchess whimpers. I cock my head toward the dressing room. Silence. I should have told Gun Guy that I always leave the key in the lock. It's mostly fourteen-karat *plated* stuff but it's too late to save that case now. He sticks the gun in his pants and scoops up a handful of necklaces, bracelets, and earrings. His eyes dart around.

"There's a bag under the counter and to your right," I say, consummate saleslady. Screw the tissue paper. He grabs one of the glossy shopping bags, jams the jewelry into it. I imagine the horror of untangling the chains. Walks over to the sweaters and shoves three fur trim cardigans into the bag. He pulls the gun out of his waistband and is already turning to leave when the dressing room door opens. Lover boy steps out oblivious. Gun Guy raises his weapon. I yell "No!" and suddenly I'm on my feet. The gun, huge and heavy, shakes in his hand. He looks pissed. He mutters "shit" just before the gun fires. BOOM! It's the loudest noise I've ever heard. The blast blows all thought from my brain. I dive back down to the floor. I'm frozen inside a white, silent fog.

My senses come back one at a time. An acrid smell. The sound of a splintering crash. I turn, see the broken mirror, shards of glass covering the floor. Seven years bad luck. For him maybe. Good luck for us. No humans hit.

Duchess still clutching the ruby cashmere blouse starts to cry. "Help me," she whispers.

Now she thinks I could help her. I put my finger to my lips and shake my head. She needs to stay quiet.

Lover boy is frozen with his hands up but Mrs. Robinson has not emerged from the dressing room. Gun Guy is at the door, thank god. He's holding the Mariana's Select Pepto pink shopping bag stuffed with jewelry and cashmere in one hand. The damn gun is in the hand with the bird tattoo. He hesitates. "Just go!" I squeak at him "You got enough. Please go." He's looking right at me. I don't look away. Can't look away.

"Don't move, Chica. Don't nobody fucking move."

The next sounds I hear are the click of the lock and the jangle of the bell as he spins out the door and takes off running. Two steps behind him, Lover boy pulls open the heavy door and follows. A hero! But no, he's not in pursuit of the bad guy. He's headed down Oak Street in the opposite direction.

Mrs. Robinson cracks open the dressing room door.

"He's gone. It's safe. You can come out now," I say.

She steps out. Without the fur coat she looks smaller and scanning the room, she looks confused "Tony?"

I cock my head toward the door. "He left."

She looks out at the empty sidewalk just for a moment. "Yes, well," she says with a wry smile and sad eyes, "He had to get back to work."

I nod.

The store seems quiet now even though Duchess is still sobbing and the Muzak version of Billy Joel's "Don't Go Changing" is blasting. I survey the mess: the open register, the smashed jewelry case, the shattered mirrors, my traumatized soon-to-be ex-customers. I help the Duchess to her feet. Gently take the crumpled blouse from her hand.

"Everything's going to be okay now," I say. My voice shakes but I'm not crying. Instead, I'm elated. I'm so high I feel like running down the street myself. But I don't move. I stand still and feel my heart beating wildly. Holy shit. I reach for the phone and dial 9-1-1.

———

After the stern white cop and his younger Black partner leave, I flip the sign on the front door to "Closed. Come Again" and shut off the lights. I call Mariana.

Her Guatemalan housekeeper answers the phone. "Sorry Miss Andrea. Miss Mariana, she is at a luncheon for the dogs."

Another charity fundraiser. I don't want to be cynical, but. "Just tell her she needs to come down to the store as soon as she can. It's an emergency."

I change the radio station to WXRT and am instantly rewarded with the comforting rasp of Warren Zevon singing *Looking for the next best thing*. The police have told me not to clean up until the insurance guy comes and takes pictures, but I can't sit still, so I start sizing the clothes racks in the front of the store where the light comes in through the plate glass windows. A loud rapping on the door makes me jump.

A stocky uniformed policeman, not one of the ones who was here before, is peering in through the glass. The name on the badge is O'Malley. I unlock the door and he says, "I have a man in the back of my patrol vehicle I'd like you to identify."

I pull on my coat and follow Officer O'Malley outside and right there at the curb is the cruiser, no lights flashing. I peer into the back seat of the car, keeping my distance. It's him all right. Guy with the gun. He appears a lot younger, smaller, and less threatening than when he was in the store, but his hands are cuffed in front and I see the tattoo. And he looks up and sees me, too. His eyes darken. I step back and turn my back to the car.

"He's the one," I say softly.

"Sure? Take your time. I'm not pressuring you."

Louder and more confidently I say, "It's him. No doubt about it. How did you know?"

"It's my experience that a young man running full speed down North Michigan Avenue wearing a hood pulled tight and carrying a bright pink bag from a lady's boutique that I myself, a well-paid police office, cannot afford to patronize, well that individual might just be a good candidate for a clotheslining. So, I . . . uh . . . halted his progress and detained him for questioning."

His partner, still behind the wheel, lets out a snort. "Knocked the loot right out of the bag."

Officer O'Malley smiles modestly.

"Do I have to come down to the station and do a lineup identification?" I ask.

O'Malley laughs. "Those damn cop shows. Civilians think they know everything 'cause they watch *Hill Street Blues*. This guy's going to jail. You don't have to see him ever again." He stomps his feet and blows on his hands. "We're escorting him to the station now. I'll have to take his haul as evidence, but you can tell your boss to come down to the 18th District Station on North Larrabee and they'll arrange for him to get his stuff back." He hands me his card.

It's her. My boss is a her but I don't bother.

As they pull away, I picture spending the next few days sitting behind the counter untangling those chains with Olivia Newton John singing in the background. Back inside the store, without taking off my coat, I write a note.

We were robbed this morning. Nobody was hurt. The police caught the guy and recovered all the merchandise. It's in their report. Sorry about the mess. The police said not to touch anything until the insurance adjusters come. You need to call both the police and the insurance company.

I read the note a few times, leave it on top of the still-open register along with Officer Munoz's card. And then I grab my purse (my twenty-four dollars still safe inside), stick my copy of today's *Tribune* under my arm, and leave. I lock the door behind me and drop the keys in my purse but as soon as I turn away, I stop, retrieve the keys, and slip them through the mail slot. Making it clear what I didn't say in the note. No more Muzak. No more rich bitch customers. I'm done.

Chapter 2

My apartment building, only a few short blocks from the Water Tower on Michigan Avenue, has no doorman but it has a bar, Streeter's, basement level. I hang on to the stair railing to avoid slipping on the steep concrete steps as I descend out of the cold sunlight and into the gloom. It takes a second for my eyes to adjust to the dim light, but I see the place is deserted except for Sam, my favorite bartender. He's cute but he isn't so cute that he thinks he's doing you a favor by pouring you a drink. He looks happy to have a customer.

"Hey, beautiful, what the fuck?" Checks his watch with a shocked look.

"I'm starving." I hold up the white bag I picked up around the corner. "Plus," I take a shaky breath. "I was robbed and shot at. So, I locked up and walked out. I think I quit, too." My eyes fill with tears.

"No way," Sam says, and he comes out from behind the bar, takes a long look, and apparently satisfied I'm in one piece, leads me gently to a stool and drops down next to me. "That totally blows."

"I'm okay," I say, spreading the contents of my lunch on the polished walnut bar to avoid his eyes. I like Sam. In fact, we tried a physical thing a couple of times a few years back. I was new in the city. Drinking until last call. His brown eyes inviting. My bed a quick three flights away. But the relationship didn't go anywhere beyond the sex and we're platonic pals now.

He says nothing. Which I appreciate. I take a bite of my hot dog. He reaches over and helps himself to one of my onion rings. Then another. Out of the corner of my eye, I watch him lick salt off his fingers. We eat together in silence. When I've finished my hot dog and the onion rings are gone, I sigh and finally turn and look at him. "Some shitty day."

Sam nods his head. "You need a drink. On me," he says and stands up and walks back behind the bar. "I shoulda already offered. Sorry. Beer?"

I wrinkle my nose. "You know I don't drink beer."

He pours a glass of the house white wine. Sets it on a napkin in front of me. "I know you went to college in Boston but you're home now and Chicago girls drink beer, Andrea. And root for the Cubs. You should."

"I'm not a big sports fan, Sam." I'm relieved to talk about something neutral. "I like movies about sports though. *Rocky. North Dallas Forty. The Brian Piccolo Story* . . . " I drop my voice as low as I can. "I *loved* Brian Piccolo."

"Stop. You'll make me cry. But it doesn't count . . . liking sports movies. It's an imperfect substitute for being a fan. A movie is a one-night stand." He pauses a second and a grin flits across his face. "Not that there's anything wrong with one-night stands. But, a true sports fan is in a committed relationship that lasts over great seasons and bad. When players come and go. Heartbreak and triumph. A true sports fan is part of something bigger than themselves—a tribe united in the search for perfection and beauty."

Sam's a good guy. Plus, he's just given me a free drink. I wait a full ten seconds before I say, "You're so full of shit.

I've been in the bleachers at Wrigley. It's all about the *beer*. Nobody there would recognize perfection and beauty if it came in a box of Cracker Jacks."

"You are sadly misguided, my child, and I can only pray for your atheist soul."

My eyes are drawn to the two-inch gold cross that hangs just below the neck of his tight black tee shirt. "You do that, Sam."

Sam tops off my glass of wine. "Seriously." He leans over the bar to peer into my face. "You okay? An armed robbery is no freakin' joke."

"I'm okay." I blink hard and gulp a large swig of wine and then manage to give him a shrug and a smile.

"So did you quit or not?"

"I left my keys."

"Shit, Mariana will take you back. Besides the getting robbed part, you seemed happy there. What's the chance you get robbed again?"

"You know what's funny? If I thought I'd get robbed every day maybe I would go back. It was the most exciting thing that's happened to me in three years."

Sam nods his head. "I get you. You're craving a little danger. You know we get a decent bar fight in here almost every night. You could waitress a few times a week. If you wore the right outfit, you'd make good money."

"Thanks but no. I don't want a dangerous job. I want one that *challenges* me."

"I'm hurt."

"I'm sorry."

We're kidding. Sam's happy to be a lifer. He gets back to work—happy hour is staring him in the face.

I pull out the *Chicago Tribune*. I've read most of it during the slow morning hours at Mariana's. That seemed like a month ago. Britain is slashing crude oil prices. Russia is

"shocked" that the US thinks they're helping to arm Nica-
ragua. Reagan is upset at something that is going on in El
Salvador that I suppose I should be paying more attention
to. The business section has a long article about interest
rates. Apparently the prime rate has hit sixteen percent and
is killing off the housing market. The Bulls beat the Bucks.
I find the relevant section and fold the paper so I can read
the want ads.

Sam flips me a pencil, then gets serious about setting up.

Tons of listing. I start with the Z's, work backward. No,
no, no, no, and more no.

And then.

Chapter 3

I get off the #36 bus, walk a block south, and spin through the enormous revolving door of a contemporary glass and steel office building. Looking good. Feeling confident. Dressed in a calf-length black skirt and beige turtleneck sweater, I smile at my reflection in the polished chrome elevator doors as I wait for them to take me up to the seventeenth floor and Mosley Securities. A place where I can use my brains is what Sam said and kept saying, glass after glass of free wine.

The middle-aged receptionist is friendly, hands me an application and a pen and ushers me into a small conference room. After a long ten minutes, a tall man with thick white hair, a hawk nose, and standard issue WASP blue eyes strides in. He's dressed in a sharp dark blue suit and a conservative tie.

I jump up and shake his hand. I'm smiling. He's not. My throat tightens and I resist the urge to pull at the neck of my sweater. Suddenly I've lost my confidence that I'm in the right place.

"Harold Stackman. Sit, please." He scans my completed application, let's out a sigh, and mutters, "Is reading really a hobby?" He puts down the paper and looks directly at me. "Philosophy major. Impressive school, too. So, Andrea Hoffman, do you know anything about the economy?"

"I had a year of economics in college. My sophomore year. A semester of micro and a semester of macro."

"Why did a philosophy major take economics?"

"I studied . . . well . . . actually, I fell in love with Ralph Waldo Emerson freshman year. And Emerson said, 'Money is, in its effects and laws, as beautiful as roses.' I had always thought money was, you know, the root of all evil, so I took some economics classes to help me understand what he meant."

"The correct quote is, 'The *love* of money is the root of all evil.' Whether that happens to be accurate, we really don't have time to debate. Just tell me if you know anything about the US economy right now."

"It's no bed of roses," I say.

Mr. Stackman smiles faintly, puffs on his cigar.

I realize he's waiting for an answer. A small nervous laugh escapes, although I know this is serious stuff. People are really hurting. "Interest rates are high, inflation rates are high, and so is unemployment. High unemployment and high inflation at the same time is unusual. They call is stagflation and, well, it's bad."

"How do you know this?"

"I read the newspaper."

"Which paper?"

"*The Chicago Tribune*."

"The Trib's crap. Read *The Wall Street Journal* every day, and Sunday get *The New York Times*. Still, not a dreadful summary of the state of things for a philosophy major who's been working in a dress shop. Why were you working there? Did Emerson have anything to say about retail?"

"Emerson had his *Guide to Prosperity*. People think he was totally against materialism but he was interested in personal

economics, so retail isn't that much of a stretch." I can tell
from Mr. Stackman's face he didn't expect an answer that
involved more philosophy. I regroup. "But mostly I was
there because I knew the owner. I had sales experience and
I needed a job. I have student loans to pay back." I leave
out a few details, like that I didn't have any money to go to
graduate school and didn't know what I would have studied
there anyway, and that I was totally burned out by the last
semester of my senior year and seriously depressed that my
ex-boyfriend had a new girlfriend and obviously didn't want
me to stay in Boston.

Mr. Stackman is giving his cigar a good workout, but I
sense he's listening. "Are you good at it? Selling dresses?"

"I guess so."

He checks his watch. "You guess so."

D+ answer. I could have said I was the store's best salesperson, being that I was the only one besides Mariana who
worked there. I could have said I could sell crack to Jimmy
Carter. While I try to think of a cleverer answer to that last
question, he asks me another one. I haven't been listening.

"Got any theories?"

"Theories?"

"How do we fix the mess the economy is in now?"

So much for this job being perfect for me. Apparently,
I'm not smart enough for this. I hadn't realized a "sales assistant" would be responsible for economic policy decisions.

"The first year of economics only introduces problems. To
come up with some solutions, I'm pretty sure I would need at
least another year." I think Mr. Stackman nods just a little bit.

"Fair enough. What do you know about the stock market?"

It's time to close this sale. "It's taken a huge drop in the
last six months," I say, and try and look concerned. "Sorry."

"Don't be. We make money either way. Do you know
anything else?"

"Buy low/sell high?" I offer. That wisdom came from my Grandpa Sam who loved studying the stock market even though he didn't have any real money to invest in it. I try to stop my leg from shaking under the desk.

Mr. Stackman seems to be waiting and when I don't elaborate, he says, "Well, you don't know much, but at least what you know isn't wrong. What's the difference between a stock and a bond?"

"A bond is a debt and stock is ownership." Ha! Got one.

"What did they tell you this job pays?"

"Nothing."

"Well, it pays more than nothing." Mr. Stackman relights his cigar with a gold monogrammed lighter.

"No," I stammer. "They *told* me nothing. The salary wasn't listed in the ad. What does the job pay?"

"The job pays twenty-two grand a year." He watches me closely.

I try for my best poker face. At the store, I was making $14,500. Twenty-two thousand dollars is the kind of money adults make. I could stop buying Suave shampoo and the store brand mac and cheese. I could have choices. I feel a little dizzy, and not from all the cigar smoke, but one thing is clear: This job is about money. I need to care about money. "I was thinking more like twenty-eight."

Mr. Stackman opens his eyes wide in surprise. "Twenty-eight? What makes you think you're worth twenty-eight, or twenty-two for that matter?"

I consciously slow my breathing and search for magic words that will make this Harold Stackman choose me. "I learn fast and I work hard," I say.

"That's the least of what I expect from an employee. Why do you think personnel thought I could use you?"

I'm cornered but not giving up. My smile returns. "I'm resourceful."

To my amazement, he bursts out laughing. Did I say something so incredibly stupid?

"Really. I've been worried you might be one of those worthless bookworm types. Frankly Miss . . . Hoffman, I'm having some trouble understanding why you're here. Had you ever heard of Mosley Securities before?"

"You had the biggest ad in Wednesday's newspaper."

"The biggest ad. Why were you looking at the ads? You had a job."

"A guy came into the store and put a gun in my face. And I had an epiphany . . . a wake-up call of sorts."

"I know what an epiphany is, Miss Hoffman. I went to college too . . . What exactly *was* yours?"

"I needed a better job."

"There are other jobs out there. You could join the circus."

"Mr. Stackman, everyone in my family is a scientist. I'm the only one among my parents and siblings who doesn't have an MD or a PhD. To them, finance *is* joining the circus. I loved philosophy in school. Learning how to think. Tackling the big questions: Is there a god? Why is there evil? But I didn't know what I wanted to do after I graduated. I forgot to tackle that big question. I had previously worked retail so I went back to a store to buy some time. Now I'm ready, really ready, to do more. I wish I could tell you I've wanted to be a stockbroker ever since I swallowed my first penny, but the truth is, I was robbed at gunpoint and quit my job and then I saw your ad and for whatever reason, it grabbed me and here I am."

Mr. Stackman stands up. The interview is apparently over.

I need to say something. "When do you think you might decide about the position?"

"I've decided already. You got the job. How's twenty-five sound?"

I laugh, can't help it, manage to nod my acceptance.

And Mr. Stackman laughs, too. This time it's a friendly laugh. Small lines crinkle at his eyes. White teeth flash. The furrows on his forehead disappear. When I came into this room, I thought he was an old man, but now I can see that he's younger than I thought—maybe fifty, maybe not even. "You're not the only one in the room who makes quick decisions. As soon as I looked at your resume, I knew you had the brains for the job. I needed to see you had the balls. Are you sure you want this? It can get unreasonably crude around here. We're not the bunch of genteel North Shore ladies you're used to working with."

I pass on a comment about those "genteel" customers. He's probably married to one. Instead, I straighten my spine and say, "I stared down a robber. I've got three older brothers. No rude behavior will unnerve me."

"Good. I believe it. I'll tell personnel you'll be starting on Monday. Be here at seven a.m. Come right up to the eighteenth floor." He pulls a slim silver case from his breast pocket. It opens with a flick and he extracts his business card and hands it to me. *Harold Stackman, Senior Vice President, Institutional Equity Department*. "Got any questions?"

"I have one question."

"Now's the time to ask it."

"Okay. What exactly am I going to do?"

Mr. Stackman answers without hesitation. "You're going to help me make money."

Chapter 4

I sleep in Saturday since I don't have to haul my ass out of bed and open the store. Not today. Not ever again. But after a leisurely morning of coffee drinking and newspaper reading—my first *New York Times*—I walk over to Mariana's to say goodbye. The doorbell jingles and Mariana, absorbed with stocking a new jewelry case, starts to say "May I . . ." but stops when she looks up and sees it's me. No smile. No concern. No apology. "Change your mind? Your keys are in the register."

"No, afraid not. I start a new job Monday but thanks for everything. Can you mail me my last check?"

She nods. "Good luck, Andrea."

I see the eye roll but I just say, "You too" as I turn and leave.

Saturday night, during dinner with two high school girl-friends, I don't mention my new job. Nor do I stop in Streeter's on Sunday to see Sam. And at no time during the weekend do I call my parents. I don't want to answer any questions or explain my decision. Instead, I spend the weekend imagining my future in Mr. Stackman's elegant oak-paneled suite, parquet floors, oriental rugs, heavy drapes on the windows, well-tended plants enriching the oxygen, a polished coffee table with an elegant fan of the latest magazines.

But Monday morning, when I exit the elevator on the eighteenth floor and walk down the hall, I don't see any offices at all. Just large open rooms. I find Mr. Stackman in the second one I pass, reading the *Wall Street Journal* at a grey metal desk. Half a dozen other desks in the room are unoccupied. Along the walls are large filing cabinets and a machine the size of a stereo cabinet nosily printing on continually spooling paper. In contrast to this drab scene, naked floor-to-ceiling windows reveal a brilliant blue sky as the day breaks over the chilly Chicago skyline. The beige carpet muffles my footsteps, so I clear my throat to signal my arrival and Mr. Stackman looks up from his paper and says, "Good morning. Welcome to the exciting world of the stock market." He tilts his head toward the desk immediately to his left. "That one is yours." It's piled with papers. I pull the chair out. It's piled with papers as well. "Research," he says. He's looking at me, head cocked. "Something different," he says.

"I'm wearing my glasses. My contact lenses didn't cooperate this morning." I tried. Multiple times. Leaving my eyes red and irritated and robbing me of time I would have spent on my hair. I am not a morning person. The five thirty a.m. alarm was torture.

"Is it ok if I . . . ?" I pantomime moving the papers to the floor so I can sit down.

He nods again and pulls out a cigarette. "The research call is going to start in a few minutes. Just listen in. If phone line one or two rings, say 'Harold Stackman's office' and take a message. If any of the other lines ring, say 'Mosley Securities' and take a message." He tosses me a pink message pad which I fail to catch. I squat to retrieve it from the floor between our desks, regretting the straight knee-length skirt I chose for today. I try to sit gracefully and slide the desk drawer open and find a pen. I pull out a yellow legal pad and write down his instructions. The phone, with six plastic buttons labeled for each line, terrifies me.

"Is this someone's desk I am using?" I say.

"No, it's all yours now. It was the library before. Those reports, that's what we sell."

"I thought you sold stocks."

Mr. Stackman removes the gold rimmed reading glasses perched on his nose and gestures at me. "This department only deals with professional money managers like banks and insurance companies. That's why we're called the 'institutional' equity department. The brokers that deal with individual investors are called 'retail' brokers. We supply our clients with information about the stock market and individual stocks and offer up recommendations. That information is in these reports. Our accounts buy and sell stocks through us and pay us a commission."

"So, these reports . . . I should be reading them?"

Mr. Stackman lights a cigarette with the end of his old one. "No, *I* should be reading them. Hopefully the clients are reading them. You should be filing them." He points to the filing cabinets.

"I'll get started right away."

"After coffee," he says.

"Should I get you some coffee?" I ask.

"No, I thought you might need some. There's coffee in the room down the hall to the right. Help yourself. You'll pass the ladies room on your way," he adds.

I take his suggestion and head to the bathroom to put in my contacts and brush my hair and then stop in the breakroom to get myself a cup of coffee. When I return, coffee in hand, the other desks are occupied. Two men sit on Harold's side of the room. One guy has dark thick hair, a long straight nose, and broad shoulders. Rocky Balboa's smarter brother. The other guy is fair with slicked back blond hair and blue eyes as light as the sky behind me. Good looking if you like the Preppie type. Which I don't. They are both in shirtsleeves with ties knotted tight. Their suit coats hang on the back of their chairs. Both younger than Mr. Stackman but way older than me. Or maybe not.

The other two desks are pushed together facing each other on the left side of the room—directly in front of me. They have a back panel about eight inches high that runs the length of the desks and is covered with square buttons each marked with a tiny name plate. Attached to the panel is a telephone handset. At the desk facing me sits a balding man shielded behind the phone bank, visible only from the nose up. The person with her back to me is turned sideways in her chair and she's rummaging through an expensive purse large enough to be a cat carrier. I'd guess she's in her late twenties and I'm immediately intimidated by her perfect makeup and Farrah Fawcett hair. She's wearing a silk blouse and slacks. I don't own a single pair of slacks. I have jeans and corduroys and overalls. I have skirts and dresses and jumpers. My mother has slacks. I'm pretty sure that when this woman stands up, these are not going to look like my mother's slacks.

"Everybody," Harold calls out. They all look at him. "This is Andrea. My new girl. Be nice."

Stallone, Preppy, and Bald guy say hello. The woman dips her head with a little unhappy smile. Her nose is tiny. She looks like a blond Jackie Kennedy or maybe the quint-essential Pan Am stewardess. I feel itchy in the L.L. Bean oxford striped blouse I thought would be perfect for this job.

A phone rings. Jackie picks up the handset and uses a pencil to push in a lit button on the board in front of her, but instead of the expected breathy girlish tone, a smoky alto voice says, "What the fuck are you calling so early for, honey?"

I hear a crackling noise and then: "Good morning. Let's get started. We have a lot to cover today." The voice is coming from a small speaker box on everybody's desk.

"New York research department," Harold says and then he gives his full attention to the notes he is taking in a spiral notebook with an elegant Mont Blanc pen.

I try to listen. The individual words are familiar . . . Xerox . . . quarterly earnings . . . disappointment . . . lower profit margins . . . higher research and development costs . . . but I'm not getting the point.

The speaker finishes and another one starts. I stare at the far end of the room where an electronic sign resembling a movie marquee runs the length of the wall. I watch its glowing numbers and letters flow by like a river of alphabet soup.

The phone never rings and after thirty-five minutes, the original speaker says, "That's all for today." Harold takes out a three-ring binder and begins to flip through it as he takes notes on a yellow pad.

Line one rings. I look at Mr. Stackman. "You get it," he says.

"Harold Stackman's office."

"Is he there?" Impatient voice. Male.

"May I tell him who's calling?"

"And who may I ask are *you*?" He somehow sounds both annoyed and amused.

"I'm Andrea Hoffman. Mr. Stackman's new assistant."

"Oh, la di da Harold has an assistant now. Well, missy, tell him Frank's on the phone."

I put my hand over the receiver and whisper to Mr. Stackman, "It's Frank."

He nods and picks up the phone and I try to hang up as quietly as possible. The phone rings again almost instantly and I tell the caller Mr. Stackman is on the phone and offer to take a message which I write down on a pink message slip and place on his desk.

When Mr. Stackman hangs up the phone, he calls me over to his desk. He holds up the message slip. "You have the worst handwriting I have ever seen. Print in block letters from now on."

"Sorry."

"Your phone," he continues, "has a 'hold' button. It's the big button that says 'hold' under it. You use it so you don't have to do a Marcel Marceau impression when someone calls and they don't hear me say 'I don't want to talk to that asshole' or hear you slam the receiver down when I pick up. When somebody calls, find out who it is. Put them on *hold*. Yell their name at me. If I want to call them back, I'll do this." He twirls his finger in the air. "If I want you to ask them to wait a minute, I'll do this." He raises his index finger. "If I just shake my head, I'm too busy to pay attention to you. Deal with it. Got it?"

"I think so."

"'Yes' would have been a better answer."

"Sorry. *Yes*."

Harold looks at his watch. "Personnel will be in now. Get down there. Any reason why you shouldn't take a drug test today?"

"I don't think so. I mean no. No reason. Unless they are looking for a little Blue Nun." I giggle.

The blond woman turns her head to look at me a minute. I knew that look from high school. It says, "You're a worthless loser."

Harold shakes his head. "Go. The sooner you go, the sooner you can come back."

I pee in a cup and then an eighty-year-old security guard whose name tag says Oscar arrives to fingerprint me. My fingerprints will be checked for a criminal record and then kept on file. I'm starting to feel important. He inks and rolls each of my fingers deliberately and slowly. "Never had a print sent back for a redo. Did you know that? I've worked here for twelve years. Never messed up a single one."

I nod politely. "Wow," I say and turn to go.

"Miss?"

I turn back. Oscar ceremoniously hands me two little packages of wipes like the ones that come with a Kentucky Fried Chicken takeout dinner. "For your fingers."

I look at my ink-stained fingertips. Oscar says, "It comes right off. Use the wipes."

As I clean off the ink, I wonder if my robber got tow-elettes when they printed him. Stupid son of a bitch. Didn't even know to bring a little black backpack to a job and walk casually. Thinking of the robbery makes me have a moment's nostalgia. Can you be nostalgic for a life that ended less than a week ago?

I turn the corner and the beautiful woman is at Mr. Stackman's desk. They don't see me coming.

She is hissing into his face: "Well, just make sure she stays the fuck away from my phones."

She sits at her desk without looking at me and immediately picks up her handset. Her sexy low voice has been replaced by a nursery school teacher's sweet as marshmallow speech. "Good morning, it's little old Charlene from Mosley." Whoever this woman really is, she's terrifying.

———

Thirty-nine. That's the number of times I've said "sorry" today. Thirty-nine times.

"May I tell Mr. Stackman who's calling?"

"Gary."

"Sorry, Gary. What firm are you with?"

"Harris Bank. Jesus. He knows me."

"Sorry. I'll let him know you're calling."

I start making a mark on my yellow legal pad every time I say it. The tracks stretch across the page right under the line where I have written:

HAROLD HAROLD HAROLD

Not because I have a teen age crush but because I'm supposed to call him Harold and not Mr. Stackman.

"Call me Harold, Andrea. Not Mr. Stackman. Not Sir. Never ever Harry. Harold."

Every time I mess that up I add another HAROLD to the row.

At noon, Harold and the other two salesmen—Rocky's brother with the totally non-Italian name of Robert Parker ("Call me Bob . . . ") and the Preppy Winston Cabot (no further instructions, so I guess I don't call him Win) stand up to leave for lunch. "Before you go, Harold, can I ask you why Charlene was so adamant about me staying away from her phones?"

"First," he says, taking off his glasses, "you're not registered. That means that by law, you're not able to take an order. If you pick up the phone and somebody barks at you 'I bid a teeny on a downtick for ten Beamer' you're going to have to say 'Gee, I can't take that order' and that's going to piss the customer off. And second, you don't know what the hell 'I bid a teeny on a downtick for fifteen Beamer' means."

"Can I get a translation of that?" I say.

"To bid is an offer to buy," he says. "A 'teeny' is a sixteenth. A 'downtick' is a lower price than the last sale." He pauses and I nod to show I'm with him so far.

"So, if the last price was 62½, they want to buy at 62 1/16. Fifteen means either fifteen hundred shares or maybe fifteen thousand shares but certainly not fifteen shares."

"Why can't I just say 'Charlene stepped away from the desk for a minute' and take a message?"

"There's no point. If a customer wants to execute a trade and we're not available, they'll just go to Merrill Lynch or Goldman Sachs." Harold replaces his glasses. The sign he's through playing teacher.

Although I've processed only about half of what he said, I clearly understand that I don't touch the trading phones.

I'm left alone with scary Charlene and the bald trader who I've heard the others call Mahoney. In between waiting for a phone to ring, I clean out my desk drawers, tossing out a pack of rock hard Juicy Fruit and a few leaking Bic pens. I find a half-smoked pack of Kools. I imagine myself pulling out a cigarette and lighting up. I've probably smoked a dozen cigarettes in my whole life, all bummed off someone else when I'm drinking. I don't not like smoking. I just don't like it enough to acquire the habit. It's something other people do. I think about putting the pack on Harold's desk but he smokes Marlboros and seems like the kind of guy who picked a brand for a reason and is loyal to it. I look up to see if anyone is watching me and then I toss the Kools in my purse. At the bottom of the drawer, I find an envelope labeled "petty cash" containing a fat wad of bills. I lay the money out on the desk and separate it into piles by denomination, turning the bills so they all face the same way. I hate messy money. $212 in well-used bills. I write the date and the amount on a piece of paper and put it in the envelope with the money. Then I write myself a note on my yellow pad. "Is there a key to this desk?" I hide the envelope inside a research report and return it to the bottom of the drawer.

About fifteen minutes later, a delivery guy shows up and drops a bag on Mahoney's desk. My nose identifies burgers, bacon, and fries. My stomach makes noises that can probably be heard all the way to the elevator bank. I hadn't asked Harold what I should do about lunch. I regret tossing out the gum. Charlene walks over to Mahoney's desk. She pulls a foil wrapped sandwich out of the bag and swears.

"Christ almighty! I told them no fries. I got a half a bag of fucking fries." She turns to me and says, "You eat these." Like it's my fault the fries exist. Making me responsible for getting rid of them. "There's a fridge with drinks in it where you got the coffee this morning. Freebies. I'm waiting for a call. Get me a Tab and you can take something for yourself." She drops the bag on my desk like it's full of dog poop and sits back down at her desk. I look at Mahoney.

"Can I bring one for you too?"

He looks shocked. "Sure. I'll have a Coke."

When I leave the room I hear them laughing but I don't turn around.

I spend the rest of the afternoon trying to organize the research reports. A check of the dates leads me to believe they haven't been touched in a year. I wonder just how important they are. I also have to wonder if filing is really more glamorous than hanging clothes. It pays better, I remind myself. It pays a *lot* better. And as soon as I get this project done, I'm sure I'll be doing more interesting things.

By two o'clock all the salesmen are back at their desks but apparently it's a slow day for everyone. During a quiet moment, Mahoney hangs up his phone and says, "Damn, John Belushi died Friday. Who had him?"

Bob, Winston, Charlene, and Harold all pull a piece of paper out of their drawers.

"I had him," says Winston.

"He was on your fucking list?" says Charlene. "He was only thirty-two."

"Fat drunk Jew that did a lot of drugs. Seemed inevitable to me," Winston said with a shrug.

I must have heard him wrong. Clearly Belushi was Italian or Greek. No way Jewish.

"Wrong," says Harold.

Thank god I'm not going to have to say it.

"He was thirty-three. Not thirty-two" Harold says. He turns to me, and mistaking the look of disgust on my face for confusion, explains. "We bet when celebrities are going to die. A death pool."

"Are you kidding me? That's gruesome," I say. "And sad. Belushi was a genius." Maybe I didn't hear Winston right. I let it go.

Harold shrugs. "It's life."

"So no one else had him? I win?" Winston says.

Much grumbling but everyone drops bills on his desk. He walks over holding out ten dollars. "Alice, you brought me luck. Welcome to Mosley."

"It's Andrea, and really . . . " I start to protest but he puts the money down on my desk. "Next time no free ride," he says. "Start your own list."

I'm kneeling by my desk sorting the energy reports into company piles when a pair of clean white sneakers stops in front of me. I look up. Male. Ash blond hair long enough to hang in his face. Twenty-seven or twenty-eight. Kind of old for a mail boy.

"Where do you want this?" he asks, indicating a bundle of mail held together with a rubber band.

"What do you usually do with it?" I rock back on my heels so I can see him better. Tall, slim, Levi's and a Talking Heads t-shirt, bored shitless but holy crap handsome.

"I usually throw it on Harold's desk but now that he has a secretary, I thought you'd want it."

"I'm not his secretary," I say, and stand up. "Andrea, Harold's sales assistant." I wait but he doesn't give me his name. "Sure, I'll take the mail from now on." I hold out my hand to take it.

He hands it to me without meeting my eyes. "Yeah. Whatever you say."

Stupid no-name kind of old to be a mail boy who thinks I'm Harold's secretary! Salesmen have sales assistants. I review my duties. I answer phones. I file. I handle the mail. Oh my god. Have I gone from being a sales clerk to becoming a *secretary*? What did Harold call it when a trade happens at a lower price? A downtick? Is that what I've done? Twenty-five grand, I remind myself. Secretaries don't make that kind of money. He's just the mail guy.

"What's your name," I call after him as he trundles his cart into the bond department.

"Allan," he says without turning around.

Which is fine with me as the view of his backside is more enjoyable than the irritating expression on his face. I watch until he disappears around the corner.

Chapter 5

I ride the bus home. It's only 4:30 but since lunch consisted of Charlene's orphaned fries, I'm starving. I make the usual stop in Jay Dogs and splurge on an Italian beef with extra peppers. Then I descend into Streeters.

Sam smiles when he sees me. Leans over the bar and gives me a quick but not exactly platonic kiss. Interesting.

"No onion rings?" he says.

"Sorry, I had fries for lunch and I'm trying to eat healthy."

Sam watches as I bite into the sandwich and the grease drips onto my napkin.

"I see that," he says. "What are you washing that down with?"

"A glass of red would be good. That sales assistant job I found last week . . . today was my first day."

"And just like that you're going to be rich."

"I don't want to be rich. I want a job where I use my brain."

"I think you'll change your mind. About the dough."

"No way. That's not me. Hating rich people is a Hoffman family tradition. My parents are the most extreme kind of liberals you can be before they just flat out call you communist. Honestly, all I need is more money coming in than going out. I just want enough so I can take care of myself."

"Some guys get turned on by independent chicks, you know."

"Are you one of those guys?" It feels good to be a little flirty.

"Usually I like to be the dude who takes care of a woman but pride myself on being flexible."

I sip my wine. "I don't think it's going to be an issue. Except for the fact that I won ten bucks on a horrible bet I didn't make, today pretty much stunk."

"Give it some time. When I started this job I didn't know a martini from a manhattan. Now look at me."

I obediently do. He does indeed look very happy.

"You know, Sam, I thought people actually *worked* at work. Turns out they talk about sports most of the day and make bets on stupid stuff they have no control over."

"Your office sounds like being in here except you get paid more and nobody spills beer on you. You're making me jealous."

People start to trickle into the bar and Sam gets busy pouring drinks for paying customers, but when he sees me start to gather my stuff, he comes over. Leans over the bar and turns on the puppy eyes.

"I get off in an hour. I could come upstairs. I'll give you a back rub while you tell me all about your big first day. Or not."

Those warm brown eyes. A few hours not thinking about messing up. A few hours not thinking.

But I need to be up before six tomorrow morning. Mr. Stackman, Harold, told me that I could come in at eight but if the job's about the research, I'm damn well not going to miss the morning research call at seven. I'll show Harold I *do* work hard and I *do* learn fast. And I'll show the mail boy too.

"That sounds like heaven, Sam, but another time. I have to get up really early."

"Holding you to that," he says, holding my gaze.

I break eye contact to fish in my bag and find three bucks to throw on the bar. Sam takes them, blows me a kiss, and rings the bell by the cash register to remind all the deadbeat drinkers that tips are appreciated.

I push past a group of familiar dental students, give them a little wave, and climb up the stairs back to the sidewalk, around the corner to the entrance for the apartments and up two flights to the third floor and my studio. My unfolded sofa bed takes up most of the room. The weekend newspapers are still spread out on the floor and yesterday's mismatched bra and panties languish on the only chair in the apartment. I snatch them up and pitch them into the corner with the rest of the dirty clothes. I kick off my shoes and squeeze around the bed to the kitchen—or what more accurately should be called the kitchen corner.

What I want is a cookie, but the box in the cupboard is empty. I toss it and eat a handful of chocolate chips straight from the bag. I turn on the TV. Flip through the channels. Alice telling Mel to "Kiss her grits." A Clint Eastwood movie on ABC. Perky Wrigley gum commercial so irritating I can't even watch it long enough to see what comes on after. Turn off the TV. I call Barbara, my best friend from high school. Time to update her on my new job but her fiancé answers and says that she's at aerobics class. Fiancé, aerobics. Barb stayed in the suburbs. I came to the city. We are moving farther and farther apart.

I really want to call my old college boyfriend. My funny, handsome, athletic, smart boyfriend who turned out to be a total asshole. Steve was an economics major in college and ended up as a junior loan officer at a bank. I was a philosophy major and I end up with a stock market job. I might need to fudge the details a little, but even so, on the sexy scale, my work situation wins. He'd be super impressed by my news.

I've been trying for the past three years to get over this need to impress him. I write him letters. "See, I got a job! See, I found an apartment! See, I'm doing great without you! Have you realized yet what an incredible mistake it was on your part not to love me?" I don't send the letters . . . well, not anymore.

I stare at the phone trying to make it ring. I want to talk to him now and not just because I have something to brag about. I just seriously miss talking to him. Man, did we talk. So many nights Steve and I sat at a table in the cafeteria after dinner. Talking. Our coffee cold. The cavernous room completely empty except for the two of us and the guy putting chairs up on the tables so he could mop the floor. I don't remember what we talked about. I do know what we weren't talking about. We weren't talking about the girlfriend he had stashed at home. We weren't talking about her because I didn't tell him I found a letter from her on his desk. "I can't wait to feel you hard and sweaty against my . . . " written in aqua ink in a loopy girlish hand. I thought my silence was noble of me. Magnanimous. You can't force someone to want to be with you. Now I see that it was stupid. Weak. Eventually it was moot. I poke around the pain a little bit. Yep, still hurts. But I miss the talking.

I rummage in my purse for the Kools I took from my desk drawer. There are matches from the Berghoff restaurant tucked in the cellophane. I tap a cigarette out of the pack and light it up. The phone rings. For an insane second, I hope.

"Sweetie, did I wake you?"

I make a face, put my hand over the mouthpiece, and take a deep drag.

"Mom, it's seven thirty-five. Why would I be sleeping now?"

I don't get an answer but I can imagine her shrug as she moves on to the real reason for her call.

"I called you at the store today and Mariana said you

weren't working there anymore. She was quite short with me. Did you get fired?"

"No. I didn't get fired. Thanks for the vote of confidence, Mom." I try to sound annoyed but I'm relieved. Mariana must not have told her about the robbery or Mom would be at my front door now and not just calling me.

"I have a new job. Mosley Securities. A stock market firm."

"Stan," my mother shouts. "It's okay. Andie has a new job. Pick up the extension."

I hear the click as my father picks up the phone. "So?" my mother says.

"I'd been bored for a while . . . and then recently, someone came into the store and persuaded me this would be a good time for a change."

"I say retail isn't good enough for you and nothing happens. Some stranger walks into the store and says it, and boom, you're a stockbroker."

"Exactly, Mom." I hold the phone away while I take a drag. "But I'm not a stockbroker yet. I'm starting as a sales assistant for a man named Harold Stackman." I know what she's going to say. I mouth the word along with her.

"Jewish?"

My mother is obsessed with who is and who isn't Jewish even though we are so far on the reform spectrum that only our attendance at High Holiday services keep us out of the non-practicing category. Of course, we participate in all the fun holidays that involve gifts or elaborate food consumption. The other parts of being Jewish—respecting the Sabbath, attending synagogue, following the laws in the Torah—we're not so picky about. We're Jews because we eat like Jews. And because, as my mother is fond of reminding me, if Hitler comes again, we'd all be dragged away by our dirty blond hair. I tell my mother Harold is pure WASP, but that he seems like a good guy.

"Well, he's lucky to have a brilliant girl like you. You might even decide you want to go to law school and study securities law. That would be fascinating. An excellent use of your brain."

"I don't know why you keep insisting I should be a lawyer."

"You were very interested in law as a child."

"I watched Perry Mason reruns every day after school when I was ten years old. That doesn't mean I wanted to be a lawyer. Maybe I wanted to be the perpetrator!"

I hear my mother sigh on the other end of the line.

"I understand," I say. "You guys made sacrifices to send me to college and philosophy wasn't what you had in mind, but you have to trust that I know what I'm doing."

"Your mother's just trying to be helpful," my father says.

"I don't need you to explain me to my own daughter, Stan. We heard the news. You can get off the phone now."

"Bye, sweetie. Good luck with the new job," my dad says.

I quickly say, "Thanks, Daddy" just before I hear my dad obediently click off.

"So what were you doing this weekend that was so important that you didn't have time to call and tell us this news?"

Mom wouldn't accept that I was doing nothing for forty-eight hours. She can't do nothing for forty-eight *seconds*. "I was shopping for new clothes for the job." Not true, but my mom loves shopping. She's the queen of the incredible bargain.

"Everything good with you guys, Mom?"

"Sure, sure. Why not? Your father made a fool of himself at the Stein's this weekend arguing with Mort about Reagan's absurd tax policies, but what else is new?"

"Mom," I interrupt her. "I go to work really early in the morning. I need to get in the shower now."

"Oh, okay." I can tell she's disappointed that I don't want to listen to her complaints about my father but I've heard this too many times before. If he went to a party and talked, he said the wrong thing. If he went to a party and didn't talk, he was anti-social. My dad is a bright and funny guy. He loves his family. He just doesn't care about impressing people. My mother takes this as a personal insult.

Suddenly, I'm exhausted.

"Congratulations, darling," Mom is saying. "Very exciting. Really. Daddy and I love you."

Love me yes but maybe not as proud of me as you would be if I had majored in biochemistry or if I went to law school. Definitely not as proud as you are of my three brothers: the doctor, the electrical engineer, and the physicist.

I hang up the phone, lift the receiver to make sure I hear a dial tone, and then smash it repeatedly into my pillow.

Chapter 6

Mahoney, the bald trader, is getting his coffee when I walk into the break room on day two. Although there's a stack of Styrofoam cups by the coffee pot, he's holding a large ceramic mug with the words "I'd rather be fishing."

"You came back," he says with a look of mock surprise. "I'm glad we didn't scare you away yesterday."

"Not at all. It's all new to me but very interesting."

He waits for me to fill a cup and we walk into the office together. He's a large bear of a man and he walks like something might be hurting him.

"Can I ask you about this?" I say and point to the phone board covered with rows of small square plastic boxes that I had seen light up.

"They're direct lines. I don't need to dial a number to reach my customers. I just punch the button. We call them keys. It saves a lot of time and sometimes, if you've got a fast moving stock, that means money."

I nod. "One other thing? When the voices come over the speaker? Who is that? And where are they?"

"We have regional offices in a bunch of cities: San Francisco, Denver, Boston, all hooked into the system so we simultaneously receive the same information. But most of the people you hear are on the trading desk in New York. Sales traders like Charlene and me, we get orders from customers and then we call them into New York to the block traders. They execute the trades by communicating with our people on the floor of the exchanges."

Out of the corner of my eye, I see Charlene sweep in and I don't want to be standing here when she walks over. I start to move away. "Thanks, Mr. Mahoney. I appreciate you taking the time."

"You'll get it. Give it a little time. Most of it's just the language. Like you're in a foreign country." He bends down, takes off his shoes, and slips his feet into a pair of sheepskin slippers from under his desk. "And Andrea, not Mister Mahoney. You make me feel old. Call me Sean or Mahoney like everybody else."

The speaker, what everybody calls the squawk box, crackles to life, and the research call begins, and like yesterday, six analysts give a five-minute rundown on important news in their industries and the changes they've made in their opinion on specific stocks. I don't so much take notes as I jot down questions. When the call is over, I turn to Harold.

"Can I ask a few questions?"

He doesn't say no so I ask.

"The guys that are talking—the analysts—they each cover just one industry, or maybe a couple of related industries, right? How do they know? Which stocks are going to go up? How do they know what's the right price for a stock?"

"Jesus, Andrea. You could have started with something easier." Harold lights a cigarette and takes off his glasses. "The very short answer is that every company, hopefully, earns a profit. The profit is divided among all the shareholders—the owners of the company. So if you had a company that earned six dollars for the year and they had three owners—three shares outstanding—then the earning per share, what we call the EPS, would be two. Six dollars divided among three owners. More realistically it's millions of dollars divided among millions of shareholders. And depending how fast the company is growing, the analyst assigns a multiple to that EPS number. Say the company is growing fast, you might be willing to pay ten times the EPS, so the stock price would be twenty dollars."

"So," I say. "The important things are earnings and growth?"

"And quality of management, amount of competition, secular demand, cyclical demand . . . "

I hold up my hand to stop him. "My second day. I'll just chew on this for a while."

Harold smiles. "Anything else?"

"The people you talk to? At your accounts? They're analysts too?"

"Sometimes. The way money managers are set up there usually is at least one portfolio manager who makes the decisions of what stock to buy and sell. It would be too hard for him to know everything about all stocks so they have analysts who specialize in certain stocks and make recommendations to the portfolio manager. So sometimes I talk to the analyst and sometimes I talk to the portfolio manager. He's more important. He pulls the trigger."

"Last thing." I say and point to a glass enclosed office on the far side of the room. The light is off but I can see it contains only a desk and two chairs. "Does someone else work here?"

"It's the cone of silence," he says. "Like on the TV show *Get Smart*? Somewhere to have a private conversation. If one is needed."

Harold puts his glasses back on and although I am curious as to what exactly necessitates a private conversation, I just say, "Okay." Harold picks up his phone.

At the end of the day, I'm reading the latest copy of Institutional Investor Magazine. It's a glossy expensive-looking publication that take a poll of all the clients and uses the information to rank all analysts by industry. This, Harold told me when he tossed me the magazine, is a very big deal. To be the number one analyst as ranked by II means big money for the analyst, prestige for the firm, and a great selling point for a salesman. It's like winning an Oscar. I see we have thirteen analysts in the top three of their industries.

Mahoney stops by Harold's desk and hands him a dozen pieces of yellow paper. "Do you think Andrea can keep track of these from now on?"

Harold looks at me and nods. "Sure. Let's keep her really busy." He takes off his glasses and motions for me to come over to his desk. He opens a notebook that sits by his phone. "These," he says, holding up the yellow papers, "are trade tickets. They have the name of the account that did the trade, the amount of stock and its price and most important, how many cents per share commission the customer paid."

I nod.

"Every day, you'll write the commission information in this book." He opens the book. "For example, the Northern sold 15,000 shares today at twelve cents a share. The Northern is my account and Mahoney did the trade so you write down eighteen hundred bucks under both our names. This is an important job. These are the numbers we get paid on. Got it?"

"You get a percentage of the commission? That's how you're paid?"

"Salesmen get fifty percent. Traders have a lot more accounts. They get twenty-five."

I say, "Yes. But won't everybody mind that I know how much business they're doing? And I know how much they're being paid? Isn't that kind of private?"

Both Mahoney and Harold laugh. "You know how people say they play the market. Nobody ever says they work the market. It's a game and every game has a way to keep score. Congratulations! You just became our official score keeper." Harold hands me the book and the tickets and I get to work.

As soon as I'm finished, Winston and Bob stop by my desk and check the numbers.

"I am gaining on you, Winston. A couple more days like this and I will crush your record from February." I'm hoping this is true. Bob is clearly the nicer guy.

"Dream on, Bobby. I've got you five out of the last six months. Accept it. I am smarter, I am better looking, and I make more money than you."

"I concede none of those points." Bob looks at me. "Which one of us is better looking?"

"I really couldn't say."

"Come on, Annie," says Winston. "You must have an opinion."

"Andrea. And yes. I do. But I really can't say . . . or I should say I *won't* say. I see no logical reason for me to pick sides. I can only say that Harold is better looking than either of you."

"Damn, did anyone ever tell you that you should be a lawyer?" Winston says.

My mother's face pops into my mind but I choose to treat this as a rhetorical question and say nothing.

Winston drops papers on my desk as he turns to leave. "My expenses from last month. I'm pretty sure the form is in your desk somewhere. You're a smart girl. You'll figure out how to do it."

I go through the receipts. Lunches at the Union League Club each and every day, dinners all over town. A trip to

St. Louis. I find the form, tally the expenses, and leave it on his desk to sign.

I'm hanging on to these new duties as proof I'm not Harold's secretary but I'm not sure how I feel about being everybody's "girl."

Chapter 7

Week two and I'm not anticipating disaster every passing second and the days start to feel less like eight hours of high anxiety and more like . . . well, like a day of work. My yellow pad no longer has Harold written all over it. My sorry tally hasn't disappeared but the number of sorrys has diminished. I come in before seven. I read the *Journal*. I bring a lunch. Best of all, I got my first check. I ran to the bank and deposited it right after the market closed. Only when I saw my new balance was I convinced it was real.

Every morning when I pass Bob Parker's desk with my coffee, he says, "Nice glasses."

I say, "Nice tie." He has a thing about ties. Everyone else is wearing thin ties. Yellow is popular. Also stripes. Maybe a subtle logo. Bob is keeping the 1970s alive. Fat ties. Bright colors. Clashing patterns. But other than this weird fashion choice, Bob's a regular guy. Wears a Seiko. Not a Rolex like the other guys do. Has a cute picture of his wife and kids on his desk. He answers his phone "Parker, here." Like the parking lot attendant would say. Bob has a sense of humor. Unlike Winston who seems to have a stick up his ass and is undoubtedly married to the kind of woman who shops at my old store. And judging from the giggly phone messages I take for him, cheats on her every chance he gets.

The phone rings at around twelve-thirty. When I say Harold is not in, the caller says, "I'm stuck at O'Hare. Give me a couple of quotes, will you dear?"

I feel a surge of power.

"Sure," I say. "Let me pick you up at another desk. I put him on hold and slide into Harold's chair to use his Quotron. The Quotron looks like a small TV set but instead of receiving television reception, the boxes show financial information. Using the attached keyboard, you can retrieve stock prices and the latest market news. I haven't touched a Quotron yet, but I've watched the news and stock quotes flash in glowing neon green on it's dark green screen. I pick up Harold's phone. "I'm ready," I say.

"IBM," he says.

I punch I-B-M into the machine and hit the enter button and the price appears. 58 ½ up a ¼.

I wish the mail guy would come by and see me doing this. Who's a secretary now?

I relay the information and my caller says, "Good . . . how's Xerox?"

I type in X-E-R-O-X. and get a message that reads *symbol not found*. "Could you hang on one second please, sir?"

I put him on hold again and see that for once Charlene isn't on the phone. "Charlene, what's the symbol for Xerox?" She doesn't turn around.

"XRX."

I punch in X-R-X and the quote magically appears and I relay the information.

"How about Sears?"

"Sorry, can you hold again?" I ask.

"How about I just tell you the symbols instead?" he says.

"That would be helpful. It's my second week."

"Well, good for you. What's your name?"

I tell him.

"Well Andrea, I'll give you some advice. Never hesitate to say you don't know something. Saves everybody a lot of time and could save someone a lot of money too."

"Yes, sir. What is the symbol for Sears?"

"S."

I give him about seven more quotes and then he says he is going to grab a martini before his flight takes off.

"Thanks for the help, Andrea. Tell old Harold that Whitney called."

"Have a good trip," I say, not knowing if Whitney is a Whitney Somebody or a Mr. Whitney.

"One last thing. Hit the quote for IBM one last time."

"It's up a half now."

"Great. Sell 5,000 shares in the main account at three quarters or better."

"I can't—" I start to say, but he's gone.

I put down the phone and write out exactly what he has said and stare at it. This is catastrophically bad. I've taken an order and I'm not allowed to take orders. It's not just an office rule, it's actually a federal law. Only people who have passed the Series 7 exam are allowed to act as a representative. In order to accept an order, I have to have a license. Harold explained this to me on day one. Right now the only license I have is my driver's license. I have no way of getting in contact with this guy and Harold is on an airplane. I think I'm going to faint. I check the quote on IBM again. It's 58 ¾. We should be selling the 5,000 shares right now. I punch in the numbers on Harold's calculator. It's almost $300,000 worth of stock. The stock ticks back to 58 ½. We missed it. Time is racing by too fast. I'm going to have to tell the one person I most don't want to tell.

"Charlene?"

She turns around slowly and waits for me to say something.

"I was giving quotes to some guy named Whitney who

was at the airport and he hung up on me but before he did, he gave me an order to sell 5,000 shares of IBM at ¾ for the main account and like I said then he hung up and—"

"Okay," she says.

Before I can ask what she thinks we should do, she picks up her phone and punches a button and says, "Hank, sell 5,000 IBM at ¾ or better."

"But I wasn't supposed to take an order. I'm not registered. I don't even know who that guy was."

"Oops. Hope you don't get in trouble for this," she says.

The squawk box crackles. "Charlene, baby, I got you 7/8 for the Beamer. Who's better than me?"

Charlene picks up the squawk phone. "Thanks." Then she turns to me. "I didn't think Whitney had 5,000 shares of IBM in the main account. Are you sure he didn't say *buy*?" She's disconcertingly calm for someone who might have just sold $300,000 worth of stock that might not exist. In fact, she's smiling. If you want to call her mirthless smirk a smile.

"Yes," I say. "I'm sure that is what he said. I think. What if I am wrong?"

Charlene shrugged. "Guess we'll find out."

I'm tearing up. I bite the inside of my lip to stop myself. Charlene rolls her eyes and turns back around to her desk. Clearly, she's been all the help she's going to be.

Now the clock seems to have stopped and I have nothing *but* time to review over and over in my mind what happened from the second I picked up the phone. I don't see how I could have done anything differently. Charlene executed the trade at a better price than the customer specified and yet, everything from the sick feeling in my stomach to the memory of Charlene's smirk when she confirmed the sale equals the feeling I'm totally hopelessly screwed.

Harold should be landing in an hour and then he'll call in. I pace behind the desks, stopping to punch in IBM on

the Quotron again and again. It's trading higher. It ticks at
59. Then 59 1/8. Then 59 again. The phone rings six times
in the next hour and it isn't Harold and it isn't Whitney and
by the time Harold calls, I'm just numb. I've gone over all
my options hundreds of times. There's the possibility that
this man was just messing with the new girl and there is no
IBM to sell. In that case, I'm going to owe the firm a lot of
money. Even if it is a good trade, I'm in trouble for trading
without a license. In every scenario I come up with, Harold
fires me for being an idiot. I blurt out the story as soon as
Harold says, "What's happening?"

"Nice," he says. "Anything else going on?"

Indifference was not among my options. "But what if I
messed up?" I try not to yell into the phone, but clearly he
isn't getting what I'm telling him. "What if someone finds
out I wasn't supposed to take the order in the first place?"

"Andrea, Whitney is unreachable and I'm five hundred
miles away. Either it's a good trade or it's not. We'll find out
tomorrow. Is anything going on I can do something about?"

"No, sir." I forgot I wasn't supposed to call him that.
He lets it slide.

"Okay then. I'll be in tomorrow around ten."

———

I sleep lousy. I never sleep lousy. Even after a gallon of coffee,
even the night before a big test, even in the past after a fight
with college boyfriend Steve or a current conversation with
my mom that leaves me with that painful feeling of disappointing her again, I can get in my bed and close my eyes and
the next thing I know the alarm is going off. But not tonight.

I review the conversation I had with Whitney over and
over again. I hear him say "Sell five thousand IBM" and
I see the smile on Charlene's face when she says "I hope
you don't get in trouble for this." I let myself hope just a

little that the trade is a good one and the day will go on like nothing happened. But I know in my heart this isn't true. I don't know much about what is going to happen when Harold gets in to the office tomorrow, but I do know, I know with total certainty, that I don't want to lose this job.

When I was in eighth grade, my guidance counselor pulled me out of my honors math class to give me a choice.

"Andrea, Mrs. Cote tells me you aren't doing well in math this year. You've always been in the honors program, but frankly, we're not sure it's for you. You could be the smartest kid in the regular math class if you'd rather switch." He didn't say it but the clear alternative was to stay the stupidest kid in honors math. He assured me that the choice was completely mine. I didn't have to think for a minute. I was staying. It wasn't like I had any interest in math. Quite the opposite. But my siblings had always been in honors math and there was no way I was going home and telling my parents I had been demoted. I'd suffered through a year of algebraic torture.

Tossing and turning in bed, I feel like once again I've officially been declared the stupidest kid in the smart class. But this time, my desire to stay has nothing to do with my family expectations. No, this time I want to stay because it's where I want to be. By some incredible accident, I've found the coolest group in school and joined their clique and I don't want to get kicked out.

The three hours before Harold comes in are torture, and when he shows up, he immediately gets on the phone with only a nod in my direction.

"Whitney, you dog. Since when are you a seller of IBM? Do you have any more behind it?"

"I thought as much. We'll take care of it. No. She's a smart girl. I told her that it was her job to help me make money. Can't blame her for trying."

I put my head down on my desk. The guy was *joking*. I messed up. I look up at the stock ticker hoping to see IBM flash by so I can see the price. I am sure as hell not going to ask Charlene.

Harold hangs up the phone and says, "Charlene, bust the IBM trade."

She turns around. "Shall I tell them why?" She is staring at me.

"You tell New York I made the mistake. Is that clear? Or do you want the desk to know that you take orders from unregistered sales assistants?"

Charlene's smile instantly fades and she twists back to pick up her phone.

"He was joking?" I ask Harold.

Harold nods. "Even if he wasn't, you shouldn't have done the trade. It was his mistake to give it to you. He should have born the consequences. Now we will."

Charlene calls over her shoulder. "Done at 3/8." Her voice is angry.

She bought the stock back at 59 3/8. We lost fifty cents a share on five thousand shares. Twenty-five hundred dollars.

Maybe even worse, Charlene already hates me for no discernible reason. Now I've gotten her in trouble and she'll hate me more. "I made Charlene do the trade. I begged her. You can take the money out of my salary," I say. "If you aren't firing me." I look down at the floor between our desks. "Am I fired?"

Harold takes the time to light a cigarette before answering me. I finally look up and he looks me right in the eye and says, "How could I fire you . . . since it was me that made the error?"

"But the money . . . " I start to say.

He holds up his hand. "Forget the money. The money's chicken-shit. Remember the lesson. Always do what's best for the firm. You'll have a lot of customers. You only have one employer."

"But isn't making the customer happy the best thing for the firm in the long run?"

"Andrea, there is a reason that I make twenty times more money than you. I'm older than you. I'm smarter than you. I know what's best for the office. Forget all the bullshit you learned in school and any business wisdom you picked up reading *Reader's Digest* in the john. It's crap. You listen to what I say and you'll learn. Now can we do some work around here?"

He gets back on the phone and I get up and go to the bathroom. It's empty as always. Hardly any women work in the whole office. I go into a stall, lock the door, put my head in my hands, and sob. I'm not upset about the spanking Harold just gave me. I deserved it. I'm just so relieved I'm not going to be fired. I'm not even going to have to pay back the money. Harold is giving me another chance. I get to stay. I pull about two feet of toilet paper from the roll and blow my nose. I should have brought my purse in with me so I could repair my mascara.

I come out of the stall and Charlene is standing by the sink. She's easily four inches taller than me and wearing three inch heels. I feel small. And awkward. "You didn't need to try and help me," she says. "I can take care of myself."

I turn on the faucet and start splashing cold water on my face. When I look up, she's gone. She didn't say it but I heard it loud and clear. "Because I'm sure as hell not helping you."

Chapter 8

You never can be sure that Chicago's not going to be hit with one last snowstorm, even after temperatures have climbed into the seventies for a few beautiful days, so a better indicator of spring is office conversation that switches from basketball and hockey to baseball and golf. These guys are desperate to get in their first round of the season.

Better weather also means New York analysts are more willing to schedule trips to Chicago, and Jim Edelweiss, our food and restaurant analyst, will be the first visitor I need to coordinate. He's ranked second in the Institutional Investor poll, so an important man. And although Harold hasn't acted any differently toward me, I can't believe that his faith in me isn't a bit wobbly from the Whitney disaster. I want the meetings to go flawlessly in order to reassure Harold he made a good decision to keep me.

Busy and with something to look forward to, a productive day turns more interesting when I have an unscheduled mail boy sighting during lunch. He's entering the elevator with a strange woman. By strange, I mean she's unknown to me, not that she's weird. Interviewing? But she doesn't look like the mailroom type. She's twenty something and wearing jeans—designer but still too casual for a job interview—and a gorgeous black cowl neck sweater too expensive for the mail room. I conclude she's the girlfriend. The mail boy having a girlfriend would explain his consistent lack of interest in me.

I'm back at my desk with a tuna on whole wheat analyzing my interest in Allan's lack of interest in me when the research department takes over the squawk box.

"Listen up. This is Peter Raskin. I'm lowering my rating on Eastman Kodak to a hold from a buy. I just got some information that leads me to believe . . . " I start to write down what he's saying. I write as fast as I can but I wish I had sent away for that correspondence course in *TV Guide* that promised "U 2 cn hv a grt jb." As soon as the squawk clicks off, I start to rewrite my hurried scribbling in a legible hand but I decide the note will look more professional if I type it. I fire up my little-used bright blue IBM Selectric and, using my two-finger hunt-and-peck method, I get the details down as fast as I can. I add the date and time on top and then run down to the mail room to Xerox three copies. I leave copies for Harold, Bob, and Winston. Charlene looks up as I walk by.

"Would you like this?" I ask.

I expect her to say something like "I am sitting right here and I'm not fucking deaf," but she holds out her hand and I give her my original and she glances at it and says, "Thanks."

Harold comes back twenty minutes later. "Next time," he says, "write the price of the stock next to the time."

"That'd be easier if I had my own Quotron," I say. His Quotron is all of two feet from my desk but I'd been expecting a little praise for my initiative. It's entirely possible that he doesn't hear me. He's already picking up his phone, so anxious to go out with this news that he doesn't even take his suit jacket off.

Just before the market closes, a maintenance guy shows up with a handcart. It has a Quotron on it. "Where does this go?" he asks. I look at Harold.

"Did you think I was a mind reader? If you need something, then ask for it. Better yet, next time just get it yourself."

"It goes here," I say to the delivery man. Then to Harold, "I want to get my registration. I want to take the exam."

"Who had six weeks?" Harold calls out.

"I win!" Mahoney says. "Pay up."

I am stunned to see Winston, Charlene, Bob, and Harold all pull out their wallets and then throw five dollar bills on his desk. "You had a bet about how long before I asked to take the Series 7?"

Harold grins at me and says, "You come in an hour early every day. You read the research instead of filing your nails at your desk. You chit-chat on the phone with the customers every chance you get. It's not a total mystery that you are more ambitious than the usual girl. In fact, I had last week. You disappointed me." He doesn't look mad. "I think the thing with Whitney spooked you or I would have had it. Call personnel and have them send you up the materials."

"Thank you," I say, picking up the phone.

"Don't thank me. Just pass the fucking test. First time."

Charlene is on her feet just minutes after the close. She picks up her handbag, which is always perfectly coordinated with that day's shoes. Today it's navy leather with enough hardware on it to bridle a pony. She walks to my desk, her lovely face expressionless. "The notes were helpful," she says. "I want a copy whenever you do them."

"No problem," I say.

"Good," she says flatly.

Not effusive praise but this is the most positive exchange we've had so far. I'm satisfied.

"These are all of them," she says, and drops the day's yellow trade tickets on my desk and turns and leaves.

I enter the trades. As always, Harold made the most money, but Bob and Winston did okay. Each banked a little more than a thousand dollars. It's funny how quickly an amount of money I thought was humongous, now seems like an ordinary day. And for doing what? Talking on the phone. Buying a client lunch. The market itself is fascinating. On any given day, it could be something economic, political, legal, or even weather-related that is driving the market up or down. But the salesmen don't need to analyze or predict stock movement. They only need to parrot what our analysts tell them to say. I can do that. And now taking the Series 7 is going to get me one step closer to getting some of those commissions for myself. It's not about the money. It's about getting in the game. I slam the book shut. Pass the test on the first try? Piece of cake.

Chapter 9

My charge, James F. Edelweis, respected Wall Street Food and Beverage analyst, arrives at the office half an hour before his first meeting. Rumpled doesn't describe him adequately. He looks like he's been playing on a dusty floor with a toddler and a golden retriever. His tie is badly knotted. His glasses are filthy—so smudged I'm shocked he can see out of them. He's tall and bulky with a round face and lots of chin. Clearly, food and restaurants hold more than a financial interest for him. He strides right over to Harold's desk to pump his hand vigorously. Harold claps him on the back.

Edelweis turns to me. "Andrea?"

He grabs for my hand with the same enthusiasm I imagine he has for the bread basket at dinner. "The meeting schedule looks better than usual. Clearly you're getting these boys organized. Glad you're on board." So much for the aloof, intellectual analyst stereotype I was working with in my head.

I smile and say, "Nice to meet you too. How can I help this morning?"

He opens his battered leather briefcase and pulls out a packet of papers. I'm pretty sure I spot an empty Snickers wrapper in there. And a not so empty bag of pretzels. He finds the document he's looking for, hands it to me. "Will you make thirty copies of this?" He turns back to Harold. "I'm going to make a few calls and then we can get going."

I happily head off to the copier. The copier is in the mail room so there is always the chance of an unscheduled Allan sighting. I don't wait for the elevator. I walk down the two flights. I pause a second in the doorway.

"I need to have some copies made!" I call into the seemingly empty room.

"Coming," says a deep voice. Not Allan. Lucas, head of the mailroom, shuffles out from the back and takes my papers away to the magic Xerox machine. I hear whirring noises and then a noise that sounds like the world's largest deck of cards being shuffled and finally the ca-chunking sounds of an industrial sized stapler. When he returns with my thick stack of papers, I instinctively raise them to my nose. Nothing. Copiers are fast but nothing beats that mimeograph smell

Harold and Jim are back from their morning client visits at eleven forty-five. I've spent most of that time staring at my Quotron and trying to figure out how to ask Harold if I can sit in on the lunch. I hand them both their messages.

"Is lunch here yet?" Harold asks.

"No, I don't think so. I'll check in the conference room."

He raises an eyebrow at me. "Where did you order it from? Maybe you should call."

I stare at him dumbly. Where did I order it from? I didn't order. Not from anywhere. I'd made Edelweiss's travel arrangements and nagged the salesmen to set up their meetings and then nagged them some more to confirm the lunch attendees so I'd know how many lunches I needed to order, then I completely forgotten that I had to do it. "I . . . "

But Harold is already on the phone, completely unaware that there's no lunch for his nineteen clients.

I have fifteen minutes. I open my top desk drawer and casually put the envelope of petty cash in my purse. I smile at Harold and walk serenely to the door. I frantically push the elevator button once I'm in the hall and try to calm down by repeating over and over *Oh my god I screwed up. I really screwed up. I am so screwed.* The closest deli is staffed by half-wits. It takes them ten minutes to make a single ham and cheese on rye. They'll never be able to put together lunch for twenty people in time. The clients are going to be *pissed*. Harold is going to be humiliated in front of an important New York analyst. I have made another major mistake. No one else is going to take the blame this time. I could save him the trouble of firing me and just go home. The elevator finally comes. The door opens, and it's Allan.

"Going down?" he asks.

"You could say that," I say as I step in. "Apparently, I was supposed to order lunch for twenty people and I failed to do so and now I need food *really fast*."

Allan just looks me over calmly.

He says, "I'll help you carry it."

"Carry what?"

"Whatever it is you figure out."

The elevator doors open, and Allan and I race out together.

When I walk in the conference room a minute after noon, Harold, Edelweiss, Bob, and Winston are already standing around talking with a dozen clients. They're all looking toward the door. I'm sure they could smell the food before they could see me. If they're surprised to see Allan, they don't show it.

"Sorry," I say. "I bet you thought you weren't getting fed, but chicken nuggets are better when they're hot." I put two giant bags down on the table against the far wall. Allan drops two more beside mine, pats me on the shoulder, and then leaves the room.

I keep up my patter. "Putting our money where our mouth is . . . or maybe I have that backwards. McDonalds *is* our number one recommendation in the restaurant sector."

Jim Edelweiss jumps right in. "I wanted you to taste the new Chicken McNuggets and decide for yourself whether McDonald's is going to be able to successfully diversify away from burgers. The numbers don't matter much if the food isn't selling."

"Food from McDonalds beats the hell out of the tired turkey sandwiches you usually give us," says the first client in line.

"Great idea, Jim," the man closest to him says.

But it was *my* idea, I think, not Jim's.

Harold taps me on the back just as I am digging the last of the little ketchup packets out of the bag. "Come on. I'll help you bring in the soda from the other room," he says.

He greets a latecomer and then is silent as we walk down the hall to the break room. When we finally reach the fridge, I grab a tray and Harold starts pulling out sodas and piling them on top. He says, "I'm the boss, Andrea. You want to pull a stunt like that you better run it by me first."

"It wasn't a stunt," I say. "I . . . forgot to order lunch. Going to McDonalds was the fastest food I could come up with."

He studies me a minute. "You're so lucky this wasn't the metal and mining analyst. I would've been furious."

I stare down at the sodas. "Are you furious anyway?"

"Angry and disappointed, Andrea." He stares down at me. A very serious and perhaps a little worried look on his face. "This could have been very bad for me. And that would have been very bad for you. I know you have loftier career plans but keep your mind on the job you have. If you want to keep it."

"Yes. Sorry. It won't happen again." I hoist the tray of sodas and trudge two steps behind Harold into the conference room. I put them down and turn to leave but Harold catches my eye and jerks his head toward a chair near the door and mouths, "Stay."

I try to focus on the talk. Why Jim likes the stock of Coca Cola and not Pepsi. Grain prices and the companies affected by their rise and fall. Trends in American eating habits. Interesting information and Edelweiss is a lively speaker but it's hard not to relive how close I came to making a fatal mistake. I slip out quietly to make a fresh pot of coffee.

When I come back, the clients are asking Edelweiss questions and I try to put the tray on the table without making too much of a disturbance.

"Your growth estimates for Archer Daniels are not that robust. Why are you recommending the stock?" asks a paisley yellow tie guy.

"My numbers are low but everybody else's are in the basement. If they come in at close to what I've got, the street will be thrilled."

I understand this well. It works with people as well as stocks. If you don't expect much, any little thing can be a positive surprise. Expecting too much? That leads to disappointment.

Ten minutes later, Harold looks at his watch and ends the meeting. I head over to the table to clean up.

"We've got to leave for a meeting at the Northern in five minutes," Harold says to Jim. "Good lunch."

"That was an excellent idea sending your girl out to get the McNuggets. I'm going to have them do that in Boston too."

Harold turns to me. I wait. The Big Time New York analyst will be surprised when Harold tells him the idea was mine. Instead, I get the surprise when all he says to me is: "Next time, bring the coffee in earlier."

At two o'clock, Charlene gets off the phone and picks up the squawk box. "Got twenty Big Mac to buy. What can you show me?"

Ten minutes later she turns around. "Andrea!"

I look up, startled.

"Watch the tape!" she orders.

I see 5,000 BP and three or four round lots of stocks I didn't know the symbols for and then I see it . . . 20,000 MCD prints at $65 3/4. McDonalds stock. I watch it travel all the way across the screen.

"That's Lincoln National's trade." One of Harold's largest accounts. "When they called it in to me they said it was payment for a delicious and informative lunch," Charlene says.

I go to the ticker machine that continuously prints the stock prices we see flow by on the electronic ticker on the wall and cut the paper that shows the McDonalds' trade.

When Harold comes back from his meeting, I hand it to him. "Lincoln National gave you this order. They said it was payment for lunch."

Harold looks at the tape. Then he takes off his glasses and points them at me. "I hope you learned a lesson today. Paying attention to things—especially the tedious things—matters. You can't always dig yourself out of a hole by being Miss Resourceful."

I force myself to look him square in the face. I nod because I can't trust myself to speak.

After a long moment, his eyes crinkle at the corners and his mouth twitches. "But damned if it didn't work today." He hands me the small piece of paper. "You should keep this. Your first trade."

My heart starts to beat again. The knot in my stomach relaxes. It's not *my* trade. I don't get any commission. The three thousand dollar commission gets credited to Harold. But hey, today I did my job. I helped my boss make money.

———

Allan's at the elevator when I'm heading home. His worried look contrasts with the serene expression of the Bob Marley image on the t-shirt he wears under his untucked button down shirt. He says, "Harold looked really mad when we walked into the conference room. Did everything go okay?"

I look around and make sure no one is behind me. "The clients loved the food and the big shot analyst happily took the credit for the idea in the meeting. And then after the meeting, the analyst graciously thanked Harold for coming up with the idea and *he* took the credit instead of telling him it was me." I sigh. "But considering the only reason I had the bright idea was because I messed up big time, yes. I think everything turned out okay."

"Good," he says. The elevator doors open. He waits for me to step in and follows.

"Can I buy you a drink?" I say. "I need a drink." I think about the cowl neck sweater girl I saw him with a few days before. "If you don't have other plans."

He considers my offer. "Where?" he says.

"Streeter's . . . on Chicago?"

"Sure."

I turn left out of the door of the building, the sky still bright and the evening air warm and humid. July only a few days away. I start walking to the bus stop when Allan stops at the curb and whistles for a cab. He holds the door open for me.

"You must be pretty thirsty," I say.

He looks confused.

"The cab instead of a bus?"

He shudders slightly. "I hate buses," he says. "My nanny left me on the bus once. She got off first and the driver took off. I was only three. I just stared out the window and watched her getting smaller and smaller. My parents fired her, of course."

"Of course," I say, unsure if this is his idea of humor.

We sit in silence until the cab crosses the Chicago River.

"So . . . " I flip through conversation topics in my mind. I don't want to ask him about college in case he didn't go. He doesn't seem like a big sports fan. He's wearing a Bob Marley t-shirt. I point to his chest and ask, "Music fan?"

He grins and says, "Ya, man. I love the music."

I glance up at the rearview mirror. Catch the Haitian cab driver's eye roll. Looking back at Allan, I don't remember ever seeing him smile before. His teeth are perfect.

"What else besides reggae?" I say.

"Jazz, blues, some rock and roll. Not top-forty."

"So disco's out?"

"Disco is far out and not in a funky way." He says this with a completely straight face. I am never playing poker with this man.

"Do you play an instrument?" I ask.

"I did. Not anymore."

He doesn't ask me any questions so we lapse into silence again.

Five minutes later, we're at the bar. I pay the driver. Allan doesn't protest.

Wednesdays at Streeter's means nickel beers until seven and the place is jumping. Both pool tables are in action and all the seats at the bar are taken. I wave to Sam as we head to an unoccupied high top near the dart board. He smiles broadly when he sees me and then the smile dims as he spots Allan behind me. Sam gets busy refilling the olives.

The waitress, a space cadet Madonna wanna-be, flounces over and plants herself in front of Allan. "What can I do you for?"

"Shot of bourbon with a beer back," he says without looking up at her.

"You want something?" the waitress asks me without taking her eyes off Allan.

"Glass of white wine, please."

As soon as she returns, Allan throws down the shot and chugs the beer while the waitress is setting down my glass. "We'll run a tab," he says. "Bring me another."

"Right away, hon." She bends to pick up his empty glass and brushes her boobs against his arm.

Allan visibly winces.

"You have a fan."

Allan rolls his eyes as he shakes his head. "Not my type."

"You gotta admit she's got some skills," I say grinning. And I have to admit she's got good taste. Allan's blue eyes, sharp cheekbones, strong jaw. Seeing him out among my neighborhood crowd, he clearly stands out.

Allan unbuttons the cuffs of his shirt and rolls up the sleeves. He rests his forearms on the tabletop and scans the room.

"And I see you have a fan as well," he says. A head jerk toward Sam at the bar. "He's been staring at you since we came in."

"Nah. That's not a thing," I say and hope that in the last few weeks I haven't given Sam the impression I want to start something up. Realizing that I have. Anxious to change the subject, I look around and catch sight of his watch. The leather of the strap is cracked and worn but the gold around the face glows even in the dim light of the bar.

"I love watches. Yours is beautiful," I say.

"A true antique. It was my grandfather's. He gave it to me when I graduated high school. He was a wonderful man." This is a lot of words from Allan. I'm amazed. I'm even more amazed when he reaches over and pushes up my left sleeve to see my watch.

"A Movado," I say. "It's nice, isn't it? It was my college graduation present from my ex-boyfriend. Not wonderful. The watch came with a note that said 'I'll never doubt we loved each other. I'll always wonder how much more we could have.' Here's a hint for him. I would have loved him more if he wasn't two-timing me."

Allan is still examining my Movado, and thank god, as I feel myself flushing bright red. I take a couple of sips of the watery wine. The fact that it's cold is the tastiest thing about it. "Sorry, that was probably more about my past than you wanted to know." I drain my glass. "But, I guess everything works out for the best, doesn't it? I didn't stay in Boston where I went to college. I came back to Chicago and here I am at fabulous Mosley Securities."

"Streeter's. You're actually at Streeter's."

My turn to eye roll. I look toward the bar. Sam is watching us. So is the waitress. I circle my finger to order another round.

The drinks arrive and also two Kamikaze shots. "Sam said these are for you," Madonna says looking directly at me for the first time. I wave at him and mouth, "Thanks." I get a curt head nod in response. Shit.

Allan doesn't wait for me. Just downs his shot with no ceremony. Finishes it with half of his beer. Six drinks so far. Impressive.

When I was in college, I hung out with the men's soccer team. Not because I particularly loved soccer but because those were the kids I was comfortable with. They were scholarship students too, Irish and Italian guys from South Boston. Guys from middle class families like mine. Allan reminds me of them. Like him, they drank a lot more than they talked. I always talk more than I drink.

"You know, I found the ad for the Mosley job sitting right in this bar," I say. No response from Allan. I try a direct question. "What were you doing before Mosley?"

He shrugs. "Some school. Travelled around. My parents got tired of me being 'unproductive' so . . . " he finishes the rest of the beer. "But you," he says with a finger point. "In early. Out late. Staring at your Quotron like it holds the answers to the mysteries of the universe. You fucking care, don't you?"

I choose to ignore what I perceive as a slightly mocking tone to his voice. "I do. I love this job. I'm pretty shocked I do, but I do. I'll have my registration in a couple of weeks."

"What does that mean? Getting your registration?"

"I take the Series 7 exam given by the Industry Regulatory Authority. I need that to be a salesman. I've been studying my ass off but it's just memorization. Nothing hard. Pass it and I can be a registered representative."

"That's your plan?"

"Absolutely. I want my own accounts." I gulp my wine. This is the first time I've said that out loud. "What about you? Where's the mail room going to launch you to?"

"No plan. I just do what they tell me." He finishes the foam in the bottom of his glass.

And I figure we're done with job talk.

My stomach rumbles. Lunch was a long time ago. "I have a frozen pizza upstairs. Interested?" I say.

Allan looks so confused I laugh.

"I live in an apartment in this building. I could heat it up if you're hungry."

Allan looks at his watch. "I have a meeting to go to but thanks." He looks toward the bar. "And I'm afraid your friend would kick my ass if I left with you." He signals our waitress for a check. She's by his side in an instant. Hands him the check.

I make a grab at it. "No. Mine." I say. "I asked you, remember?"

"When you pass that big-deal test, you can buy the drinks. I got this." He glances briefly at the check and then pulls a bunch of wrinkled bills from his pocket. No wallet. He hands the money to the waitress and she smiles broadly.

"You come back soon." Hands him a slip of paper. Fingernails painted red and filed sharp.

Allan makes a noncommittal sound and turns his back on her. As he stands, I think I see him wobble ever so slightly. To me, "What's your name again?"

"Andrea?" He's drunker than I thought.

"No! I'm not an idiot. Your last name."

"Hoffman."

He taps his finger to his forehead. "I remember seeing that on an envelope or two."

"And your last name?" I ask.

He shakes his head and then looks over at Sam who is, again, looking at us. "See you tomorrow, Hoffman." And then he swoops down and kisses me firmly on the lips. Lingers just a second. Comes off grinning. Tilts his head toward the bar and says softly, "I win." And turns and walks out.

What the hell! I watch until I see him exit the building and get off my stool and head to the bar. Pretty unsteady from two glasses of wine and the Kamikaze. Sam does not look happy to see me. I point a thumb toward the door. "That's a guy from work. Named Allan."

"Whatever you say," Sam gets busy drying a beer mug.

"Thanks for the shots," I say. Get no response but a blank stare. Feel the color rise in my face. I'm not apologizing for bringing a paying customer into the bar. Sam's not my boyfriend.

Upstairs, I make the frozen pizza. While it's cooking, I stop and remove the slip of ticker tape from my wallet, find the Scotch tape in the junk drawer, and tape the small piece of paper to the fridge under the ten dollar bill I won my first day. I step back to admire the scene, stumbling against the bed. I put a finger to my lips. Where Allan's lips had been. Pretty interesting day.

Chapter 10

*P*er Harold's suggestion, I've been spending every Saturday afternoon of the last five months on my couch reading *Barron's*, a weekly newspaper devoted to economic news and market analysis, trying to improve my finance knowledge. This week, I pick it up at Union Station before I hop on the Burlington Northern train. I'm headed to Downers Grove—the suburb I grew up in, twenty-six miles southwest of Chicago. It's Mom's birthday and tucked in a pocket in my purse is a small box—no wrapping paper. Just a fat gold ribbon tied into a perfect bow. Inside the box, a pair of emerald and pearl earrings to match her green eyes.

I step off the train and immediately hear my oldest brother Jake yell, "Over here! Hey, pinhead." He's standing with my younger brother, Mark, by the family Dodge Dart. They're waving like I'm a kid getting off the bus from summer camp.

"Can you believe Pete gets to bag this gig?" Jake shouts. A few heads turn his way. I hustle over. Peter, the brilliant young surgeon, the youngest brother, couldn't get away from his Milwaukee hospital for the day even though it's Mom's sixtieth birthday.

"We should have been doctors, Jake," I say. No hug from either of them.

"A PhD in electrical engineering. Some moms would be more impressed."

Jake, wearing a faded MIT sweatshirt, pouts like a child even though he turned thirty-four last month.

"Pete's always been the favorite," Mark says. He's the brother who looks most like me. We could both pass for Irish with our fair hair and green eyes.

"Give me a break. Mom thinks you're all royalty. Her brilliant boys. I'm sure the phone lines are hot from the amount of time she's spent bragging about you coming home."

I imitate my mother. "Jake's flying in from California with his wife and my grandson. Mark's making the drive down from Lansing with Geena and the baby. I told them not to bother but they insisted."

"I guess you taking a train in from the city doesn't count," Jake says.

"True." I don't have kids, I don't have a husband. I don't have a PhD. I'm a girl. I don't count."

As soon as we get back to the house, the same house where my three brothers and I were all raised, my brothers grab beers and settle on the screened-in porch talking with my father about an article they had all read in *Scientific American*. No sports small talk for this crowd. I try and spend all of my time in the kitchen so I can avoid my sisters-in-law Rachel and Geena and their fascinating conversations about toddler poop. Not to mention avoiding the actual toddlers. Although the other grown-ups seem fascinated by baby Taylor's efforts to hold things in her tiny hands and examine them, I'm missing the thrill of it. Josh, aged five, is a miniature of his father and seems to think that attending kindergarten at a Montessori school means he's way smarter than me.

"Did you know, Aunt Andrea, that fish breath water through their gills?"

"I did know that, Nephew Josh."

"Why do you call me that?"

"Why do you call me *Aunt* Andrea?"

He launches a miniature dump truck at my head.

I hurry back to the kitchen.

"Did you see how I fixed the couch?" Mom asks.

I take a dish towel out of her hand. "How about you let me do the dishes? Get you out of this hot kitchen on your birthday! You can join Rachel and Geena in the living room."

"If my daughters-in-law have anything to share with me, they can come in."

I nod my agreement but don't want to go there. Instead: "Yes, the couch looks amazing. Magic Marker really is magic."

"Hints from Heloise in the Trib. You should read her." She hands me a pot to put away, says, "Do you ever hear from that Steve character anymore?"

I don't have to try hard to figure out why my Mother connects our threadbare couch with my college boyfriend. The crappy couch reminds her of all the money that went to paying my tuition.

"Not for a long, long time," I tell her.

"Are you dating anyone new?" Mom's hands are in the silverware drawer but her eyes are on me.

"You'd be the first to know," I say. Mercifully, it's time for cake.

I hurry upstairs to retrieve my mom's birthday present. Out of habit, I had left my purse in my bedroom but clearly my room isn't mine anymore. A portable crib is set up for baby Taylor and little Josh will be sleeping in my old twin bed tonight. I'll be going back to my apartment. Pushing aside Taylor's diaper bag and my nephew's Hot Wheels carrying case, I smooth my orange batik bedspread and sit down to listen. Creaky bathroom door. The high-pitched whine the plumbing makes when the hot water runs. So many years of tagging after my brothers. Begging them to let me play. "You can play," they'd say, "but tomorrow you have to be our slave." When they got older they didn't want me around at all—except when their friends came over so they could make fun of me. "Oh, look! Here's old tub of lard. Little lead balloon."

I shift my gaze from the worn green rug, to the yellowing peace sign poster, to my reflection in the full length mirror hanging on the bedroom door. I'm not twelve. Not fat. Not a loser. I see a young woman with a great haircut wearing stylish clothes. I stand up to go downstairs for cake, the elegantly wrapped present in hand.

The presents wait until after we've eaten the cake my mother insisted on baking for herself. I hang on to my small box for Mom to open last. Dad gives her yet another cookbook. Jake has wrapped up a tube of Bengay to go with the gardening tools he bought her. Mark gives her a gigantic sweatshirt that says *University of Michigan Mom* on the front. Whenever my brothers buy Mom clothes, they are always huge. I don't know why they do this. Her personality's large but by any measure, my mother's a small woman.

I had called Pete last week and told him he was buying Mom a silk scarf. I bought it at Marshall Fields, wrapped it, and gave it to my father for the hand off.

"I don't know where he finds the time to be so thoughtful," Mom says, choosing to ignore the absence of a signed card.

I avoid meeting anyone's eyes.

"Do you know what I love?" she says as she folds the wrapping paper that surrounds her. "I love it that my boys didn't delegate the present-buying. You definitely picked these out yourself." She gives them both a kiss. Skips Dad.

I hand her my present. Her eyes light up when she opens the box. "These are lovely, Andrea. But probably way too expensive. You should be saving your money."

When she leaves the room to try them on, Jake walks behind me on the couch and punches me in the arm—hard. He whispers in my ear.

"Way to make the rest of us look bad, pinhead."

My father gets up and starts burning the wrapping paper in the fireplace. It's ninety degrees out but we pay for garbage pickup by the bag and my dad's all about saving money. He's a chemist at Argonne National Laboratory, a government-owned scientific research facility, a job he loves but not one that pays well. That cheap streak of his? It put my brothers and I through college without a ton of student loans.

My brothers, their wives, and the children form little closed subsets in the room. I sit alone on the threadbare couch wondering if maybe I made a wrong choice. Maybe the earrings were too ostentatious. Maybe we weren't the kind of family that gave gifts like this. We were the kind of family that gave each other books and tools and useful things. I thought giving my mom an extravagant gift would make me feel successful. I naively thought my family might be impressed. But leave it to Jake to make me feel like the family idiot once again.

Chapter 11

I stride across the polished lobby this morning, enjoying the click-click of my new Etienne Aigner high heels. Screw my judgmental family. I like this job and I'm good at it.

I wait impatiently for the elevator. My good mood intensifies as I catch one of the bond brokers checking out my legs as we ride up in the elevator together, but it's replaced with confusion the second I enter the office. There's Allan, wearing a navy suit, a creamy white shirt, and a maroon and blue striped tie sitting at the sales desk next to Winston. The mail guy is reading the *Wall Street Journal*. He looks up when I come in.

"You got a haircut," I say.

Allan says nothing. He runs a hand through his newly tamed hair.

"Allan's going to be working with us from now on," Harold says.

"With us?" I repeat. Still not getting this.

"You work for me," Harold said. "Just do your job."

Allan seems to have decided that this conversation is between Harold and me and he goes back to reading the paper. Harold hands me a memo. He has his "I am the boss face" on and I know better than to say more. I scan the page quickly: *As part of the ongoing staff development program, trainee assignments are being rotated. Lloyd Young will transfer from the back office to the bond trading desk, Sam Owens will leave bonds and work as a runner on the options floor, and Allan Mosley will end his rotation in the distribution department and will be a sales trainee in the institutional equity department.* I read and reread the words. I haven't had my coffee yet so I'm slow but I'd have to be an imbecile not to understand. My confusion is replaced with rage. Allan *Mosley*. I've been at this job for six months and no one has mentioned that the mail guy is a Mosley. I spent an hour and a half drinking with him and he didn't mention his name was Mosley. I bet that was fun for him. Slumming. Something to talk to his polo team buddies about over martinis at the club. The story about the nanny and the bus? I *laughed*. Derisively. I told him I wanted to be a salesman and he showed no reaction at all. And now he's got a suit on and he's sitting at a sales desk.

I spend the morning doing my goddamn job.

When Harold announces he has a meeting upstairs, Allan comes over and sits in his chair. AJM is monogrammed on the pocket of his beautifully pressed and starched shirt. Are all his shirts monogrammed? Did I miss that detail when the shirts were wrinkled?

Allan runs his hands through his hair. He probably paid a fortune for that cut.

"This is why I don't like people to know," he says to me. "They act weird."

"Allan, I think I'm perfectly justified in acting weird. This information might have come up last week. I feel really stupid." I am trying to talk softly so Charlene doesn't hear me.

Allan doesn't follow my lead. In a normal tone of voice, he says, "Yeah, well. I'm sorry I guess. You're not the first woman to think I'm an asshole. It was nice that you didn't know. And just for the record, they told me about the switch on Friday. I didn't tell you because I knew you'd be mad. But I didn't really know why you'd be mad so I didn't . . . I didn't say . . . " His voice trails off.

"I'll clue you in then. I'm mad because you let me believe you were working in the mail room when really you were in the management training program. I'm mad because I told you I wanted to be a salesman and you've slid right into my spot and I'm mad because I was starting to think that hard work got you somewhere in this business and now I see that's silly and naïve. It's who you know and always will be."

Charlene's not on the phone. She has her face turned toward her Quotron but I am sure she's listening. It's probably been great fun for her to watch me work my ass off and ingratiate myself with everybody for nothing.

"I only admit that I wasn't totally honest with you," Allan continues. "But it's in no way true that I asked for this job. I don't even want to work here. My family expects it. I wasn't given a choice." He stands up. Tugs at his tie. Looks like he would rather bolt toward the door, but when I start in again, he sighs and sits back down.

"I just want to be clear that I didn't know." I say. "Your last name. Remember, I even asked you at the bar. I don't want you to think I was . . . like . . . you know . . . after you. I mean I've seen you with your girlfriend and all."

"My girlfriend?"

"The tall girl with the short black hair I see you getting into the elevator with."

He looks confused for a minute and then he looks annoyed. "God, Andrea, that's my father's secretary. His office is on the twenty-fifth floor. He sends her to fetch me sometimes when he can't track me down."

Something else to feel stupid about.

Allan stands up again. "You believe what you want to believe. I'll be gone soon. My next rotation will send me to New York."

"Is that what you want?"

"I thought I told you already. What I want has nothing to do with it."

It doesn't look that way from where I am sitting but I nod and start moving papers around. Allan waits a full minute to make sure we're done and then creeps back to his new desk.

The day gets worse. Early in the afternoon, I pick up a call for Bob Parker.

"Bob's not here. Can I take a message?"

"Is this Andrea?" Male voice, pitched kind of high.

"It is."

"Well, this is Frank Kennedy. I was at the Edelweiss luncheon."

I try not to groan. I've heard Bob and Harold talk about this guy. He's a giant mooch. He's getting a divorce and would accept an invitation to hear cats howl Gilbert and Sullivan if it involved free booze and kept him from his empty apartment. I'm pretty sure I can picture him— salmon colored shirt with a white collar, cheap un-shined shoes, too-short tie.

I say, "Can I get you some follow-up information on any of Jim's stocks?"

"No, actually I wanted to ask you a question because, you know, you're cute as a bug's ear."

I hold my breath.

"Would you go out with me sometime?"

Go out with him? He's ancient. Late thirties. Divorced. And he's clearly kind of a dick. "Still there?" he asks, and I realize I haven't answered him.

No way, I think. But.

"I guess so," I say. I know Bob and Harold don't like him but I don't know if he's an important client. I'm afraid to piss him off.

"Saturday night?"

No reasonable excuse pops into my head.

"I guess so," I say.

Harold, who apparently has heard enough of the conversation to figure it out, looks furious when I hang up. "Who was that?"

"Kennedy from Allstate."

"Did that asshole ask you out?"

"Yes."

"Do you want to go out with him?"

"No, but . . . "

"Why didn't you just say no?"

"I don't know. He's a client. I didn't know how to just say no."

"Jesus, Andrea. Call that creep back right now and tell him you're not going out with him. How can someone so smart be so dumb?"

Harold picks up his phone but I just stare at mine. I'm a fool for saying yes and now I have to make a bigger fool of myself by calling back. He's not even Harold's client. I'm not sure why this is Harold's business.

I try to concoct a plausible excuse to give Franklin Kennedy. I decide to go with "I just checked my calendar and I completely forgot I have to go to a wedding this Saturday night." If he asks for a different night, this time I'll be prepared to say I'll have to get back to him.

Before I pick up the phone to call Kennedy back, my phone rings. I pick it up and crisply give the standard Mosely Securities greeting.

It's Charlene. She says, "Nice phone manner. Don't give Kennedy any half-assed excuses. Come right out and tell him that since you're new, you didn't know sales assistants aren't allowed to date clients." Why is she calling me? She could have just turned around.

"You can't let these scumbag clients take advantage of you. If you want to be a salesman, act like one and not a silly schoolgirl. Time to grow up." The phone goes dead.

I don't know if this another one of Charlene's nasty tricks but I dial the number and decide to play it exactly as she told me to.

When I explain why I'm calling, he doesn't sound surprised. I'm guessing I'm not the first cute bug's ear he's tried this on.

"I hope I didn't get you into trouble," he says.

"Not yet," I say. "I think that's why they have this policy."

He laughs hard and loud. A donkey bray. I hold the phone slightly away from my ear.

"You're a funny one. I sure am sorry you can't go out with me. Want to sneak around?"

I express extreme regret.

"Just fooling," he says. "But you should be careful. You don't want to give off the wrong impression."

"Well, gee," I say, "I sure do appreciate your advice." I write *asshole* over and over on my yellow pad.

"See you around," he says.

"Not if I see you first."

He's braying again as I hang up. I stare at Charlene's back. I call her direct line.

"Did it," I say. "Thanks."

She hangs up without saying anything but I see her nod her head slightly.

At noon, Winston stands up and clears his throat. When he sees we're all looking at him, he says, "I'm taking our new team member to my club for lunch." He looks right at me. "Angie, will you tell anyone that calls I'll be back by 1:30?"

I don't bother to correct him for the hundredth time. He knows my name. He's just an ass.

I see a flush creep up Allan's neck. He writes something down and folds the paper before he stands up and slips on his suit jacket.

On his way out, he drops the paper on my desk before he follows Winston to the elevator.

When he is out of sight, I unfold it and read, "I'd rather be having lunch with you."

Chapter 12

I start looking for a new apartment in July and when my lease is up at the end of the month, I move from my sweltering studio to a nicer one bedroom in a small brownstone a dozen blocks north, air conditioners in both the bedroom and the living room. Cranking it up and wearing a sweater in my living room during heat waves makes me feel rich beyond my wildest dreams.

But even going from cool apartment to cool office, there is no getting around the fact that this is summer and I'm working five days a week wearing sticky pantyhose. True, the guys wear suits and ties, but the guys take a lot of days off to golf. I come in every day.

And while each broiling hot day of this summer drags on interminably, the season itself rushes by and I haven't followed up on my plans to go up to Ravinia for a concert, stop in to Streeter's and see if Sam wants to go to a Cubs game with me, reread *The Great Gatsby* down at the Oak Street beach, or spend a hot Sunday afternoon in the cool galleries at the Art Institute. Mostly I work all day and go home and watch TV at night. Weekends, I'm studying for the Series 7 exam.

The most interesting thing about this summer is the relentless flow of news. The Falklands War, the Israeli-Lebanon War, Penn Square Bank going bust, and the country in the worst depression since 1929. The market, which I had been expecting to continue its slide in the face of all these depressing events, actually seems to love this kind of misery and has reversed the six-year bear market and risen ten percent.

I'm learning that stocks don't care what happened in the past. They don't even care what is happening now. The market is totally fixated on what happens next and I'm starting to see the value in this way of thinking.

I take the exam on the second Saturday of August in a large classroom at the Chicago Board of Trade building with twenty other hopefuls. One other woman. It's long but it's not tricky and I leave feeling good.

Harold gets an interoffice envelope mid-morning. Scans the contents and tosses it to me. "You passed. Congratulations."

I'd been confidant but still a rush of relief sweeps over me. And joy. "Do I get some accounts now?"

"No. You get to buy drinks at the Tower Club after the close. Be patient about the accounts."

I can't stop smiling. This means someday, I'll get my own accounts. I know it does. On the way to the bathroom, I stop by Allan's desk. "I did it. Passed on the first try."

"Never a doubt in my mind," he said.

Mahoney, Harold, Bob, Allan, and even Charlene and Winston join me at The Tower Club, a restaurant located not at the top of the building but in the lobby, after the close. It's early and there's plenty of room around the polished ebony bar.

Attempting to be sophisticated, I order a whiskey sour.

Harold turns to the bartender. "Give her a Dewars with a splash. No fruit drinks, Andrea. This isn't a bar mitzvah."

Drinking. Something else I am going to have to get better at. My scotch tastes like burnt floor cleaner but no one seems to notice I'm making a slow go at it. Except Charlene. She raises her glass of clear liquid when I glance her way.

"Maybe try vodka, next time."

I'm afraid she's mocking me but then she gives a little head nod and adds, "Good job on the 7, girl" before she resumes her conversation with the bartender.

Winston, a more likable guy with a few drinks in him, surprises me by revealing that there was no betting action on my passing the test. Nobody wanted the other side. I'm touched by their faith. One by one they drift out, leaving me the biggest bar bill I've ever paid but I'm happy to do it.

Allan hangs around to walk out with me. Now that I'm registered and Allan is not, I should be his senior. But he's an assistant salesman and I'm still a sales assistant. The difference being that he doesn't file, gets paid more, and is in line for a permanent sales position. And then there's the other small detail. He's a Mosley and most likely will be my boss one day. But job jealousy aside, I do like Allan even though he's weird. When we hit the sidewalk, he stops.

"I forgot something inside. Thanks for the drink." He turns back and disappears through the revolving doors. Gone. The kiss in the bar? The nice note about lunch? I expected follow-up. But it's like they never happened.

Chapter 13

Grey clouds hover outside the windows. In a few weeks, those clouds will drop snow but it's unusually warm for early December and today's forecast is for rain. I love the office on a rainy day. The sound of the rain pelting against the windows mixing with the hum of the machines. The green symbols on the Quotrons glow just a little brighter on the black screen without the sun streaming in.

I walk into an empty room. Suit coats hang on the back of Winston's, Allan's, Bob's, and Harold's chairs. Newspapers neatly folded on their desks. Charlene's handbag, black patent leather with beige leather trim, is tucked under her station. Mahoney's slippers are lined up under his desk, the surface of his desk is clean except for a piece of paper taped to his phone console: "Gone fishing." He's spending a week in a rustic cabin on Lake Seminole in Georgia. When he left on Friday, he looked positively giddy—babbling about topwater frogs and lipless crankbaits. I'm confused about why anyone voluntarily goes to Georgia and totally ignorant about the joys of bass fishing but I'm happy he was so happy. I wander into the break room and find everyone there. They wave their mugs at me in greeting. It's weekend recap time.

"So anyway," Bob's saying, today's tie a veritable vomit of purple and green, "there must have been seven guys there all named Bob." He turns to me. "My wife's cousin's wedding. In Milwaukee." He resumes the story. "So you know how it is. It's too confusing with all these Bobs. Pretty soon they're all getting a new name. The really tall guy is now being referred to as Tall Bob and the groom's friend is now Best Man Bob. All the Bobs get nicknames but me. I'm just Bob. It's not like I didn't try but nothing stuck. At the end of the night, I'm still just Bob."

Winston asks, "Open bar?"

"Just kegs and jug wine."

"Barbaric." Winston shudders.

"It was Milwaukee."

Charlene, wearing a navy linen shift dress that perfectly fits on her tall slim frame, says, "At least you weren't Dead Drunk Bob or Fat Ass Bob." Taking Bob's stories seriously was her way of being nice to him. He had two accounts that gave her lots of business.

"Just Bob," Bob says again and walks morosely back to his desk.

At ten-thirty, Charlene motions Harold to follow her into the glass-enclosed office. It's the first time I've seen anyone set foot in there. Against the pouring rain, the little room glows. Charlene, perched on the desk, waves her hands emphatically. Harold sits on one of the chairs with his back to me. I scan my memory of the last few days but I can't come up with anything that I've done to set her off. What do they have to talk about that the rest of us shouldn't hear?

Harold pats Charlene's arm on his way out and heads straight to my desk. Crap. I'm wrong. I have done something. My stomach tightens up and I set my teeth together hard.

"Did anyone from the Harris bank call?"

"While you were talking to Charlene? No, no one called."

"If anyone calls from the Harris, I want you to get me off the phone. Immediately."

So it wasn't about me. I need to be less paranoid.

Whenever his phone rings, Charlene turns around to look at Harold. He shakes his head and she turns back to her desk. I notice she's not making calls and when someone calls her, she responds efficiently and goes back to staring at the lights on her board.

The squawk from New York. The unmistakable New York accent of the head block trader: "Chicago? I'm holding my dick here. Anything?"

Charlene picks it up. "Stay hard, Jay. Nothing yet."

Charlene turns around for the hundredth time. "Harold, can you call them or something?"

"I left a message for the analyst to call me the minute he gets out of the meeting."

At noon, Harold tells me to go get him a ham and swiss on rye from the deli in the lobby. This is the first time since I've been here that Harold has not gone out to lunch.

When I get back, I ask him if the call he'd been waiting for has come in.

"Not a goddamned word." He thanks me for the sandwich but he doesn't eat it. It sits on his desk next to this morning's cold coffee. I'm enjoying a large mouthful of my tuna sandwich when the phone rings. Harold's line. Charlene swivels. It rings again. Harold is just looking at it. "Want me to get it?" I ask, half choking.

"Lucky three," he says and picks it up after the next ring. "Harold Stackman . . . OK . . . I understand." He hangs up the phone and lights another cigarette even though he has one still burning in his ashtray. "Charlene, darling," he pauses. She looks ready to spring at him. He inhales and says, "Fasten your seat belt. The committee says 'go.' They're walking it to the desk right now."

She's already turning around, asking, "Does it have my name on it?"

"It's yours to lose."

Harold unwraps his sandwich and inhales it like he's starving.

Charlene picks up her phone and hits the direct line to the New York trading desk. "Jay, it's on. I need to say something *now*."

She hangs up from New York and picks up the direct line to the Harris bank. One deep breath and when they answer, she's casual as shorts at a funeral.

"Hey, we got a red light special over here. We're a size buyer of all the banks." She hangs up. "Let's see what that brings back. It ought to take them a minute or two." She's on her feet and headed to the door. "I have to pee and once this gets going, my butt's not leaving this chair."

Harold shakes his head. "Learn to piss in a bottle like guys do. If you miss this call . . . " But he's talking to an empty doorway.

Winston shakes his head. "Charlene really doesn't look like the kind of woman who even has a bladder."

"I'm trying to eat my lunch here," I say.

"Shit." Harold screams, staring at Charlene's desk. Harold never screams.

The Harris light is blinking.

I look at the door. Charlene's not rounding the corner. I see panic on Harold's face.

They'll just call someone else, I think. I've been told this a hundred times. *They'll just call someone else*.

The light's still on. Harold isn't moving. Charlene isn't coming. I jump out of my chair, trip over my garbage can, and smash my elbow on the edge of her desk, but I manage to grab the phone and push the Harris key. "Hi, there," I say.

I hear a man say "Charlene?" and I say "Choking . . . just a second" in a strangled voice that I don't have to fake. I cough a little too, and then I see Charlene fly back across the room. She rips the phone out of my hand, pushes me aside with a hip check, and clears her throat to provide some continuity before she says, "All better, sugar. I got so excited when I saw your light go on, I swallowed my gum. What can I do for you?"

It's already been two hours since the first phone call and Charlene's been glued to her phone negotiating between her client and our New York traders. Harold paces behind his desk and finishes a pack of cigarettes and starts a new one. When he leaves the room to pace the hall for a change, I empty his overflowing ashtray. Then I go and get Charlene a Tab. The other guys stay on their phones. There's nothing they can do to help and plenty of things they can do to be annoying. Best to stay out of the way.

At two-twenty-five, I see Charlene nod and hang up. She bows her head, still and quiet. Finally, she sighs and gives herself a little shake and turns to face Harold. Her blue eyes are filled with tears, a sight I thought I'd never see. She shrugs and Harold nods.

"You did your best, kiddo," he says.

Charlene turns back to her desk, picks up the squawk box, and yells so loud I think they could have heard it in New York without the electronics. "Print it you cock-sucking mother fuckers. It's done!"

Harold leaps up from his desk and the trash can goes over for the second time today as he hurtles toward Charlene, grabs her out of her chair, and swings her around like a toddler. Winston and Bob come over and hug her and Allan stands awkwardly by me and we all look up at the ticker. The squawk crackles. It's the head trader, Jay. "Mosley humps one and all. Hang on to your balls and watch the tape. A beautiful fucking sight!" And together we watch in silence as the numbers and letters travel all the way across the screen.

One million shares of First National Bank of New York sold and one million shares of Colgate bought to replace it. Bob lets out a long whistle and the shouting begins. We're all jumping up and down and yelling and then as word spreads to the retail office, we can hear them down the hall too. The story comes across the newswire. Mosley Securities prints the biggest block trade ever in the history of the New York Stock Exchange.

Charlene looks over to me but I'm busy answering the phones, which are going berserk. Her eyes land on Allan standing by my desk.

"Go," she says to him. "Liquor store. Champagne. Now."

She starts to fumble in her purse for her wallet but Allan holds up his hand and shakes his head. Slips into his Burberry raincoat, grabs his big black umbrella, and takes off like he is used to being ordered around.

The next time I look up from the phones, he's back with four bottles of Dom Perignon and a sleeve of plastic glasses. He sets everything on Mahoney's empty desk. Poor Mahoney sitting in a row boat in the middle of a lake oblivious to all this, happy because he caught a ten-pound big mouthed bass.

Harold puts down his phone and pops the cork on the first bottle. He pours out six glasses and then holds his high.

"To Charlene," he says. "A fabulous trader and a magnificent woman." He bends from the waist in a courtly bow.

Charlene blushes. Blushes! "Ah, you'd say the same of Lizzie Borden if she made you money but hey, nice trade, you old fart." Charlene clinks with him and finishes half her Champagne in one swallow. Then she lowers her glass and turns to me, "Didn't I tell you to keep the fuck away from my phones?"

Oh shit. "I don't know what got into me," I say. "I saw the light and I just . . . "

"Well, fuck that shit!" Charlene cries. "You're my best bitch now!" She rams her glass against mine and spills the rest of her Champagne over the both of us, all the men laughing.

Harold pulls his checkbook out of his briefcase. He writes the information quickly and tears the check off and hands it to me. Andrea Hoffman. One thousand dollars.

The paper trembles in my hand. My voice cracks. "You must be joking. A thousand dollars? I can't take this."

"Sure you can. Get yourself some acting lessons," he says. "That was the worst impression of Charlene I've ever heard." I start to shake my head and hand it back to him but he says, "Take it. A bonus. I figure I made about fifty grand today because you answered the phone. Be a man, Andrea. Just take it."

"If it makes you happy," I say, putting it in my pocket. We all drink more champagne. The head of the Chicago office shows up. He drinks, too. Harold's phone rings and I break away from the group to answer it.

"Harold, you need to take this one."

Harold comes over and picks up his phone.

I rejoin the group. They look at me with curiosity.

"His wife?" Bob asks.

I look toward Allan. "Your dad."

We all end up down at the Tower Club. Leaning against the black bar, his silver hair aglow from the reflected light from the wall of backlit premium liquor, Harold is clearly the host. He's smoking a huge cigar and drinking a martini with olives the size of walnuts.

"Whiskey Sour, Andrea?" he asks.

"This isn't a damn bar mitzvah," I say.

Everyone laughs. Harold hands me a Dewar's. My first sip is delicious. Charlene is drinking a vodka tonic. She looks different than she does in the office. She's smiling a real smile—the kind that means you're happy and not just planning something evil. The guys hover around her. When they talk, they lean toward her to make sure she's listening. I hadn't realized how young Winston and Bob are. Barely thirty. Allan, holding a highball instead of a beer, looks like he belongs in this group. When Charlene talks, the men seem to stop breathing. Except for Allan. Whenever I look at him, he's looking at me. I bum a cigarette off Winston, and Allan steps in to light it for me. He doesn't step back and now he's close enough that if I shift my weight I can brush up against him.

Some traders come in from First National and then some from the Illinois State Board and they offer congratulations and get free drinks and they're followed by guys from Bear Sterns and Dean Witter and eventually all the newcomers surround Harold and Charlene. Allan and I are pushed further from the group.

"Want to sit down?" he asks.

"I might not be able to get up again. The cleaning staff will find me here in the morning," I say and drop onto the soft grey leather of the booth.

A waitress delivers more drinks and I look up to see Harold scanning the room. He spots me and his eyes flick to Allan and back to me. Perhaps a slight raise of his eyebrows before he turns back to face the group of traders.

I sip my drink, perfectly happy for once not to be making conversation. The last time I felt so elated was after Brandeis won the NCAA soccer championship. Division three but still a huge thrill. I was at a post-game party with a huge crowd of people, pure joy. Granted it was grain alcohol punch enhanced happiness. Old boyfriend Steve, not yet an asshole, was so wrecked.

"We should get married," he slurred.

"Ask me when you're sober," I said. But of course he never did.

Allan leans in close to my ear. It's gotten very loud in here. I get a whiff of his aftershave. Woodsy. Unexpected. "What'cha thinking?" he says.

"My asshole ex-boyfriend. I was thinking about how much I wish I could tell him about this."

"Why?"

"Well, it's not like this is going to mean anything to my family. I haven't discovered a new trans-uranium element. And my high school friends? It would sound like bragging."

"But it's not obnoxious to tell the college dick?"

"Of course! That's the point. He would understand how historic this day was for me and he'd be crazy-ass jealous. He'd burn with envy."

Allan raises his glass and tips it toward mine. "To revenge!"

I lift my glass. Take a drink. Sigh. "I don't think I can finish this one," I say.

"Nonsense," Allan says. "It's a sin to leave a drink unfinished." He motions for me to join him on his side of the booth. I get up and slide in. Our backs to the crowd.

He pulls a small bottle out of his pocket and a tiny silver spoon. "Let's get you back in the party." He holds the spoon heaping with white powder under my nose. I inhale. A small amount of powder falls on the table and Allan dips his finger in it and then puts his finger in my mouth and rubs it against my gums. Bitter. My gums tingle where he touched them. I shudder slightly and then grin as my head starts to sparkle.

"You good?" he asks before he helps himself.

I turn my head and scan the room. No one is looking our way. I laugh. "Yes, I'm good. Pretty fucking great." I toss down the rest of the scotch.

"We should get you out of here," he says, putting his little brown bottle back in his pocket. Pushing me gently out of the booth.

We make our way back to the bar. The goodbyes take time, as Charlene insists on introducing me to everyone around her. It's a big crowd. All of them happy to meet the girl who answered the phone. I'm smiling too much. They're too drunk to care.

Harold pats me on the head. "Get in on time tomorrow. Pros play hurt."

I nod and leave the bar, concentrating on placing one foot in front of the other.

The rain has slowed to a drizzle. Allan flags the cab and when it stops, I open the door, drop in, and he gets in and sits down practically on top of me.

"Where to?" the driver asks. I glance at the name on his license. Lots of vowels. Greek maybe.

"We're not sure yet. Why don't you just head north up Wells and we'll decide," Allan says.

The driver drops the flag. I see his smile in the rearview mirror. The radio on low. Bobby Darrin massacring *If I was a Carpenter*.

"107 Cedar street." I say.

Allan says, "I thought you lived on Chicago Avenue." He shakes his head. "Anyway, you're not going home. We need to get some food into you."

"I'm not hungry." The coke. "And I moved. Like three months ago. We're on a need-to-know basis, Allan. I mean, I don't know where you live."

I turn my head to give Allan a good long look. His tie is off. A second shirt button is undone. His pupils are huge in the dim light of the cab. I giggle.

"What's funny?" he asks.

"Your pupils," I say.

He puts a hand under my chin and tilts my head up. Looks close. "Yours too."

I can feel every place our legs and hips are touching. I put my hands on Allan's chest, feeling hard muscle under the smooth cool fabric of his expensive shirt. The smell of his aftershave mixes with our boozy breath. I want to stay in the back seat of this cab forever.

The cab crosses over the Chicago River and the cab driver asks, "Any consensus on your destination yet?" New song. Better one. *Ferry across the Mersey*.

"I'm drunk," I inform him.

"Do you need me to pull over?"

"No, I'm not sick. Just tispy . . . *tip*sy."

The driver checks me out in the mirror. Nods and then returns his eyes to the road just in time to see the brake lights of the Chevy Impala in front of us illuminate and he slams his brakes to keep from driving right up into its spacious trunk. I land on top of Allan on the floor of the taxi.

"Sorry folks. Everybody okay back there?"

"We're good," Allan says. "Why don't you just . . . "

"I know. I'll just keep driving."

I shift so we're nearly nose to nose. I'm confused as to why Allan seems perfectly comfortable lying on the filthy floor of this cab, headed nowhere with shitty old pop music playing on the radio. And why isn't he trying to kiss me? So fucking annoying. I push myself back onto the seat, concentrating on avoiding kneeing him in the nuts.

"Just to be clear," I say, "I'm not sure I like you all that much. You stole my fucking job right from under my fucking nose, you Mosley shit head."

He joins me on the bench. Farther away now. "I'm flattered by your honesty," he says. "Also a bit shocked by your new vocabulary. But I'm not stealing your job. In three months I'll be transferred to bonds or move to New York and Jesus, Hoffman." He pauses. "Don't you know that everybody in the office loves you?"

It's really much too warm in this cab. My head is spinning. "Really? Do *you* love me? Cause I'm not interested in going out to eat with you right now. Right now, I want to take you home. I live at 107 Cedar Street." I tap on the glass to make sure the driver heard me. "Got that?" I lean close to Allan and whisper. "I want us to get naked and fall into my bed and . . . "

"Andrea!" Allan touches my lips with his index finger. "Stop. You don't like me. You just said so. You really don't want to sleep with me."

I nod vigorously. "I do. I really do. Since the first time I saw you. Fucking mail boy. You're so god. damn. good. looking."

"No," he says. "You're really drunk. It was an exciting day and I probably shouldn't have given you the . . . "

It's ridiculously fucking hot in this cab. Allan's voice is starting to sound extremely far away. I close my eyes to try and focus on his words, but . . .

Chapter 14

I wake up as hung over as I have ever been in my life—thumping head, burning eyes, fat tongue, dead dog breath, and for some reason my left big toe is throbbing. But even though I wake up nauseous and exhausted with no memory of how I ended up in my own bed, I don't wake up mortified because I wake up alone.

So, incapacitated or not, after an ice-cold shower and a double Alka-Seltzer, I'm in the office a full thirty seconds before seven and so is everybody else. Allan looks relieved that I showed up. I shoot him an apologetic look. I'm not sure what I'm apologizing for but the last thing I remember was me in the cab begging him to rock my world. He waves me off and gives me a thumbs up. A thumbs up? What is that supposed to mean? I catch Charlene observing our exchange with a little smile. She looks fresh and well-rested, wearing a rose-colored blouse that perfectly matches her lipstick. Wearing gray to match my skin tone was not a wise fashion choice. I look as dead as I feel. The office is library quiet. The boys have their heads buried in their newspapers but I suspect they're suffering from their own health calamities. Harold did his best to help by bringing in a dozen donuts and a jumbo bottle of aspirin—leaving them on Mahoney's empty desk for everyone's consumption. By the time I get to the goodies, I'm left with the choice between plain, coconut, and a jelly cruller with a hunk taken out of it. Clearly the early bird gets the chocolate.

I wait until Harold finishes his morning calls and then I pull out the check.

"This was a joke, right?"

Harold takes his time lighting a cigarette before he says, "You've heard of the Super Bowl, yes?"

"Football. Yes. I know about the Super Bowl."

"When they hand out Super Bowl rings, everybody on the team gets one. Not just the starters. Everybody on the team—the players, the coaching staff, even the water boy. You're on the winning team, Andrea." He stares me down, making sure I get what he's saying. I nod, and satisfied he adds, "And now you need to get to work. I want to see those trade tallies."

I try to focus and add up all the numbers. Winston and Bob are going to be ecstatic to see that they had customers who participated in the big trade as well—buying pieces of what Harold's client was selling and vice versa. The numbers I write down for Charlene and Harold are truly staggering. Two million shares at nine cents a share totals $180,000 dollars! I don't know how their share is going to be divvied up but they each made more money yesterday than I will this year. When I'm finished, I just stare at my Quotron trying to imagine what I would do with that kind of cash. A cruise in Greece or replace Mom's couch? With that kind of money, I could do both. I pick up the phone and call my mom at work.

She answers with a short, "Helen Hoffman. Can I help you?"

"Hi, Mom. How's it going?" I give her a chance to talk before I hit her with my big trade news.

"Not great. It's finally happened. Your father's just been fired . . . laid off . . . however I'm supposed to say it."

I'm shocked but I'm not shocked. The news reports about Reagan cutting the budget for pure scientific research have been circulating for months and my mother's been hounding my father like Lady Macbeth to try and protect himself.

"Poor Dad," I say. "He loves that job so much."

"Well, if he loved it so much, he should have done somethings to make sure he kept it . . . like moved into weapons research. Plenty of money for those guys. Sid and Stan didn't get let go."

"Is he home? Should I call?"

"He has three months to finish up his project and look for another job so no, he's not home. He's at the lab."

"I'm really sorry, Mom. I can help. I want to. All that tuition you paid. I've always considered it a loan. I'll start paying it back."

After a brief silence she says, "Maybe now would be a good time for that."

"Check's in the mail," I say, trying to sound cheerful but thrown by the fact she didn't even try to resist my offer.

I hear voices in her office. "I should go," she says. "Were you calling for a reason, Andrea? Is everything alright?"

"Everything's fine," I say. "I'm fine. Work's fine. Just checking in."

"That's nice," she says. "I'm glad your little job is turning out to be fun."

———

At the end of the day, Allan stops by Harold's desk.

"I'm flying to New York tonight. I'll have to miss work tomorrow."

"Everything okay?" Harold says.

"It's a family thing—a command performance. I'll be in Monday."

Harold nods and goes back to his phone calls.

Allan stops in front of my desk. I raise my eyebrows and wait but he stays silent.

"Have a good trip," I say.

"I guess," he says, and turns and leaves the office.

All day long I'd been dreaming about getting home and falling into bed, but now the day is done and I'm in a cab, I change my mind. I tell the driver to go to Chicago and Wabash. It's been a long time since my last visit to Streeter's.

The place, decked out with lights and fake pine boughs for Christmas, is mobbed with Northwestern's law and med students since it's Thursday night with half-priced pitchers until nine. I push through the crowd toward the bar and feel a little out of place in my suit and heeled boots among the blue jeans and sneakers. I see Sam drawing beers behind the bar.

"I'll take one of those when you have a second," I say.

If he's surprised to see me, he doesn't show it. "We've missed you around here," he says.

"I've missed you too, but work's been busy and . . . I moved." I feel a little disloyal saying it.

He delivers the beer, shouts over the crowd noise. "They must have a good beauty parlor in your new neighborhood. Your hair style got an upgrade."

"Yeah," I say, "that's what happens when you get an office job."

". . . and the switch to beer? Job related as well?"

"Nah, I'm just trying to impress you."

A waitress I've never seen signals Sam that she's got drink orders and Sam moves down to the end of the bar.

I don't really want the beer, but I sip at it as I look around. The guy next to me jostles my elbow and then apologizes profusely.

"Sorry. Hope I didn't spill anything on you. That's a really nice suit."

He's not completely unattractive. His straight, unnaturally white teeth lead me to believe he's a dental student. He's wearing a Blackhawks t-shirt. And flip-flops. In December.

"No big deal. It's crowded in here." I turn back to the bar.

"I'm George," he says to the back of my head.

I try to catch Sam's eye to come save me. He's got a half-filled beer glass in his hand but he's stopped the pour to listen to a girl sitting in front of him in tight jeans with long blond hair. I could try and fool myself that he's so close to her because it's loud in here but there is no denying that he's looking at her the same way he always looked at my onion rings. I can sense George still standing next to me. The juke box is playing *Rock the Casbah,* which is my second least favorite rock song ever and I really don't have the stomach to drink this beer. I pick up my briefcase.

"Leaving so soon?" George the dental student hockey fan says.

"I have a date," I say. I try to smile at him. He's harmless, but he's just too late. A year or two ago, I would've been interested. Now, hanging around in this bar talking to someone who's still in school is a lot less appealing than a couple more Tylenol and a takeout box of Popeye's fried chicken. I need to get home. I have work tomorrow.

I fish a twenty dollar bill out of my purse and leave it on the bar. I hope Sam realizes it's from me. A small payback for all the freebies in the past.

The bouncer opens the door for me. "Stay safe out there," he says as I exit the bar, head up the street and on to my new neighborhood.

Chapter 15

Since I started this job, the stock market has been on a tear. The Dow Jones Industrial Average, a group of thirty stocks that represent the market as a whole, was at 820 when I started in March. Nine months, it's fluctuating around 1000. Personally, I don't own a single share of stock but the strong market is definitely putting me and everyone else in a holiday mood. And when the office and the clients are happy, I'm happy. Today Winston arrived wearing red corduroy pants and a green sweater with a pine tree motif. Bob came in white wool slacks and a blue snowflake patterned turtleneck.

"Is the circus in town?" Charlene says as she passes them on the way to the break room.

"The client Christmas luncheon at my club. My clients are counting on it."

"Yes, well hopefully they'll be paying for it too. Market closes at three-thirty, boys. Make sure they get their orders in."

When only the smell of her perfume remains in the room, Winston says, "Can you imagine being married to her? Ball-busting from morning to night."

By mid-morning, I'm reading an industry report about rate increases for electric utilities when Charlene stands up and stretches.

"I've got to take a pit stop. Grab my phones for me, will you, Andrea?"

I look at Harold, in a charcoal grey suit and tie, to see if he can give me a hint as to whether she is joking or not, but he just shrugs.

"Sure thing," I say. I stare at the phones and pray no keys light up, and yet, two minutes later when Charlene reappears, I'm a little disappointed to tell her no one called.

At two o'clock with just an hour and a half of trading to go, I happen to look up at the news tape. Oil prices flash by. A volume update and then . . . *Shearson to acquire Mosley Securities.* Harold's on the phone.

"Harold!" I wave and point. Harold reads the headline and quickly ends his call.

The office is completely silent. The three of us stare at the tape even though the news story is gone. No phones are ringing. The silence extends into the retail bull pen and through the bond department. No sounds float down the hall. I look at Allan's empty desk. He's in New York on family business. Selling the family business. Did he know this when he left?

"What does this mean? We're being bought by Shearson? Are we all rich?" I ask Harold, hopeful.

"No, we're not all rich," he says. "Allan and the whole goddamn Mosley family are rich. I guess I should say richer. The rest of us? We're all just fucked."

Chapter 16

After the Mosley merger was announced, the phones went crazy. Everybody called wanting to know what we knew, which was nothing. But after a day or two, the phones stopped ringing. Mosley was history. Shearson bought the company for the investment banking relationships and the high asset retail clients. They already had a fully stocked institutional equity division. Our salesmen and traders were, in most areas, redundant and one by one they found other jobs and packed up and left. Harold, Bob, and Charlene went as a package deal to Kendall-Fitzgerald, a medium sized firm that was looking to set up a regional office in Chicago. Non-producing personnel—that would be me since I didn't have any accounts assigned to me yet—weren't part of the deal. Harold took nothing that didn't fit in his briefcase and was out the door ten minutes after he called New York to tell him that he was quitting. I got a handshake and a "Good Luck" and was left sitting furious and terrified at my desk in the rapidly emptying office. I didn't know what was going to happen to me and I had no one to ask.

Charlene was apparently not big on goodbyes. When I got to the office the next morning, she had already come, cleaned out her desk, and left. She called later in the day.

"Did I leave my black patent leather Charles Jourdans under my desk?"

I stood up and looked.

"No, I don't see them," I said.

"Shit," she said, and hung up the phone.

Bob Parker came in later in the morning to pack. Not wearing a tie. On his way out, he stopped by my desk and thanked me for my help. Bob was, as my mother would say, a mensch.

Mahoney took his slippers, his "I'd rather be fishing" mug, and a fat lump sum payment and retired.

"This is a young man's game," he said. He was a classy old guy and I was sad to see him go.

Winston decided he could make more money as a broker for his rich friends and he went over to Shearson's retail office. I wasn't sad to see *him* go.

The good news is that it's been weeks and no one has gotten around to firing me. Christmas and New Year's came and went and my paycheck keeps showing up, so I come in and sit at my desk in the empty room and answer the occasional phone call. Sitting alone in the glass room, I've finished *Madame Bovary* and *The Grapes of Wrath*, two books I'd promised myself I'd read if I had the time. *Moby Dick* waits but I hope that something happens to me soon, because honestly, I'm sick of this self-improvement plan and would rather be talking to clients about paper and forest product stocks. Sometimes Allan comes in and sits in Harold's chair and we talk. I gather that the deal put some serious cash into his trust fund.

"Aren't you going to go work at Shearson?" I ask.

"Dad's on the board and they gave him some bullshit title and a plush office but I wasn't part of the deal."

"You can apply for a job at another brokerage firm," I suggest.

"Don't be ridiculous. Apply for a job?" he says. "Doing what?" We both stare at the ticker. All those trades being done by someone else.

"*You* could apply to another brokerage firm," he points out to me. "You're the one who's registered. You know plenty of clients who would give you a recommendation."

"I'll do that if I need to," I say. "I'm waiting to see what Shearson has in mind for me."

Allan opens Harold's desk drawer. Rummages among the dry pens and dull pencils. Looking for God know what. I've already taken everything useful. "I guess I'll run the Foundation," he finally says.

"What exactly does that mean?"

"My family set up a charity with some of the money we made off the merger. First off, the money has to be invested and eventually there will be decisions that need to be made about who gets the grants. It wouldn't just be me. There's a board of directors, of course."

"Holy shit," I say. "And you'd do what exactly?"

"Dad wants me to be the Executive Director."

"You'd run the whole thing? The most responsible thing my father ever asked me to do was put gas in the car. Why are you still sitting here?"

Allan brushes his hair out of his face. He hasn't been bothering with the suit and tie since the merger. He's back to his mail boy jeans and wrinkled shirts. "Scared shitless," he says.

"I'm sure you can handle the job. You're a smart guy. Not that you make it obvious."

"I know I can do the job," Allan says. "I've been a junior board member on our other foundation since I was thirteen. My parents have a Kennedy fixation. You know, 'From those who have been given much, much is expected'. No, I can do it. I'll be good at it."

"So what's the problem? You're going to get paid to invest money and give it away. What a great job. You'll make people happy. You'll be a real life Santa Claus."

"Andrea, do you have a big Thanksgiving dinner?"

"Damn if you aren't the king of the land of non sequiturs," I say. "And yes, pretty big."

"Do you have a separate table for the kids?"

"You bet we do, and I'm still sitting at it. I'm twenty-five years old and still at the kids' table. It's humiliating."

Allan shakes his head. "We have huge Thanksgiving dinners. The adults sit in the dining room and the table is spectacular. Mother goes all out with the towering flower arrangements, gleaming silver, the pressed Irish linens, the Wedgwood dishes and the Waterford glassware. The help serves in white gloves." He pauses. "Mom gives them a complete dinner to take home when we—when they are done for the night." He searches my face to gauge my reaction. I shrug. I do think it's crappy to make people work on Thanksgiving but it's not his fault. He rubs the day-old beard on his chin and continues, "Lit candles in tall candelabras. I know it's decadent but it's also really beautiful." His turn to shrug. "Anyway, the kids eat off a buffet in the conservatory and just generally run amok. When I was younger, I would eat fast and then perch on the stairs where I could get a good view of the grown-ups. I couldn't wait to be there. They looked so sophisticated, so important. But now it's my turn and I'm not ready. All of a sudden the folks at the grown-up table seem trapped there, and it's the kids running around the house who seem like the lucky ones. I just thought I'd have more time. I feel like as soon as I take this job, I'm done. Locked in. Fun's over."

Now I'm also shaking my head. We must look like a couple of metronomes. I'm a little stuck on the fact they have a conservatory like they live in the house from the

game of Clue but I get past it and say, "Allan, it's an opportunity. An awesome opportunity. Don't be such an ass.
You'll still have your whole life ahead of you. It's just a
job. You're not joining the priesthood. But if it really isn't
something you are interested in, don't do it."

Allan looks at his watch which I've learned is a Patek
Philippe worth more than a studio condo in a decent neighborhood. "Let's go drink," he says.

"What the hell," I say. "Cocktails. For sure. I need the
practice."

Chapter 17

I t's only a three block walk from Mosely to the Shearson offices on south LaSalle Street, but I trudge down the sidewalk like a dead man walking. I didn't want it to last—this employment limbo I'm in—but now that the personnel department has summoned me to their offices, I'm terrified. This could be my last day. I should have been actively looking for something else. Asking clients about job opportunities. Putting together a resume. Why had I thought waiting was my best option?

I check the building numbers and find the address I need on a classic Burnham and Root building from the late 1800s. Instead of chrome and glass, the elevators are paneled in dark wood. The walls of the corridors are hung with paintings of rural American landscapes in heavy gilded frames. The reception area's furniture is ornate and somewhat uncomfortable. The lighting is subdued. A small, tasteful fresh flower arrangement sits on the reception desk. All the nearby doors are closed.

The woman from personnel who takes me into her office is not much older than me but she dresses like she's middle-aged. Black suit, high collar blouse. Her hair is pulled back in a wide black velvet barrette and her sturdy black shoes with the one-inch heels are what we call in my house bubbe shukh—grandmother shoes. I'm pretty sure she's judging me by my burgundy snakeskin slingbacks. Not a great choice for a snowy day.

We settle in her office and she starts her routine. She smiles (coolly) and we shake hands (limply). We exchange names. She examines the manila folder that holds my employment record. Finally, she looks up and asks what it is I would like to do at Shearson.

"I'd like a job as an institutional salesman. I have my Series 7 license and I've been backing up the salesmen in my office, so I am familiar with all the regional accounts. Of course, I expect that I'd start out as a back-up again and work my way up."

"Let's start with the typing test," she says.

I push back on this plan. "I know my current job title is Sales Assistant but I have significantly expanded my duties at Mosley and I think it would be more correct to say I have been a Sales *Associate* for the last few months. I make calls to clients and attend meetings . . . " I lean forward in my chair and look directly into her eyes, "I see this merger as a good opportunity for me to advance."

"We all have to start somewhere," she says. She smiles again and this time I see a bit of lettuce stuck in between her upper canine and incisor teeth. She hands me a blank piece of paper and gives me a minute to practice. Maybe if the Equal Rights Amendment hadn't died just this summer, I'd have had a stronger case. I stuff the paper in the big blue IBM Selectric, flip the power switch, and start to type. My fingers fly over the keys.

CRAP. I am not a fucking secretary I don't get piad to type I am not interesssttted in this shhit shit i wonder when the lasttime they gave a godddamn male a tyoing test

Ms. Cain pulls the paper out of the typewriter and looks at it before I can snatch it back or explain myself. She's taking enough time to read it through twice and for me to regret being such a wise-ass. She crumples it up and tosses it with a high arch into a wastepaper basket a good fifteen feet away. She walks over to her door and closes it and then sits down in the chair across from me and grins. I'm stupefied. It's like when Pinocchio becomes a real boy.

"Did you ever hear about that woman from Harvard Business School who went to Goldman Sachs for an interview and they wanted her to take a typing test?" she asks.

I shake my head.

"She naturally refused and the guy said, 'What's the matter? Can't you type?' And she said, 'Of course I can type. I can screw too, but I'm not ever going to do either of those things for a living.' Ballsy, huh?"

I laugh. "I wonder if they gave her a job," I say.

"No way. They're chauvinist pigs around there. Here too. No offense, I hope. About making you do the typing. They insist I give all females the typing test. I'll say you passed."

I'm offered the job as sales assistant for the manager of the Shearson Institutional Equity department. "What happened to his last assistant?" I ask hopefully. "Was she promoted?"

"Maternity leave."

I accept. It's the same job I started with Harold. But as soon as I meet my new boss, I know this guy isn't Harold. And I'm not the girl from the dress shop anymore. Now I recognize a downtick when I see one.

PART TWO

Chapter 18

"Andrea?" My boss is out of his office and standing by the desk I use on the trading floor.

"I need you to run over to Marshall Fields and pick up a box of Frango Mints."

I don't explain that I am making sales calls. I don't ask why he needs them. If this is a personal errand, I'll be pissed but I'll do it anyway. I've been trying hard to make Shearson work for me for fifteen months. I call one more client and tell them we are lowering our rating on Proctor and Gamble from buy to hold before I pull on my coat and my woolen hat and grab my gloves. Outside the building, my eyes sting from the icy winds that make the Loop in February such an ass-kicking experience. I raise my hand at the curb for a taxi and a Yellow Cab stops in front of me. Regretting I didn't change out of my shoes and into my boots, I wait as it discharges its passenger.

"Could that be Andrea Hoffman buried somewhere in that pile of outerwear?"

Harold Stackman! He wears only a topcoat and leather gloves. No hat or scarf. No heavy boots. He tells the driver to wait before he slams the taxi door. Chivalrous as always.

He's grown a thick white mustache. It suits him and I tell him so.

"I'll just assume that you look pretty good yourself," he says. "I hear you've been busy. Backing up some big accounts for that lazy bastard you work for."

I don't challenge his assessment. "I do. And I have some small accounts of my own. With more to come." So they promised. I try to smile even though I'm freezing.

He says, "And yet I smell discontent." He reaches into his pocket and pulls out the silver card case I've seen so many times before. Hands me his card. "I want you to come work with us at Kendall-Fitz."

"No discontent. I'm happy at Shearson." On rare occasions.

"We need you. Come up to the office after the close tomorrow. We'll talk."

I glance at the card before I put it into my pocket. Harold's a Senior Vice President now.

"I don't know if that will be a very good use of your time but I'll come talk," I say.

The driver taps his horn. "You want this cab or what, lady?"

Harold opens the door for me. "You better get going. I've got a meeting and your nose is starting to drip."

———

The address on Harold's card leads me to the corner of Dearborn and Washington. The space at street level is significantly set back from the sidewalk on all sides, so the entire fifteen-story building appears to be balancing atop a small glass box. The box is home to a Sansabelt slacks store, tacky. I peer in the plate glass window. There are no customers inside. The salesman is reading *Life* behind the cash register. I walk on to the entrance, push through the revolving door, and enter a poorly lit lobby with a worn linoleum floor. When I get out of the elevator, I'm in another poorly lit hallway. There's carpeting up here but it's threadbare and no longer an identifiable color. There's no reception desk. I walk twenty feet to the end of the hall. The signs indicate that I have found the bathrooms. I walk back down the hall to the opposite end and find an open doorway with a small sign that says "Kendall-Fitzgerald." I'd think it was a third-tier shop at best, but I've asked a few clients about the firm and they all assured me it was a respected player with a good trading desk and quality research.

I walk into an open room enclosed on two sides by the same type of floor-to-ceiling windows of the shop below.

"Welcome to my mess," Harold calls out as soon as he sees me standing in the doorway. Stacks of paper cover nearly every level surface in the room. Old newspapers, piles of research reports, used up yellow legal pads, computer printout sheets, trade tickets, memos, notices, magazines, and crumpled pink "while you were out" slips. There's no stock ticker on the wall. No need. All that information is on our Quotron's these days.

I hopscotch over sections of the floor where the carpet tiles are missing. The metal floor underneath looks slick. In a spot near the wall, the metal square is also absent and I can see that what I am walking on conceals a veritable snake pit of phone cables and electrical cords. I've never thought to wonder where all the cords were.

A large poster is tacked to the wall. It pictures a cross-eyed dandy with one arm around a blond bimbo and the other draped across the hood of a large, classic Rolls Royce parked in front of a stately mansion. The caption reads "Don't Confuse Brains with a Bull Market" and someone has written on it "This means you, Danny boy."

I say, "So this is why you need me. To start filing again?"

"Don't judge a book by its cover. We like it this way. It's homey and it keeps costs down. More for me."

I seriously doubt that he likes it this way. His desk is as immaculate as ever. I look toward the windows where I see the familiar boards covered in square keys. The trading desk. Paper clip chains dangle from the ceiling with small plastic figures attached to them like charms . . . a G.I. Joe, a Gumby, a topless hula dancer amateurishly and immaturely tattooed with ball point pen. The office looks and smells pretty much like a kid's room, the parents on an extended vacation. It's hard to imagine Charlene sitting there.

"Does Charlene still work here?" I ask.

"Happy as a lark. But anxious to have you back on the team." Harold's mustache is twitching just a little. His blue eyes haven't left my face. He cares what I'm thinking about this place.

Harold points at an empty chair. "Sit. So how much money are you making these days?"

I sit. "Jeez, boss. Don't we go through some pleasantries first? How's Blythe?"

"Still married to me. I didn't ask you over here to chit-chat. Are you making $35,000 yet? Commission or straight salary?"

"I got a raise to $31,000. Technically, I'll be getting commissions if I ever get some trades."

"You call some of your own accounts, right?"

I suspect that Harold knows the answer to these questions or I wouldn't be sitting in this office right now. "I have some very small accounts and I back up all four salesmen. I still cart analysts around. I still order lunch."

"The salesmen? Are they any good? Are you learning a lot from them?" Harold is leaning back in his chair and blowing smoke from his cigar up to a hole in the ceiling where one of the acoustical tiles is missing.

"I feel like I should say everyone's brilliant. But William, the office manager? He's an asshole. Thinks women should only be nurses and teachers. Resents it every time I try to show some initiative. The other guys are indifferent. They like having backup and someone to do grunt work. I don't think they have enough imagination to see me as a threat."

"Got favorite stocks?"

I feel a lot more comfortable talking about stocks. "IBM's been on my list forever. Also Allied Products." Harold nods. It's a local company. "And I like the toy companies. Mattel. Tonka."

The sky darkens and the lights come on in the buildings outside the windows. The office starts to look less like a train wreck and more like a Hopper painting.

"All good picks. I can pay you $35,000 base salary and you'll get paid commissions on the same schedule as the rest of us, Andrea. Once a month. Thirty percent of gross. The accounts aren't great but there'll be commissions for sure. You can earn fifty-thousand dollars easy with this package. Frankly, it's been over a year. I thought you'd have been here asking me for this by now." He stops to take another pull on his cigar.

I shake my head. "Didn't think that was an option. You walked out the door at Mosley and left me to fend for myself."

The glasses come off. Words of wisdom coming. He says, "You needed more experience. And I didn't need you here then. I need you here now. What do you say?"

I look around. Try to imagine myself here. "Shearson has done a lot for me. Keeping me on after the merger. I know the product. I like the analysts. I don't know if this is a good time for me to make a move."

A phone rings on a distant desk. Harold ignores it. Shrugs. "If you're not interested in making the move, I'm not going to put a gun to your head."

"That's usually what it takes," I say. I'm standing up to leave when a tall man, his coat open and an enormous orange and blue striped scarf wound around his neck, comes running into the room. I know who this is.

"Forgot my frigging keys again." He skids to a stop just short of knocking me down. He looks at Harold. "She showed!"

"Andrea, this is Daniel Theodore Johnson. Fine salesman. Questionable human being."

Dan Johnson's about five years older than me and could pose for a picture of the "All American Boy," snub nose, blue eyes, dimples, and straw colored thick hair. He grins at me. He has a crooked front tooth.

He snaps his fingers. "I *do* know you," he says. "I saw you at the First National thing. The party for their new office."

"I'm shocked you remember I was there. You were working that room like you were running for mayor."

"Would you vote for me?" He doesn't wait for an answer. "You were huddled with their boy genius auto analyst. Are you kids dating?"

"No way. Not even friends."

"Not even friends." He shakes his head and grins. "A woman needs a man like a fish needs a bicycle. Pretty good quote, huh? Well, one thing I know. You're not a dyke. I'm a pretty good judge of that."

Harold is vigorously shaking his head. He says, "What the hell! I'm trying to hire this girl, Danny. Help me or get your keys and go the hell home."

"Sure thing, boss." Dan drops to bended, popping knee in front of me. With his face close to mine, I smell the booze. He says, "Andie. May I call you Andie? Come work with us. I've heard that you're a great salesman . . . saleswoman?. . . salesperson . . . fuck whatever . . . a super smart chick and people like you. Together we'll make a lot of money and have a lot of fun and . . . " He thinks for a minute. "Nope, that's it. We need you and we offer money and fun. That pretty much says it all." He raises his eyebrows to make his whole face a question mark. "Please?"

"Excellent sales technique." I'm trying to be cool but I'm flattered by his speech and can't help grinning back at him. His twinkling eyes—delighted at meeting me, or maybe just lit with the fire of a scotch or three—leave my face and focus on the floor for a second. "Scorc! Lost no more." He grabs his keys from under the desk and is gone in a flash, racing toward the elevators.

"Running back," says Harold. "Huge college football star." As if this explains anything.

Funny, all of a sudden, I don't remember why I should stay at Shearson. I'll make more money here and I could use it: I'm still supporting Mom and Dad. I sit and ask Harold questions about specific accounts. I want to be sure it's the job details and not Johnson's dimples, flattery, and corny bullshit about money and fun that makes me want to work here. After all, Mosely was fun too . . . until the day it was over.

"I have a question," I say.

"Now's the time to ask it," Harold says.

"At Shearson, they made me Assistant Vice President. Can I keep that title?"

"No, Andrea, over here you can't be a fucking Assistant Vice President."

I think about how I'm going to make my argument. I want to make this move but not if it's another downtick in any way.

Harold sits up in his chair and stubs out his cigar. "You'll be a Vice President, Andrea. Your days of being an assistant *anything* are over."

I feel a rush of gratitude. Maybe it's even love for this man. I force myself to stay in the chair and not pop up and hug him. Trying to keep a shit eating grin off my face, I say, "Okay then. I'm in, boss." I lose the battle with the grin. "Thanks."

Harold puts his glasses back on looking very pleased. "See you on Monday." He picks up his lighter and puts it in his suit coat pocket. "We'll clear you a space!"

I head for the door, bundling up my outerwear.

"One last thing," Harold calls after me. "Buy yourself a good coat."

"This coat is very warm," I say.

"I don't give a crap about warm. Buy yourself a coat that makes you feel like a Vice President. Go to Marshall Fields. The fifth floor."

———

I feel guilty about giving my boss three days' notice instead of two weeks.

"Leave today. Whenever you've packed up your stuff," he says when I tell him. Not at all angry. That's the way it's done in a financial firm. If you're leaving—whether you're fired or quitting, out the door you go.

So I leave, stop in personnel on my way out to save him the trouble and go straight to Marshall Fields and wander around on the fourth floor for a while looking for the up escalator. I finally ask a sales clerk.

"No escalator to the fifth floor, miss. You have to take the elevator."

The elevator doors open into a luxurious cocoon. Soft lighting. Plush carpeting. Flower arrangements of white roses and fragrant lilies. A tall, blond woman who is dressed much more elegantly than I am glides over to where I am rooted. "May I help you?" she asks.

"I'm looking for a dress coat," I say. "But I don't see any." In fact, there was hardly any clothing displayed on the floor at all.

"I'll get you set up in a dressing room and I'll bring some coats for you to try," she says.

I follow her to a room the size of Mariana's store. There are huge windows with a view of the city, two armchairs, and a small couch. A carafe of water, a plate of butter cookies, fresh fruit, and a crystal candy dish full of Frango mints arranged on the mahogany coffee table. Vivaldi's "Four Seasons" plays softly in the background. "Would you like coffee, or perhaps you would prefer tea?" the woman asks me before she glides out. *Now this,* I think as I wait for my saleswoman to return, *is a shopping experience.*

Twenty minutes later I'm buying a cashmere wool blend full length coat with a sheared beaver collar that makes me look taller and slimmer and quite Presbyterian. My hands tremble as I relinquish my Marshall Field's credit card.

"I know you'll enjoy this coat for many years to come. It's a judicious investment," my new friend says. "Do come again."

I leave the fifth floor with my four figure "investment" in an elaborate box and half a dozen of the mints wrapped in a tissue and stashed in my purse.

Chapter 19

APRIL 1985

After a year plus, the messy chaos of the Kendall-Fitz office seems normal to me. 1983, the year I spent enduring the stuffy formality of Shearson, is only a sad, blurry memory. Except for the twenty percent rise in the Dow Jones Industrial Average. That part was fun. The markets have been see-sawing and now we're back at 1260, a level we've seen before, but as Harold is fond of saying, we make money in both up and down markets. And that's been true around here. Kendall-Fitz is not a giant firm like Merrill Lynch or Goldman Sachs, but it's been growing rapidly. We have five regional sales offices, a decent investment banking department feeding us Initial Public Offerings, and thirty-five equity analysts, twenty of whom are ranked at or near the top of their industries. Harold is still very much the team leader and it's great working with Just Bob again. Daniel Theodore Johnson? More complicated. He's hot and I hate that I think so. And Charlene? Shockingly, we've become friends. The get drinks together, go to the movies, discuss our periods kind of friends. I like her and hard as it is for me to believe, she totally likes me.

This morning, I drag into the office and drop my coat on the back of my chair. I'll hang it up later. First, I need coffee. Harold looks up from the *Wall Street Journal*. Looks to be about to say something to me but changes his mind and just gives me a nod. Dan, studying the sports page of the *Sun Times* doesn't bother to look up as I pass by his desk. Bob's at the coffee pot when I get there.

"Your tie," I say, throwing an arm across my eyes. "It's so bright!"

"Your eyes," he responds. "They are so bloodshot!"

Charlene, wearing cashmere in pastel blue, looks up as I pass the trading desk. She's wearing her blond hair straight and bobbed just below her chin these days. She looks fabulous.

"You look like shit this morning," she says.

"Thanks," I say. "I feel worse than I look."

"Good for you!" she says. "If you need anything, let me know."

"Hey, Hoffman, you on the phone?" Johnny Mac, the senior trader is standing across the aisle and on the far side of the double row of desks. If Mahoney, the senior trader at Mosley, was a kindly teddy bear, Johnny is more the terrifying grizzly. At six foot four inches, his deep voice carries easily over both the distance and the normal din of a crowded sales and trading department twenty minutes before the stock market opening. All the desks in the room practically touch. Which is good so that everybody hears everything. Which is also bad cause everybody always hears everything.

I raise my hands above my shoulders like a gun is aimed at me so that he can see I'm not holding a phone, and I turn my head slowly. He always sounds grumpy so it's impossible to tell if he has good or bad news for me.

"What'd you do? Give that Richie Rich Guy a hummer at dinner last night?"

He means Allan Mosley. Mosley Foundation, which has grown rapidly since he became its chief almost three years ago, is one of my biggest accounts. It turns out Allan's a very savvy investor and as the nonprofit's assets have grown and his ability to do good with the money has expanded, so has his enthusiasm for the family business. Last night I took Allan to Nick's Fishmarket, one of the best restaurants in the Loop, and we consumed large but unequal amounts of beer, scotch, and champagne, and then indulged in an Armagnac while we waited the extra twenty minutes for Nick's signature soufflé for two. Which was way too rich after all that alcohol. But delicious. With a stage four hangover, I don't feel like bellowing back a reply. I stare at him dumbly, conscious of the undivided attention of the entire office.

"Well, you did something right, you little shit," he says, scooping a trade ticket and waving it at me as he continues our private conversation at ninety-two decibels across the crowded room.

"That prick you dined with just sent in an order to buy 250,000 shares of Monsanto."

"Really?" I push myself out of my chair and walk carefully over to Johnny Mac's desk. I peer over his shoulder to look at the trade ticket he's just written out.

"You don't believe me? Get the fuck out of here. I got work to do." He fires a jellybean projectile to encourage my retreat. A sharp sting as it hits my shoulder and drops to the floor. It's a red one, my favorite. I pick it up quickly so as not to expose my backside to further attack, pop it in my mouth, and keep moving.

"All you salesmen ever care about is how many cents a share you're gonna get."

"Saleswomen," I correct from the relative safety of my desk.

"Sales-bitch. In my book, you ain't a woman until you grow some tits," he growls, but he's got a smile of sorts on his craggy face as he picks up the shout-down and announces to all Kendall-Fitzgerald offices across the country that he has 250,000 shares of Monsanto to buy. I do the math quickly in my head. Even at eight cents a share it's a twenty-thousand dollar trade. Six thousand pre-tax bucks in my pocket.

Charlene spins around in her chair. She sits across from Johnny—on the side closer to the sales desks. "Babe! Nice order. Proud of you."

She's interrupted by a deep sandpaper voice with a heavy New York accent blasting out of the squawk box. The voice comes from our main office high atop the World Trade Center in New York. The voice is the voice of God. Well, in reality, the voice is the voice of Neil Kent, head of all trading and sales activity. But everyone calls him God.

"OK, you humps and humpettes. We finally got a decent piece of merchandise in here. You'd better pick up those phones and find us some schmucks to sell us this stock. If we buy this off the floor and I find out one of your customers is the seller of this shit," he pauses for emphasis, "I'll find you, I'll rip your fucking face off, and then I'll fire your ass." The box falls silent.

Charlene turns back to her phones and gets to work She knows which of her customers hold large Monsanto positions and hits the button for each of them in turn.

"Hi honey, it's Charlene. I got a need for Monsanto. Big. Big. Got anything for me?"

I head to the ladies' room, taking the now empty coffee carafe with me. No dedicated break room in this office. Just a table in the corner for the coffee pot. Mini fridge underneath it for the milk. A tiny freezer compartment just big enough for two ice cube trays. It's not my job to make coffee anymore. That would fall to awkward Erin Yutz, the junior trader on the trading desk. She does all of the clerical work for the traders in addition to having a few insignificant accounts—some of them my insignificant accounts. I hear her now, small tentative voice, doggedly calling her clients.

"Uh, it's Erin Yutz from Kendall-Fitzgerald. I would like to buy a large amount of Monsanto."

So she'll be busy for a while and I need more coffee. I could, theoretically, ask Mary Consuelo Pineda—Harold's secretary. But Mary Consuelo, just nineteen years old and the size of a banty rooster with the temperament to match, responds to requests grudgingly and in her own sweet time.

I fill the pot myself and am back at my desk with a fresh cup of black coffee as I watch the market open.

"So did you blow him at the restaurant or in the cab?" Daniel T. Johnson asks.

It amazes me that when I started this job, I had a crush on Dan. True, he's irresistibly attractive and charismatic with a "Volulez vous coucher avec moi" smile. But he's a classic jock. Too confident of his own abilities. He relies on his talents and puts out too little effort. Is dismissive of people who are a little different. That includes me.

"Do you need some pointers, Danny? Are your blowjobs just not paying off these days? Try more tongue and less teeth."

The sad truth is Allan would rather drink with me than have me get anywhere near his precious family jewels. He sent me this trade because I'm a damn good saleswoman. My previous attempts to make this relationship anything more than platonic have always ended up with me home alone with my vibrator. I've accepted the fact that we're always going to be just friends. He respects me, but . . .

I turn from Dan and begin rummaging in my purse. In the bottom left-hand corner, I find two white pills. Aspirin. Maybe No-doze. Possibly just mints. I roll them between my thumb and forefinger to remove some of the old Kleenex fuzz and although this doesn't result in a positive ID, I go ahead and pop them in my mouth. Yes! Aspirins and they're burning the hell out of my tongue. I take a swig of my coffee to wash them down. Jesus Christ! Still hot. My eyes bug, my face contorts and my body shakes like a wet dog. It's just past 8:30 a.m. This is going to be a great day. I reach for my phone to start making my calls.

———

Harold, tipped all the way back in his chair, polished brogues on his desk, lit cigarette in hand, catches my eye in a break between his steady stream of phone calls.

"Did you talk with Allan about the Monsanto idea last night?"

Early in the evening, I remember talking about the new leader of the Soviet Union Mikhail Gorbachev, the environmental and regulatory consequences of the Bhopal chemical plant disaster, and the ending of the ban on interracial marriage in South Africa. The Mosley Foundation has an international investing focus and these things are important to Allan. During dinner, the conversation moved to domestic topics. Particularly drug stocks and cutting edge medical technology. I confess that at times I was doing more talking than Allan was. But after dinner, we moved on to topics closer to Allan's heart. Like music and the new British Invasion. The Cure. Tears for Fears. Murray Head. Murray Head? To refresh my memory Allan had launched into the chorus of *One Night in Bangkok*. Oh yes, *that* Murray Head. And then just saying Murray Head made us giggle like girl scouts and somehow this prompted a rant from Allan about women wearing their hair ratted up so large they look like they've stuck their fingers in an electric socket. Terribly low class, you know. Although Allan doesn't think of himself as a rich guy who grew up in a mansion with a conservatory, he so is. A successful evening of client relationship building, but I don't recall recommending Monsanto during any of those conversations. In fact, when I called and thanked him for the trade this morning, I'm pretty sure that was the first time I said Monsanto to him in any context. But that's how the business works. A client allocates commissions to you based on your ideas, but they don't necessarily give you the exact trade you recommended. And let's face it, sometimes you get a trade because you took them golfing (well, not me) or got them Bulls tickets or told them a particularly good dirty joke that day.

"Oh yeah," I lie easily. "We've been working on this idea for some time now." Harold's cigar smoke is accumulating into a cloud over my head.

"That–a-girl. Just like I taught you." Harold catches Dan rolling his eyes.

"Watch out Danny. I might give Andrea some of your problem accounts."

Daniel narrows his eyes looking for a fight but he sees that Harold is smiling and he relaxes. Harold loves his lazy ass.

"I could try something completely new. I could pay some attention to them," I say.

Bob Parker, his desk just to the left of Dan's, licks the tip of his finger and draws a point in the air for me.

Dan turns to Bob, "Et tu, Brutus? You're a guy. I need you to have my back."

Bob shrugs, "I don't get involved in the war of the sexes, kids. My wife won't let me."

Both Dan and I groan. "Why is this a sex thing?" I say.

Harold sits up in his chair. Stubs off the cigarette. "This should be a—get back to making research calls—thing."

Everybody obediently picks up their phones.

I have a medicinal greasy bacon cheeseburger for lunch and start feeling mostly human again. But the day is still going by much too slowly. I stare at my Quotron and think about scarfing down some Fig Newtons without the energy to walk to the vending machine.

The market closes at four in New York, three o'clock here. Soon after, we're done. Johnny Mac stops by the sales desks on the way out the door.

"Who's stopping by the Cohasset tonight?"

He means me.

"Half an hour." Big commission today means I'm buying. I shuffle some papers around on my desk like I have some important work to finish up.

Dan puts on his suit jacket and tightens his tie. Charlene and Johnny have already headed to the elevator. "Coming Harold?" he asks.

"I'll stop by and have one. Just to make sure you get on the five-fifteen train."

"Yeah, good." Turns to Mary Consuelo, "If my wife calls, tell her I'm on the five forty-five at the latest."

Charlene sticks her head back in the room. "What's taking you so long, dickhead?"

"Coming! And it's Monsieur Dickhead, s'il vous plaît."

"He's ridiculous," I say to no one in particular.

Harold takes his glasses off and I sense a lecture coming but he just says, "It wouldn't hurt you to be more like him."

"Right," I say, head turned so Harold doesn't see my eye roll. I pick up my purse and inform Mary Consuelo, "I'll be in the ladies' room buffing up if anyone calls for me."

"Good luck with that," she says cheerfully. Whether that's a comment on the likelihood of me getting a phone call or the difficulty of making myself look any better, I'm not quite sure. But I'm guessing it's the later. Mary Consuelo is always in full war paint, her dark brown hair teased and sprayed to maximum volume. As I pass her desk, I hear her ask Harold, "Can I leave a little early today? I have to find a dress from my niece's confirmation on Sunday."

"What's wrong with Saturday? You can't shop on Saturday? Today I let you leave early and tomorrow you . . . "

I didn't hear the end of the conversation but I've heard one pretty similar to it every day of every week. Harold and Consuelo's work relationship is a never ending series of negotiations.

"Do me a big favor," he frequently begs her, "help me pretend we run a professional office here."

"Okay. I'm ready to go," I announce. Glasses off. Contacts in. Hair brushed. A little makeup.

"Just Bob? Can I buy you one?" Bob rarely joins us. It's too bad because he can tell a damn good story when he wants to, and he doesn't live that far from me so we can share a cab home.

"Not tonight. Thanks anyway. Don't do anything I wouldn't do."

I don't bother to say anything to Erin. She has paperwork to finish up and besides, she's terrified of Johnny and Charlene. I should have sympathy for her since at one time in my life I was terrified of Charlene myself, but for some reason her timidity just pisses me off.

I stand up and start walking out without so much as a glance at the mess on my desk. "Let's go, boss. Maybe on the walk over, given the shit I hear daily in the office, you could explain to me why in a million years I would ever want to get married."

"You need a daddy for your babies," Mary Consuelo calls after us. She's desperate to have a kid. "Two by twenty-two," she says. A husband not as critical.

"Maybe I don't want kids. Not everybody has to have them."

Harold puts his hand on the small of my back and pushes me gently toward the elevator. "You will. Husband, kids, a dog. All of it. I know you better than you know yourself."

I shake my head. "All I know right now is I want a drink."

Chapter 20

*H*alfway between the swank offices on LaSalle Street and the huge commuter train station along Canal is a dark, cramped tavern called the Cohasset Inn. Smelling like the floors haven't had a good cleaning since World War II, the Inn has been serving watery cocktails, sour wine, and warm beers for over fifty years. They only employ waitresses who are busty, dog-faced, and cranky. Only hire bartenders who are Irish. The bathrooms are poorly lit which is probably a blessing. In winter, the toilet seats are cold as bus stop benches.

Certainly, there are nicer bars in Chicago. Hell, there are nicer bars on the same block. Restaurants that have a "happy hour" and serve complimentary mini-meatballs, egg rolls, and cocktail wienies. Saloons that always put a napkin under your beverage and give you a clean glass with your bottle of beer. And in all those other drinking establishments, it's better than even money you'll find a roll of toilet paper in every stall. Sometimes we do go to those places, but mostly we feel at home at the Coh.

When Harold and I push through the crowd, we're pleased to discover the advance team has secured two wobbly tables with excellent proximity to the bar. Dan and Charlene are deep in conversation and don't look up, but Johnny does.

"We're just talking about you, Hoffman," Johnny says, "Grab a beverage and come sit down."

Harold drops in to the empty seat by Johnny, who's talking with a man named Patrick O'Neil. Older. Not Telly Savalas bald but his slicked back hair shows a lot of scalp. Broad shoulders in an expensive suit. I know who he is. He works for Kendall-Fitz at the Board of Trade—something to do with options—but he's way too important to be a floor trader. At Kendall-Fitz functions, Patrick hangs out with the big dogs. And I can tell by Johnny's posture and expression that this is a guy he respects. The only empty chair is on Patrick's left, so I hand Harold the martini I just got for him, shrug off my coat, and sit down.

Patrick clinks his beer bottle against my Dewar's. Locks eyes on mine. "I've been informed you're buying. Thanks for the drink, Andrea." High wattage smile.

It's easy to see why this guy is a big shot. Not handsome but charisma like a movie star.

"You're welcome," I say. He knows my name.

"God was asking about the salesman on the Monsanto trade," Johnny says.

"And you said?" I say.

Dan and Charlene stop their side conversation to listen.

"It's a simple question. I told him it was you."

"Okay." I shrug like this is of little interest to me.

"He's like: 'Big trade for a little broad.'"

"Why the hell would he think I'm little?"

Charlene, her lipstick perfect even after her second vodka rocks, says, "You are. Tiny. Face it. Size four on your most bloated day."

Dan chimes in, "Yeah, I've taken dumps bigger than you."

Charlene gives him "the look." "Yes, I'm sure you have."

Johnny laughs out loud, showing off his legendary mattress-sized tongue. "He knows everything, Hoffman. Including what you weigh and what you ate for lunch today. It's why they call him God. He's just signaling that he knows you're alive."

Butterflies, excitement or fear, I don't know. God, the head of all equity sales and trading operations, is really, really good at his job, which is to make sure the rest of us make Kendall-Fitz an ungodly amount of money. A brilliant guy. But a weird guy. He doesn't come out of his office. Like, *never*. He has a private bathroom, two-way glass in his office window, and a devoted secretary who handles his interactions with the world.

I say, "Will God ever come out here?"

"He never has," Patrick O'Neil says. "And I've never had a meeting with him in New York. Johnny? Harold?"

They both shake their heads.

"He says that he can know someone better if he never meets them. People in the New York office don't even see him," Harold says.

"I don't get it," I say.

"He doesn't care if you do or you don't," Johnny says.

"I care about another drink." Dan says, lifting his empty Heineken bottle.

Everybody is in on another round. My bill is going to be huge.

"Patrick, buddy. How about playoff tickets? You got a source?" Dan says.

I see the slightest flinch in Patrick's expression. I'm thinking he doesn't consider Dan a buddy. "I got a guy. Sure. Amazing seats." Patrick says. "They'll cost you, though."

"They'll cost Kendall-Fitz," Dan says. "I'm taking clients and expensing them. Obviously."

"No! I thought you were taking your wife," Johnny says and laughs derisively.

"Women like basketball," I say. "Maybe she wants to go. Maybe your clients' wives want to go too."

"Not my wife," Dan says. "She doesn't know a foul shot from a touchdown. Patrick? Your wife like sports?"

Patrick has a wife. Interesting. He doesn't wear a wedding ring.

"Is shopping a sport?" he says.

The men laugh. Not Charlene or me.

I speak up. "How can anyone not like the Bulls? Michael Jordan. Leading scorer. Leading rebounder. Most likely to be named Rookie of the Year. Who wouldn't want to see him play?"

"99% of all fucking broads," Dan says.

"You're an asshole, Dan. You know?" I say. Then remember Mr. O'Neil is here.

"Lighten up, you two," Charlene says. "You remind me of my little brother and sister. Always scrapping."

She looks at her Rolex. It's as infectious as a yawn, and everyone starts looking at their watches as well.

Harold starts gathering up his things. "Let's go. I blew my promise to get you on the five-fifteen and we're going to miss the five forty-five, but we have a shot at the six- o-six."

"Might even have time to pick up a couple beers at the station for the ride." Dan leans over, gives Charlene a quick and sloppy kiss, and moves quickly out of slapping range.

She scowls. Dabs at her lips with a cocktail napkin. "Andrea's right. You're an asshole. And you need some Binaca."

Harold and Dan head toward the door. Only Harold thanks me for the drinks.

I figure this is a good time to make a long overdue trip to the bathroom. When I get back, Johnny and Charlene are also gone. I stop at the bar, throw down my American

Express card, and fearlessly pay my three figure tab. Then walk over to retrieve my coat.

Patrick O'Neil, alone at the table, jumps up and pulls out a chair. His suit jacket is off, his tie is loose, and the sleeves on his monogrammed dress shirt are rolled up. I start to say that I need to go but he just points to a fresh Dewars on the table. "For you," he says. "My treat."

It's barely six and I have nowhere to go but home and nothing to do when I get there but a third drink is bound to make me stupid and I'm pretty sure this guy is not someone I want to be stupid with.

I sit.

He raises his glass to mine. "So, how much money did you make today?" Casually. Like this is a reasonable thing to ask a near stranger.

I stammer out the trade details. "250,000 shares. Eight and a half cents a share. My cut will pay for about eight month's rent. Even after this bar bill."

"I'm impressed," he says. "Not a lot of people even know what an institutional salesman is. How did you end up doing this? Is your dad in this business or something?"

"I just got lucky. Nobody in my family is in any kind of business." I explain my green sheep status.

"You're funny," he says. And now he's saying something but the people at the table next to us have started singing *My Way* along with the jukebox so I can't hear what it is. I lean closer to him in time to hear, "And pretty."

Flustered, I look down at the table and mumble "Thanks." I've never been good at accepting compliments. I look up and he's still looking at me. I shake my head. "Honestly, the lighting is terrible in here."

"I doubt it's doing anything for me." He's still smiling but his eyes seem to be asking me a question.

"I'm sure a guy like you couldn't care less about being pretty."

"What do you think a guy like me cares about?" His tone is casual but it makes me nervous.

"I'll be honest with you," I say. "I don't know a lot of guys like you."

"And what kind of guy do you think I am?"

An easier question. Emboldened by my third drink I say, "I think you're a big shot."

Mr. O'Neil laughs. "You got that exactly right. I'm a big shot. And the new head of equity sales? Your new boss? Charlie Finnegan. He's a friend of mine."

"He's from Chicago?"

"No. Boston. But we worked together at Merrill for a few years. In New York. He's a good guy. In fact, we had a long telephone conversation the other day. I think he's going to like you." O'Neil's eyes are again locked onto mine. "I'm going to make sure of it."

My heart rate speeds up. Is this an offer or a negotiation?

A guy in shirt sleeves stops at the table. "How's it going, Patrick?"

Patrick reaches up and pats the man's arm. "Good to see you, Nick. Let's grab lunch soon."

"I'd like that," this Nick guy says. "Give my best to Julie and the kids." His eyes flick to me and immediately away. He gives a nod and heads to the bar.

"It's too noisy to talk strategy in here," Mr. O'Neil stands up. Towering over me. "We're leaving."

"I don't know, Mr. O'Neil. I have to . . . "

"Jesus. Don't call me Mr. O'Neil. I'm not that fucking old." He smiles when he says it but he sucks in his stomach and I hope he hasn't noticed that I saw him do it.

"Not *old*." I make a face to indicate how ridiculous that is. "I'm just . . . you know, well, you're too important of a

man for me to call by his first name. Without an invitation."
As soon as I say this, I cringe. Girly voice. Kiss ass tone. So
not me.

But Mr. Important seems pleased to hear this. "Well,
I'm saying you should. It's Patrick from now on, okay? Let's
grab some dinner."

Patrick O'Neil wants to have dinner with me. Because I
am the kind of woman who does big block trades or because
he wants to sleep with me? At this point, believing either
seems egotistical. Saying no seems wrong. Insulting. And
face it, I'm curious. Very curious. I stand up and put on my
raincoat. Patrick pulls my hair out from under the collar.
His fingers brush the back of my neck. Accidentally? A shiver
travels down my spine. He puts a hand to the small of my
back and gently but undeniably pushes me toward the door.

We wait on the sidewalk for a taxi to appear and he looks
down at me. Staring. Like there's something he's trying to
figure. The hand on my back has moved to my elbow.

"What exactly do you do for Kendall-Fisk?" I ask.

"Managing director in charge of all derivative products."

"Wow," I say. A managing director is one step above
Harold's senior vice president level. I feel a flash of panic.
This guy is way out of my league. My stomach tightens. This
is a mistake. "I know very little about derivatives."

He flags down a yellow taxi and holds the door for me. His
eyes on my legs as I scoot over to the far side of the seat. He gets
in, shuts the door. "Ambassador East," he says to the driver.

A hotel. I try and keep my face calm but my heartrate
skyrockets.

"I love the Pump Room," he says. "Fabulous oysters
Rockefeller. Okay with you?"

I want to laugh. The Pump Room. An elegant restaurant *in* the Ambassador East Hotel. I've never eaten there
but the bar is legendary. "Yes. Great."

He pats my knee. "Good. You know, people think deriva-tives are difficult. They think they're a legal form of gambling. But they're not. They're the future. You'll come and visit me at the Options Exchange. You'll get the idea right away and it'll give you a real edge with your clients—giving them risk hedging strategies."

"That'd be great," I say. "I'd really enjoy that."

"I'd make sure you'd enjoy it," he says, and then raises his hands. "Whoa. I'm not sure that came out the way I intended."

I laugh nervously. Wish I could act . . . less like an idiot.

"But maybe it did," he says. That look on his face again. Hunger?

"You'll need one of these," he says, and reaches into his breast pocket and pulls out his card case to give me one of his business cards. I see a pink piece of paper taped to the silver case. He stares at it, shaking his head.

"Jesus Fucking Christ. I totally forgot." He points to the note. "My boy has a basketball game." He checks his watch. His face tight. Mr. Charming is gone. He's all busi-ness. "Okay. I can do this." He knocks on the partition. "Guy, how'd you like a fare to Glencoe?"

"Fine by me. I've got enough gas. It's double the meter, though."

"I need you to let the girl out." The taxi pulls to the curb and stops. "I'm going to call you tomorrow and we're going to go for dinner soon. The Pump Room or wherever you'd like."

He starts to pull a bill out his wallet. "You can catch another cab from here, right?"

I wave off the cash. "I'm good. Really. Big trade today, remember?"

"I remember," he says. "Congratulations." He reaches out and pulls me to him. Kisses me open mouthed. With tongue. I'm shocked. Also not shocked. I don't kiss back but I don't push him away. He pulls back and grins at me. "See you soon."

I watch the taxi pull away and stand a minute on the sidewalk. I'm tempted to walk back to the Cohasset as if returning there could give me a clue as to what just happened. When I left the office, Just Bob told me not to do anything he wouldn't do. I'm pretty sure this was one of those things.

Chapter 21

The phone rings while I'm watching *Highway to Heaven*. I startle and look around like someone has caught me picking my nose.

"Hello, darling. You weren't sleeping, were you?"

Does she have to ask me this every time she calls? "Mom, it's only seven. My bed time's been eight-thirty ever since I turned ten."

"OK, smarty pants. You just sounded a little sleepy. Have you been getting enough rest, dear?"

"More than enough rest. Really. How are you doing?"

"Everything out here is great. I talked to the boys this weekend. They're all fine. Busy. You know."

"Oh, yes." I don't know, since my brothers and I aren't big on keeping up with one another. Mom moves on. "What's new?"

I don't think "I'm becoming an alcoholic" is an answer she's prepared for, so I tell her I had the biggest trade in the office this week.

"That's my girl. I'm sure you are the best salesperson they have. They're lucky to have you. I hope they know that."

I'd like to hear her say "Daddy and I are lucky to have you. I hope you know that." But I've given up expecting it to happen.

"I was at Dr. Mitchell's office the other day," Mom says.

"Toothache?" I prompt.

"Just a cleaning, but he wanted me to ask you if you know anything about a little stock called BioNext?"

"Never heard of it, Mom."

"Oh? The doctor said it was very hot."

I sigh. Three years and Mom still doesn't understand what I do. I try again. "I work with institutional clients. They only buy bigger stocks. These little tech names are for individuals. It's a totally different business. Try asking the dentist about your liver next time you're in his chair and see what he knows."

I walk around my apartment with the cordless phone tucked between my ear and shoulder, picking up items that clearly don't belong in the living room (my pantyhose and underwear for starters) and transfer them back to where they belong. After depositing the laundry on the floor in the south corner of my bedroom, I stop by the coffee table and pick up an empty wine glass for the return trip to the kitchen.

Mom is on a new topic. "Can you come home for dinner Saturday night?"

This is totally a trick question. If I say "no" I'll get the guilt lecture on why I don't ever make time for them. But, if I say "yes" I will get the inquisition into why I don't have a date. And why don't I? Weekends I often entertain clients. Dinner and center orchestra seats at a play or concert. But not every weekend. Those other weekends? Perched on a bar stool. Why don't those hours of drinking with guys I randomly meet turn into a call and a date? I'd like to think the men are unimaginative, too boring, but I worry that I'm too . . . something. Successful? I sense talking about my job scares them away. Fuck 'em if that's true. What else am I going to talk about?

It's still early in the week. I say "maybe" to give me enough time to come up with a plausible excuse in a day or so.

"So, we can have lunch . . . " she persists.

"This week is out and next week I'm going to Indianapolis to meet some new customers."

"That'll be nice. Are they nice?"

If "nice" means do they pay me a lot of money, then no. "Well, like I said, they're new."

"Will you have time to call Aunt Marion and Uncle Jerry while you're there? They're in Indiana you know."

"Mom, they live in Lafayette. That's closer to Chicago than to Indianapolis."

"So you won't call them." Silence and then she laughs. "That's fine with me. I never liked them."

"I'll keep that information to myself, Mom."

"I'm sure it will be a great trip and you'll sell a ton of stock."

"Glad you two are fine," I say. Even though that question hadn't been asked and answered. "Not everyone would be able to handle things as well as you guys are." "Things" in this case referred to the fact that the only job my dad was able to get was one that required him to work downstate during the week and live in a shitty apartment with a stranger and then have a long train ride each way on the weekends so Mom could keep the car. This arrangement sucked the most for Dad. Mom seemed to be enjoying her extra freedom. Sometimes, when I was pushing a stock because they were laying off people and thus saving costs and improving their earnings, I thought about how each of those laid off workers was a person like my dad.

"I gotta hang up now," I say. "The timer just went off in the kitchen."

"Oh, are you making dinner, sweetie?" Having to eat is always a good excuse for anything in our family.

"No, I'm making chocolate chip cookies to take into the office." If you're going to lie, you might as well make it a whopper.

The phone rings seconds after I set it down. It's Charlene. We don't do girl talk in the office. We both think it's better if the guys don't know we're friends.

"You've been on the phone forever. How was it?"

I walk halfway into the kitchen with the phone before I remember the cookie story is totally fictitious. I take a crab cake from Monday night's doggie bag out of the fridge, sniff it, and go ahead and put it in the oven.

"How was what?"

"Don't play dumb bitch with me. Patrick. I saw the way he looked at you at the Coh. I'm sorry I left you. I should've dragged you into the bathroom and warned you about him."

"Warned me? Whatever do you mean? Do you think he had some kind of designs on me?"

"Still haven't taken those acting lessons Harold wanted to pay for, eh? Your southern outrage accent is terrible."

"Nothing happened." I don't mention the kiss in the cab. "He's old, not particularly good looking, and married. But, I'll be honest with you I was kind of interested. There's clearly something sexy about him."

"It's called 'power.'"

"I guess. He got me all hot and bothered with talk about helping me get some better accounts and teaching me about options. He made me feel smart and . . special."

"You are smart and special, honey Just . . . "

"Yes. I know. He uses that bullshit with a lot of girls. But . . . "

I stop. She waits. I torture her.

"For god's sake, Andrea, we've established you wanted to sleep with him but you didn't. Just tell me what happened."

"Fine. I agreed go to dinner with him. I was flattered, curious, a tiny bit intoxicated, and totally famished. We got into the cab and suddenly he remembered he had to hightail it home for some kid thing. Commandeered the taxi and sped off with me standing like a forgotten shopping bag left on the sidewalk."

Charlene laughs. "Sorry. Not funny but . . . "

"I know." I laugh too. "He's not an evil man. He made the cab come to a complete stop before he opened the door and threw me out."

"He'll try again, you know."

"That's not going to happen. He's already forgotten about me. He said he'd call today to reschedule and he didn't."

"Of course he didn't. That would've looked too needy. He's a busy important man. You are supposed to be grateful when he finally calls. And he will. Trust me. He's got an itch and he's gonna want to scratch it eventually."

"Well thanks. Now I'm picturing an angry rash on his balls. Very sexy."

I hear coughing on Charlene's end of the line.

"Dammit Andrea, you just made me spit out a mouthful of a very expensive Cabernet."

"Sorry about that," I say, actually pleased with myself. "Okay. You're probably not wrong. He was looking to get laid. I wasn't exactly saying no. I guess I should have but it didn't seem like the worst idea at the time. Anyway, he changed his mind. End of the story."

"It's *your* story. You do whatever works for you. Do you want to go see *9 ½ Weeks* on Friday night?" she asks. "I think it's playing at Water Tower."

"It's like X-rated. People will think we're queer," I say.

"Like I give a shit," she says.

"I know. You really don't. It's amazing. People's opinions don't register on your radar."

Charlene laughs.

But I'm serious. "Is it weird that I care? I want people to think I'm nice. Especially strangers. It's important to me that the cab driver, my waiter, the ticket taker at the movies . . . all these people should think I'm nice." I take a breath and continue. "*Being* nice, like not sleeping with some other woman's husband because he might help my career, that's not so important to me. "

"So, the movie?"

"Sure. I'll even let you hold my hand in line."

When we hang up, I put a pickle on the plate and eat the two day old crab cake. Living large.

Chapter 22

Even with a job as great as this one, some days work sucks and today is one of those day. I really don't feel like calling anyone or reading research or doing anything remotely productive, but the problem with working at a desk next to all the other desks in an open office is that you can't shut your door and avoid the world, or put your head down on your desk and take a little cat nap, or even spend a great deal of time staring off into space trying to sort out your life without someone walking by and slapping you upside the head or punching you in the shoulder or just yelling "Earth to Andrea!" in your ear.

Right now I need to escape the fishbowl and I head for the green lumpy couch in the women's bathroom. I've been horizontal for ten minutes when Charlene comes in.

"That couch is so gross, honey," Charlene says as she heads for the middle stall.

"I'm hiding," I confess.

"What's the matter? Cramps? I can give you a nice little pill to make those go away."

"No, not cramps. I'm just generally miserable."

Charlene comes out of the stall and looks at me in the mirror as she washes her hands.

"You need to get laid."

Mary Consuelo bursts in, breathless with an important message, but possibly just covering up the fact that she was listening outside the door for the last god knows how long.

"There's graduate students here from the University of Wisconsin MBA program. Harold wants you to speak to them. He's too busy."

Charlene digs in her handbag and silently hands me her hair brush. Then she pulls out her Chanel makeup bag and leaves it on the side of the sink. "I've got to get back to the desk. Use what you need."

I dig through the cremes and powders and sticks and brushes until I find a concealer, eyeliner, and mascara to apply. After a moment's hesitation, I add a swipe of lipstick. Putting everything back, I spot the small brown bottle and the tiny silver spoon. Charlene said to use what I need so I help myself to a small hit and, feeling much better, I return to my desk to pick up my suit jacket.

Harold, on the phone, mouths "thanks." Harold hates talking to MBAs. I've done this for him before.

Dan looks up from his Quotron as I pass. "Want me to come in at the end and do the money thing again?"

"I hate the money thing," I say.

"I know. That's why I'll do it. And you know, college babes."

I would've never asked him but . . . "Okay. Sure. Give me about fifteen minutes."

The conference room is not quite as shabby as the trading room but it's a long way from plush. Thirteen students from the University of Wisconsin Business School are sitting in silence around our oval faux oak conference table when I come in. They look up expectantly and the disappointment shows on their faces as I approach the table.

"I know you were expecting to meet with Harold Stackman, our sales manager. He's unavoidably unavailable. My name is Andrea Hoffman and I've been an institutional sales-man for almost five years." This is, I know, an egregious exaggeration of my work history, but I'm selling the firm and to do that I've got to sell myself. "I'm happy to talk with you about the institutional sales business or any other aspect of the business—trading, analysis, investment banking—that you'd like to talk about." I glance around the room to see if they are suitably in awe of me yet. I'd have to say no.

"What brings you to Kendall-Fitz?" I circle around the table, pausing behind a beefy blond boy with the dull eyes. A few students manage to give me cautious smiles, but they sit silent.

"Maybe," I say, on the move again, "maybe you've heard MBA's are getting $50,000 just to walk in the door." I see a "tell me something I don't know" look on the face of a surly frat boy in a cheap brown suit. Sitting next to him is a gorgeous woman—redhead in a blue suit and high-necked white blouse. Dan is going to like her. On the other side of her, someone that catches my eye—dark hair a bit unruly, lots of eyelashes framing attentive green eyes, a little older than the rest of the kids.

"This is your opportunity to jump in and say that you're here because you want my job!" A few people smile but nobody raises a hand, speaks up, or slides a resume my way. Maybe I should've asked Mary Consuelo to bring in coffee. These visitors look like they could use a stimulant. Too late now so I push on. "Okay. I'll assume you're just here on a simple fact-finding tour so maybe it would be best if I tell you why *I'm* here."

"You drew the short straw," says a preppy looking blond guy who I guess will be going to work with his father. He shoots his cuff and I notice his Rolex just the way he wants me to. I slide back my sleeve casually so he can see that on my left wrist is my Movado *and* a thick gold bracelet I bought at Tiffany.

"Where would I rather be? You guys are such great company." I keep my face blank and this time I get a more genuine laugh from the group. "But I'll tell you why I'm an institutional salesman. I'm here because I love money. I don't mean that I love to make money, although that doesn't suck either, but I love money in the way that Ralph Waldo Emerson loved money: 'Money is, in its effects and laws, as beautiful as roses.' When I was in college, I thought I'd understand what he meant if I took some economics classes. But I didn't really get it until I started this job. *This* is where you see that in action. The beautiful laws and effects of money. Allocating capital. Shifting risk. Correcting hubris. Every morning I come to work and the laws and the effects of money create a new market. That new market creates winners and losers. I find that exciting. Figuring out who those winners and losers are going to be and making sure my clients profit."

Clearly, I'm not translating my sense of excitement to anyone else in the room. I see one pencil tapper, a yawner, kids glancing up to check the clock on the wall.

But then one of the students raises his hand like this is an actual class. It's the hunky dark haired guy.

"Ask away," I say.

"More of a statement," he says. He has a warm baritone voice with maybe a hint of a New York accent. "Emerson did not love money. He found it an expression of value and therefore at the heart of altruism."

Now all eyes are on me. Fuck. I could be back at my desk making calls right now instead of trying to impress a dozen dipshits.

"But, I get what you're saying," the good looking but now annoying student continues. "Capitalism at work right before your eyes. Cool!"

A few of the students nod their heads.

"I made almost $162,000 in my first twelve months here," I blurt out. "That's about ten times the average income of a college-educated American today."

All heads turned in my direction. Eyes on me. Now I have their attention. Shallow bastards. And I'm no better.

The Preppy blond jerk lets out a whistle. "And I bet the men make more, right?"

I picture myself punching him in his smug face.

The red headed woman says, "Jesus, Brock. Way to be an asshole."

I smile at her and shrug. "It's true. They've all been here longer and they do make more money than me. A lot more. I'm not going to lie to you. This isn't a business that makes it easy to be a woman."

Dan knocks on the open door and then strides up to the table and slaps me on the back. Never been so happy to see him.

"Very nice, Andie! I'm sure you all enjoyed hearing her speech. It's fascinating why people buy and sell stocks. There can be real satisfaction in outguessing the herd. I'm Daniel Johnson and I like the excitement of this job too. In fact it was pretty damn exciting to be sitting in the Kendall-Fitz box at the stadium last night. Box seats directly behind the bench. Best way to see a hockey game, that's for damn sure. And I love money too. Not Andie's theoretical, market moving money. I like this kind of money." He reaches in his pocket and throws down a handful of twenty dollar bills. He's staring directly at the redhead just like I knew he would. She blushes slightly and it softens her face which only makes the severe suit look sexier. I clear my throat to keep Dan on track.

"Money in this job is there for the taking but you got to take it. No one gives it to you." He looks around the table and at the money. "That's a lot of beer money. Who wants it? Who goes after what they want? Who in this room has some balls?"

A chair pushes back. A guy stands up. He's at least six-five and reaches effortlessly across the table to slap a massive hand on top of the bills. And unlike anyone else in this room, unlike anyone else I have seen in this office this week or any other week, he's Black. "I do. I want it." He is staring at Dan. "I'm going to be rich."

"Yeah, man!" Dan says. "That's what I am talking about." He waits a second and then says, "Now give it back."

The students hoot and hiss. The big guy doesn't move his hand.

Dan nods his head. "I tell you what. I'll trade you for it. I get my two hundred bucks and you get an all-expenses-paid trip to New York City for a job interview."

The guy scoops up the money and hands it to Dan. "Good deal." They shake.

We take a few questions and then wrap it up. Dan and I stand side by side in the doorway shaking hands as the students file out. "Good luck man, go for the money," Dan says. He slips the lovely lady his card when he shakes her hand. Smooth.

"If you can't imagine anything else being this exciting, be sure you get us your resume," I add. The dark-haired Emerson expert hangs back. He stops in front of us.

"Well, which one of you is right?" he asks. "Love or money?"

We look at each other and grin.

"She is." Dan says. "You really have to love this market crap or you might as well be selling cars."

"Ah, you're probably right," I say to Dan. "You have to love the money," *or need the money*, I think, "or you won't last a week in this business."

"Seems a bit insane," the student says.

"It works for us," I say. "Maybe we should change the whole pitch. If you like the idea of working in a mental institution . . ."

"But you hate that hospital smell," Dan continues. "Come work at Kendall – Fitz."

"Catchy," the guy says. He hands me a card. Doesn't give one to Dan.

Dan asks, "Where are you going next?"

"Goldman Sachs."

"Be careful over there, man," Dan says.

"Why?"

"They're big on teamwork. Don't try and be a hero."

The room is empty and I turn to Dan. "Thanks for coming in. I was sucking. But since when do you have the authority to give away trips to New York?"

"For such a smart girl, you're so ignorant. I can't believe you didn't recognize him. The guy is Carl Ritchie. All-American center four years in a row. He would be playing in the NBA but for a blown knee. The customers will eat that shit up. New York will hire him in a minute."

"I hope they do hire him. That would shake things up around here. Jesus, Johnny will go nuts around the guy. How would he contain himself?"

"I imagine when confronted with a 240-pound guy who is one hundred percent muscle, it might be fairly easy for him to refrain from making racist jokes."

"Another good point for you. You're on a roll. Did you see the size of that guy's hands?"

Dan raises his eyebrows at me and has a smile on his face. "So you're a hand man, huh? I learn something new about you."

"Well, some people say that if your hand is bigger than your face, it's a sign of intelligence."

Dan fans out his fingers and holds his hand in front of his face to check.

Quick as I can, I push his hand so he slaps himself in the face. Old sibling trick.

"Guess it's not true in all cases," I say, and spin out of reach before he can retaliate.

"Very immature behavior!" He grins. "Kind of turned me on."

Getting along is not impossible for us but it's awkward. If we were actually friends what else in the universe would have to change? I head to the door.

"If anyone asks, I'm picking up some cash." I say.

When I get back from the bank, my phone is ringing and I pick it up to hear a deep male voice say, "Hoffman, it's Jack Keith."

I'm silent while I wait for a bell to go off in my head that will signal to me the identity of this Jack Keith person.

"I gave you my card about thirty minutes ago. You're not doing a lot for my ego."

"Yes," I recover. Green eyes guy. "Of course." I fish the card out of my pocket and look at it. "But I figured you'd be at Goldman right now," I say, feeling lame.

"Turns out," he says, "that they have telephones over here."

"I'd heard that," I say. "What can I do for you?" I ask, thinking that perhaps he left something in the conference room.

"I'd like you to go out to dinner with me tonight."

"Um, wow. Nice offer but ah . . . " His green eyes were interesting. Challenging me on the Emerson quote was rude. "I've already got some plans."

"You sure? My basketball pal went for the money but I think the most valuable thing in that conference room was you."

My stomach does a flip flop. And a flush starts up my neck. When was the last time a man said something like that to me?

"I really don't like pushy guys. If you're interested in getting a job here, send your resume to Harold Stackman. As for a date? Sorry. Can't." I say.

"I'm not pushy. I'm honest. I don't want a job. I think I'm clear about what I want. I'll call again when I have more time."

I wait to hear the click before I hang up the phone, then toss his card into my top drawer and turn my attention to my messages.

My phone rings. It's Charlene.

"How'd that go?"

"Dan gave away a trip to New York to some big Black dude."

"Carl Ritchie. I saw him in the hall. He's hot. Hope we hire him."

"And one of the students asked me out to dinner."

"And?"

"I said no, of course."

I write No No No until Nos covers two lines of my yellow pad.

"Was he hideous?"

"Actually, he was pretty hunky in a Matt Dillon kind of way."

"Oh for God's sake, Andrea. Why not? Maybe he's a great guy. You might fall in love, get married, and have a couple of cute kids together."

"That would be exactly the reason I didn't say yes. We'd have a couple of bratty kids and I'd give up this amazing job and then he'd start cheating on me and we'd get a divorce and I'd be screwed. Like Dan's wife's going to be some-day soon." I look over and catch Dan working a toothpick between his teeth as he talks on the phone. "But I probably shouldn't have been quite so curt with him. After all, he's interviewing in town. Chances are, he'll end up a client."

Charlene just huffs. "Well since you're not busy tonight, come over to my apartment. I've got to clean. I need company and you clearly need an attitude adjustment. Bring wine."

———

At five-thirty, I set out for Charlene's apartment, a modern high rise a block from the lake a short four block walk east from my place. I enter the marble lobby and spot the now familiar doorman behind an enormous cherry wood desk shaded by a veritable forest of fichus trees. His blond mullet, poufy on the top and shaggy in the back, contrasts with the blazer he's clearly trapped inside. He's using two pencils to tap out a drum solo on the desk and when he sees me, he drops the sticks and grins. Green gum visible between his teeth and lips.

"Hey, you're Miss Mason's friend, right?"

I nod.

"What's your name, again?"

"Adrienne," I say.

"Yeah. Adrienne. Like in *Rocky*." He points toward the elevators. "I'll let her know you're on the way up."

When the elevators open on the thirty-second floor, Charlene is standing barefoot in the hall by her open door.

"Adrienne? Your saloon alias, I presume." She rattles the ice cubes in her drink. She's wearing crisply ironed jeans and a spotless white t-shirt. Bare feet. Her hair is pulled back from her face with a white stretchy headband and she looks a lot younger and less formidable than she does in the office. I'd guess that she's a few years past thirty but even though we've gotten to be more than just work friends, I would never be bold enough to ask her age.

I stop in the doorway. Every time I come here I have to restrain myself from saying "holy shit." The apartment is a stunner. Featured last year in *Design Magazine*.

"I thought you said you had to clean. Everything looks perfect."

"Clean?" Charlene hoots. "Honey, maids clean. That's their job. My job is to trade stocks. If they promise not to do my job, I promise not to do theirs. Do you mean to tell me you don't have a cleaning lady?"

"My whole apartment is about the size of your living room. I don't really need a maid."

"So your apartment is clean? Right now?"

Charlene takes my silence as her answer. "I'll give you the number of my cleaning service."

As we talk, we pass through the entry hall to the dining room, down two steps to the sunken living room. The drapes are open and I look out onto the balcony that overlooks Lincoln Park with a clear view of the Lake beyond. There's more furniture out there than I have in my entire apartment.

"What can I get you to drink?" She opens a cabinet stocked like the premium shelf behind the bar at Morton's. Heavy crystal glassware gleams besides a silver ice bucket.

"Scotch, please." I hand her the bag I'm still hanging on to.

She opens it and puts the bottle of California Chardonnay in the mini fridge tucked behind the cabinet door. "Excellent choice. We'll just let it chill slightly before we open it."

I take the generous scotch she pours and then plop onto the enormous white leather sectional couch that surrounds a square glass coffee table. Four straight lines of cocaine are neatly arranged on its gleaming surface. Two silver straws complete the tableau. Charlene picks up the straw and neatly kills two lines. She offers me the other straw.

I'm a coke mooch. Have been ever since Allan offered me my first hit. I take it whenever offered. I love that sharp smart sparkly feeling it gives me but I've never bought any for myself. It would make my life easy in a way I don't feel I deserve. Like having a cleaning lady. I lean in and kill the lines.

"This is the only way to get a boring job done," Charlene says, working on a refreshed vodka.

"And that boring job is?"

"Closet cleaning. But it can wait. Let's get back to your housing situation. Do you own or rent?"

"I rent."

"Well, there's the problem right there. You're never going to care about something you don't own. How much money do you have in the bank?"

Awkward. I answer: "Not a lot."

"Bitch! You can't kid a kidder. You made more than eighty grand last year, you're doubling that now, and you spend almost nothing, so I'm guessing you have at least a hundred grand tucked away."

"I've got $92,000 not counting my IRA." When I say it out loud, it does seem like a big chunk of change.

Charlene sighs and makes the face that I haven't seen since the days at Mosley when I was such a disappointment to her "The game is not over when you make the money, Andrea."

"You're saying I should be spending more." I am spending it. Just not where she can see. My parents have gone from resisting my monthly checks, to grudgingly accepting them, to eagerly anticipating them. They need a new roof. The car is about to give up the ghost. My improving finances and their depleted savings seem to be a perfect fit. My brothers all have an excuse why they can't chip in. Jake's house needs a new roof of its own. Mark's having a second kid. Pete's still paying off those med school loans. All great excuses and yet . . . . But, it's fine. I can handle it. Why should it sit in the bank when Mom and Dad can use it?

"I'm saying you should be spending, investing, spreading it around. You don't want to be the next Hetty Green."

"Who?"

"Legendary female investor during the early 1900s. Called the Witch of Wall Street. The richest woman in the world in her day. But also a legendary cheapskate. Look her up." Charlene stands up. "Come on. We're taking a field trip."

Charlene picks up a set of keys from a small table by her front door. Still barefoot, we head to the elevator and down to apartment six F. When she turns on the lights, I can see it's empty. "A friend of mine used to live here," she explains. "He was transferred to London."

One bedroom, one and a half baths. Hardwood floors throughout. Balcony off the living room.

"His company's selling the apartment and they want to get rid of it fast. They're asking $120,000 but I bet they'd take $109,000. Twenty percent down would be about $22,000. You can do this easy."

I could do this. I walk from room to room. My kitchen, my living room, my bathroom with a whirlpool tub. I go out on my little porch. The view is of the treetops and not the lake, but I can imagine a chaise lounge and a book on a summer day.

"Interest rates are so high right now. The mortgage would be almost fifteen percent," I say.

"That's why the apartment is cheap. You'd refinance when they come down. And the value of the apartment will go up."

She hands me the keys. I lock the door. It feels right.

We head back upstairs and she chops out two more lines for us. Then opens the bottle of wine I brought. Pours two full glasses.

Charlene didn't go to college, but she's smart. More than just street smart. She reads voraciously and numbers and math concepts are easy for her. Plus she understands people, especially men. And she's right about the apartment.

Owning a house, that would seem wrong. Married people own houses. But a condo would be different. It would make financial sense. Of course I need to buy an apartment. And I definitely want to get some of this coke. Just to keep around. Just for emergencies.

"I need some of this, Charlene. Where do you get it?"

She looks at me like I must be joking.

"Your secretary, Mary Consuelo sells it. Didn't you know?"

Nope. I didn't know. "That big cross she wears . . . I thought . . . you know. She's kind of . .."

"Andrea," Charlene shakes her head. "Sometimes . . ." An eye roll but she's smiling. "Up. I asked you here for a reason. It's time to tackle the closet."

Full of coke-induced energy and enthusiasm, I head for the bedroom and sit on the bed next to the night table where Charlene has set her Chardonnay. I spy a copy of *The Man who Mistook his wife for a Hat* and *Bright Lights Big City*. I'm about to ask about them when Charlene throws open her closet door.

"Tada!"

Double bars on the left side of the closet hold blouses on the top and skirts and pants on the bottom. They are arranged by color and then from lightest to darkest shade. The back wall has a single bar with dresses and suits. The right wall has no bars, only shelves. On the shelves are handbags, square wicker baskets, and dozens of shoe and boot boxes.

"I guess I'm a little obsessive," she says. "When I was growing up, my mom wouldn't let us go to the bathroom in the morning until we passed room inspection. Bed made and everything in its place. Not that I had anything to organize. We were so poor we barely could pay attention. A pair of sneakers and a pair of church shoes. My one church dress and some hand-me-down jeans and t-shirts. Kept it all in a cardboard box. But you better believe I decorated the hell out of that box."

"We were pretty poor too," I say. *Not dirt poor*, I think. *Suburban poor*.

"I bet you had a closet though."

Okay. She wins. I had a closet. But it did have lot of hand-me-downs in it. "Anyway," I move on, "I thought you said you had to clean this up. It's already perfect."

"Not clean it up. Clean it *out*. I want to buy some new things for the spring and I have to make some room. Some of these things I haven't worn in years." She pulls a silk blouse off the rack that is a gorgeous shade of night sky blue. "Like this. I never wear anything like this anymore."

"But it's beautiful," I say.

"The sleeves are way too full. Makes me look like a fucking pirate. I used to alter things. Take up the hems. Add darts. Take out pleats. Change buttons. But I don't sew anymore."

"You don't have the time?"

"I don't need to. I didn't do it because it was fun. When I first came up to Chicago from Indiana, I'd go to a thrift store and look for something with a designer label in it that I could mess around with. Like Scarlett and the drapes."

She pulls out six more blouses and begins to ruthlessly weed out the pants and skirts. Before long, I am dwarfed by the enormous pile of clothes on the bed next to me.

"Okay, I'm done. Is there is anything you want before I take it to Goodwill for the next trailer trash reject to find?" She follows my eyes. "Not the blue blouse. You're no fucking pirate either."

I try some things just because trying on clothes is fun. Besides the height difference, she has "a big rack" that Johnny is so fond of pointing out that I am lacking. But we agree on a few things that fit. She points out that I need to upgrade my underwear.

"Children wear underwear, Andrea. Women wear lingerie."

This could turn out to be an insanely expensive evening. I'd already brought over a pricey bottle of wine and now my shopping list includes an apartment, a maid to clean it, some fancy lingerie, and a personal supply of cocaine. I've been thinking I'm a twenty-eight-year-old extraordinary success but now I see I've gotten complacent. Time to hurdle up to another level.

The door man seems even happier to see me when I step out of the elevator.

"Yo, Adrienne." He motions me over to the desk. His uniform jacket is hanging on the back of the chair. His short sleeve shirt exposes muscled biceps and ropey forearms.

"I'm going on break." He opens his palm to show me a tightly rolled joint. He cocks his head toward a door behind him. "Join me."

I'm still buzzing from the blow. Judgment perhaps slightly impaired from the scotch and wine combination, it makes sense to me that a little weed will help me sleep. Plus Charlene has shown me I'm more than what I've been giving myself credit for. Time to act like one of the guys. So I say yes and follow him into the back. There's a couch and a table with a small television on it. A kitchenette area. He switches on a cheap radio. He reminds me his name is Raymond. We sit on the couch and pass the joint back and forth while he explains that this is only his part-time gig. He's got a band. *The Dream Weavers*. They have a gig this weekend at a bar in Uptown. Did I want to come? He'll put me on the list. What's my last name? I tell him it's Mosley. Adrienne Mosley. He tells me I'm pretty and soon we're kissing. His hand working its way into my jeans. His other hand unzips his polyblend slacks and guides my hand onto his hard cock. He's got skills and I come quick. A minute later, he grabs a fist full of Kleenex and finishes. Jumps up and puts himself back together. Break's over. He pulls a Pepsi out of the fridge and turns toward the door.

"Can I call you a cab?" he says. The doorman again.

The room is hot. My head is fuzzy. I need some air. "No, I'm fine. I'll walk."

"Don't forget Saturday, Adrienne."

"For sure," I say and give him a little wave. Ten minutes later I'm opening my front door with no memory of the walk I've just had. I set down my bag of new old clothes and drink a full glass of water and pop two Tylenol. I yawn and glance at the clock. Still early enough for me to get a full eight hours of sleep. I head to the bedroom, shedding clothes as I go, figuring my future maid will pick them up.

Chapter 23

I'm wearing the coral cashmere sweater Charlene gave me under my favorite Albert Nipon charcoal grey suit and I feel surprisingly ready for a good day at work. Perhaps an amalgamation of single malt scotch, white wine, coke, and weed is the perfect combination for me. The doorman thing—tacky—he had a mullet! But not mortifying. Who was going to know? I'll pass on buying the apartment in that building though.

Charlene's wrapped up with a big Kodak position she is trying to buy in a strengthening market. She nods when I pass by, smiles when she sees the sweater, but immediately turns back to her task.

Dan looks at me quizzically, like something is going on he should know about but can't remember. He probably smells Charlene's perfume lingering in the sweater.

"You look nice," he says. "Did I forget we have an analyst in town?"

"Maybe I have a date later."

"Do you?"

"None of your business."

Wearing Charlene's hand-me-down sweater must be giving me some of her chutzpah because I decide this is a good day to try and call portfolio managers who never call me back and sell them Genetech, a high priced but exciting biotech company our biotech analyst loves. I successfully connect with an elusive downstate portfolio manager and am well into my pitch when I see my second line light up.

"So, have you considered adding a position in your growth fund?" I ask, giving myself a break to look up at Mary Consuelo and see who's calling.

"Steve," Mary Consuelo calls out with a shrug.

I know a bunch of Steves—a couple of analysts, one portfolio manager, and a trader in our New York office—but none of them are more important than the guy I am talking to right now, so I twirl my finger. I see her nod and I go back to paying full attention to the conversation at hand. To my surprise, he asks me a few questions and then actually says thank you. "Call me again when you have other ideas along these lines. You're on the right track."

I hang up and do a little dance still sitting at my desk. *I am on the right track!* It's not a trade, but from a guy as tough as this one, it's a benediction. I'm on a roll and I keep dialing. It's midmorning before I get a chance to go to the bathroom. When I come out of the stall, Mary Consuelo is washing her hands.

"Hey," I say. "I've been meaning to ask you something."

"I know. Charlene already put your order in. Go get me four hundred dollars. I'll have your shit by the close."

I've got four hundred dollars but four hundred dollars is a lot of money to snort up my nose. But I can't say "never mind." Consuelo will think I am a loser. This has been quite a couple of days. Best commission week ever. Attracted the attention of an important new "friend" in the business. Gave a hand job to a sexy stranger and then slept like a baby. And now I am buying drugs from my secretary because if I don't she'll think badly of me.

"That Steve guy who called earlier," she says, "he seemed pretty shocked you wouldn't pick up."

"Did you get a number?"

"No, he just said it was Steve from college in town for a meeting and he'd call you back at the end of the day." She's smirking at me. She loves to store up bits of our private lives like a junior J Edgar Hoover and I instantly regret the coke buy.

"Oh, that Steve," I say, and even though my heart is pounding in my chest I add, "he's not a big deal."

"He thinks he is," she says, and she smiles at me as she heads out the door. "I need the money, like, right now." She's not smiling anymore. "Cash."

I run across the street to my bank all the while hearing the voice in my head saying, *Steve called. Steve called. Steve called.* Back at my desk, I wait until everyone is busy and I transfer the twenties into an envelope. I get up and hand the envelope to my new drug dealer and hesitate at her desk for a fraction of a second.

"No, he didn't call back yet," she says.

"I wasn't asking." Mary Consuelo raises her eyebrows and I cut my losses and walk back to my desk.

The market has been closed for twenty minutes and no Steve. He said he'd call at the end of the day. It's the end of the day for me. I decide to give him one hour. I've waited six years for this call but I can't sit here all night. If he misses me, he could call me at home. My number's listed. Which makes me wonder how he got this number.

She picks up on the first ring. "Helen Hoffman speaking."

"Hey, Mom."

"My darling. What a pleasant surprise. What's new?"

"I was calling to ask *you* that. For instance, have you gotten any strange phone calls lately?"

"Didn't I tell you? I'm sure I told you that boy called looking for your phone number a few nights ago."

"You know, it's funny but in fact you didn't tell me. I'm kind of surprised you gave him my work number."

"He caught me off guard. I was watching *Murder, She Wrote* and I didn't want to miss any clues so I just gave him the number and hung up. I was going to call you after the show but it was late and I know you go to bed early."

"Thanks, Mom. That's very thoughtful of you."

"Should I have not given him the number? What did he want?"

"I don't know what he wants because I didn't pick up when he called today because I wasn't expecting his call. But it's okay. It's no big deal."

Steve was afraid of my Mom, so if he called her, he really wants to get ahold of me. Why?

Mary Consuelo gets a phone call and she talks loudly and rapidly in Spanish. She hangs up and heads out. I hear the elevator chime and a minute later she walks directly to my desk and drops a small bag from Walgreen's. Sings out "Drug delivery" and sits back down.

I look around, panicked, but nobody seems to be paying any attention to our transaction. "Thanks for taking care of that," I say.

"Don't mention it," she replies.

You can count on the fact that I won't if you don't, I think.

I stare at the bag. I'd love to take a trip to the bathroom but then I might miss the call. I need help making time pass. A Bob story would help.

"Hey, Just Bob!" I call to him, "What happened yesterday when you flew out of here like a fireman headed to a three alarm?" Johnny and Charlene are long gone but Harold and Dan are still in the office and I know they'll want to hear this. They look up just like I knew they would.

Bob puts down his pen. "Can't take your eyes off me, can you? You watch my every move."

I roll my eyes. "You slammed down your phone, yelled 'shit,' and stomped out."

"I was on a rescue mission. Yesterday, my wife, Judy . . . "

"As opposed to your *other* wife, Bertha," Dan says.

Bob just shakes his head and keeps going. "Judy was mugged. I get a call from the desk sergeant at the Harrison Avenue police station. There's a guy who hangs out in front of fancy places ladies go to have their nails done. The police speculate that he identifies ladies with wet nails by the way they hold their hands. You know, elbows bent, their arms close to their sides and their hands straight out in front of them with the fingers spread wide apart—like a platypus." He demonstrates.

I look down. My nails look bad. The cuticles are a mess. I should get a manicure. Bob continues. "It seems gals would rather die than ruin a fresh manicure, so the mugger essentially just walks up and lifts the handbags right off their shoulders."

Harold lets out a low whistle of appreciation. "No overhead. High margins. Maybe we should find this guy and bring his operation public."

"Boss, do you ever think you might be too obsessed with this business?" I say.

Harold shrugs and relights his afternoon cigar.

Dan looks a little concerned. "She wasn't hurt was she?"

"Not a scratch on her but really, only my wife could get mugged by a white guy on Michigan Avenue in front of a hundred other people at two-thirty in the afternoon."

"Well, thank god for that," Dan says. "Did you ever hear about the time Patrick O'Neil was mugged on a business trip in Denver? Some spic—no offense Mary Consuelo . . . "

Mary Consuelo narrows her coal black eyes at him. Offense clearly taken.

". . .pointed a gun at his head in the hotel parking lot."

"So what happened?" I ask casually.

"He cooperated. Gave him his watch and wallet. The cocksucker ran away. Then Pat calls his wife and says 'Honey, I was robbed at gunpoint' and you know what Mrs. O'Neil says to the father of her children?"

I shake my head.

"'What'd they get?' Nice, huh? Not 'Are you okay?' Or even 'Oh my sweet Jesus!' Cold as ice. *'What'd they get?'*"

So more evidence about why Patrick wanted to have dinner with me. His wife is a shrew. I would never be that way. About Patrick. Even though he hasn't called.

"So, what'd they get?" I ask Bob.

Bob is jubilant. "Actually, the guy got nothing. Judy says that after a manicure she doesn't want to ruin her nails fishing around in her bag for her wallet and keys so she keeps those in her pocket. The guy chucked the bag in a trash can two blocks away and all the other crap you guys keep in your purse was still in there when the cops found it." Now he is almost giggling. "The only thing the guy took was what he must have thought was a credit card case."

"And what was it?" Harold says.

"Photo album of the family at Starved Rock. Can you imagine? He opens it up and instead of Judy's gold card, there's the whole Parker family smiling at him like *Fuck you, buddy*! I almost feel sorry for the schmuck."

Everybody is laughing so hard I almost miss the phone.

"Andrea Hoffman."

"Well, what do you know? The big shot answers her own phone."

The voice is so familiar and yet it's so strange to be hearing it. "I sent my secretary home early so she could stop and pick up my dry cleaning and drop it off at my apartment." I wait a second to see if Steve laughs. I don't hear anything but breathing and it makes me wonder if my mother talked to him longer than she let on. Maybe she did a little bragging? "So you're in Chicago?"

"I'm at a convention at the Conrad Hilton."

"Nice place," I say. He can't see me wrinkling my nose.

"I have time for a drink," Steve says. "How about you? Do you have time to see an old friend?"

"Depends on when and where," I say.

"People here are saying that the bar at Nick's Fishmarket is nice. Have you heard of it? I can leave now and be there in fifteen minutes."

Nick's is good. They know me. I'll have home field advantage. "That works for me," I say. "I'll see you there."

I hang up and stare at the phone. He wants to see me. I lean over in my chair and run my hand up my leg. It feels scratchy through my pantyhose. Damn my mother. A little advance warning would have been helpful. I can hear her asking, "What difference does it make if your legs are shaved? Are you planning on jumping into bed with him?" Maybe. That part of our relationship was always good. I wish I'd had time to follow Charlene's advice about lingerie.

Nick's is less than a five minute walk from my office, so that gives me ten minutes to fix my hair and put on some makeup. I head to the ladies room with my purse and my Walgreens bag. When I get back to my desk, buffed up and fortified with a miniscule snort of the coke—just enough to make me feel bold—I see that Harold has taken the bottle of Glenfiddich out of his desk drawer and he and the boys are having a drink.

"Join us, Andrea," he offers.

"I'd love to," I say, "but I have to head over to Nick's for one."

"You *do* have a date," Dan says. "I knew it when I saw what you were wearing this morning."

"So I look good?" I can't help but ask.

"Compared to who?" Dan says, sounding exactly like one of my brothers, but I can see in his eyes that he thinks I do.

"You look nice," Harold says. "You look classy."

"Thanks, Harold. Takes one to know one."

Harold pours another generous shot into Dan and Bob's coffee mugs that double as highball glasses. He waves the bottle in my direction before he puts it down.

"I can pour you a short one."

I quickly look to Dan and wait. Jokes about my height are his specialty.

"Pass," he grins. "But I want it noted for the record that I showed some self-restraint."

"Duly noted," I say.

I'm tempted to stay and have just one drink. I could tell them where I'm going. Get some manly advice about how to handle myself. They'd be the first ones to tell me to show up late. Make it seem like I don't care.

Dan is puffing on a cigar. He must have coerced Harold into giving up one of his Macanudos. Bob's tie is off and his shirt is opened a few buttons. What is it about those Italian guys and their chest hair? No surprise, Mary Consuelo bolted the second the clock struck quitting time.

The sunlight is starting to fade from the sky. The office phones are silent.

Downstairs, the Sansabelt store is closing. I hear the clank of the metal crate that covers the plate glass windows. The sidewalks will be packed with people heading home. Showing up at Nick's late is one thing. Showing up sweaty from a seven block sprint is another. I should go. We sit around the office after hours, drinking and shooting the shit like this at least once a week. I'll stay the next time.

"You boys should go home soon." I say and pick up my briefcase. I pause at the door and look back at Harold, Dan, and Just Bob, their faces bright from the scotch and the reflected green glow of their Quotron screens. Bob makes a little shooing motion with his free hand. "We expect to hear a story tomorrow," he says.

"Fat chance," I say. But maybe. I wave and walk out pretty sure they'll be there until the sky turns dark. None of them seem to be in a hurry to go home. In fact, from where I stand, this feels pretty much like home right here.

Chapter 24

*C*hicago is a city situated on the shores of Lake Michigan and so it seems logical that a restaurant called Nick's Fishmarket would be sitting at the end of a long pier with wide plank floors, fish nets and life preservers hung on sea blue walls. Throw in a stuffed pelican or two decorating the bar. But in fact, Nick's sits just a few blocks from my office in the heart of the Loop, deep in the ground under the First National Bank Plaza. I force myself to walk those seven blocks slowly. I need to arrive last. I don't think I could bear to sit and wait for Steve to show up.

As I stroll, I remember Steve's one visit out here when were in college. A long weekend over the summer break. We had come into the city on a hot and humid July day and taken pictures in front of the Picasso, the Buckingham fountain, the bronze lions in front of the Art Institute, and as we sunned at Oak Street Beach. A day I designed to make Steve fall in love with Chicago. And as I turned the corner to arrive at the restaurant, I realized we'd been here too. Not to eat at Nick's, of course. We were on a hot dogs budget that day but we had come to see the Plaza and dip our feet in the fountain as we gazed at the Marc Chagall Mural. Jesus. So much history.

Six minutes fashionably late, I enter the small elevator that takes me to Nick's. When the doors open, I step into the thickly carpeted bar and stop to let my eyes adjust to the dim light. I catch a familiar whiff of Aramis and look to my left to see a good looking man in a blue pinstripe suit. I remember Steve as being taller but I didn't wear heels back then.

"Andrea?"

There is no mistaking the voice. It sends me back six years in an instant and I'm on campus; in the library, in front of my dorm, down at the pool and a hundred other places where I had heard Steve call my name. I drop my briefcase and open my arms for a hug. A stronger whiff of his after shave. Even with his suit jacket on, I sense he's kept his athlete's body. I step back. Happy to see he hasn't fixed the slight gap in his teeth.

He speaks first. "I can't believe that's you. Are you wearing lipstick? You look fantastic. Your mom said you were doing really well but I . . . "

"She didn't tell me you called. Your folks okay?" I had adored his parents and they had loved me back.

"Talked to them yesterday. They said to tell you hi."

I take off my coat and Steve takes it out of my hand. A slight eyebrow raise as he notices the Burberry lining before he hands it off to the coat check girl. I reach for my claim check but he pockets it. The coat check girl gestures to my briefcase.

"Would you like me to hold on to that too?"

"I'll keep this, thanks."

Steve puts his hand on the small of my back and steers me toward a high top table in the bar.

"Sorry about the short notice. I didn't want to give you a lot of time to think of a good excuse not to see me."

"Are you kidding? Why would you think that I wouldn't want to see you?" Maybe because of a drunken phone call I made a few years ago to dredge up some of our past? I'd ended my rant with sloppy sniffles saying I never wanted to see him, talk to him, or even think about him ever again. Not elaborating my reasons. That would have been too humiliating.

"I'm glad you called," I say.

"I remember the Chagall outside. That was a fun trip," he says.

"That was a long time ago. You have a good memory," I say.

"Yes, because it was a good memory," he says.

I don't answer him, afraid he might hear the catch in my throat. I haven't been crazy all these years.

The light is better here at the table than in the foyer and I see his huge blond college jewfro is gone. His hair darker and cut close to his head. It makes his cheekbones more prominent and throws focus onto his dark brown eyes. I spend so much time looking at blue-eyed men in this business, I had forgotten the appeal of warm dark eyes.

I need a drink. I signal the bartender and he says something to the waiter in front of him who turns and heads right over.

"Sorry, Miss Hoffman, I didn't see you come in. What can I get you and your guest?"

"Hey, Frankie. It's okay. I'm not working tonight. This is an old friend of mine."

"Well, any friend of yours in a friend of mine. Welcome to Nick's," he says. "Dewar's for you?"

"Sure. Steve?"

"Glass of a Napa Valley Cabernet if you have it. If all you have by the glass is a house red, I'd rather drink a Heineken."

"We're famous for our wine list, sir. I'm sure you'll be impressed with tonight's selection," Frankie says, and heads back to the bar, lips pursed.

"I guess you come here a lot, *Miss Hoffman?*" Steve says. "You didn't mention that when I suggested the place." I guess he expected that I'd be impressed to be having a drink at such a swanky establishment, but I'm not the same girl he took to the Playboy Club using his father's key almost a decade ago.

I shrug. "My office is close by. Drinking and eating is sort of part of my job. The clients like it here."

"I never imagined you'd end up in finance. I had you pegged for teaching or maybe social work." Steve shakes his head. "The suit, the lipstick, a Burberry raincoat, a leather briefcase. I'm sorry. It takes a little getting used to."

I laugh. "I still have overalls. My family thinks I'm a capitalist pig but my coworkers think I'm a communist. Funny about perceptions, eh?"

Frankie arrives with our drinks. He places Steve's glass down carefully. "Stag's Leap 1979. Not the '78 which is truly exceptional, but still I'm sure you'll find it acceptable." He leaves without waiting for Steve's reply.

I watch while Steve swirls his glass and then sniffs the wine before taking a tiny sip and letting it sit in his mouth with his eyes closed for a moment before swallowing. I've seen him guzzle Boone's Farm and I take a gulp of my drink to keep from laughing at this behavior. "Tell me what you are doing now."

Steve's only too willing to talk about his life in Boston. He owns a two bedroom condo with a view of the harbor. He has season tickets to the Red Sox. He belongs to a really posh tennis club. He has dinner every Friday night at his parents' house. He has a few real estate deals going with his dad—apartment properties they renovate and rent.

While I drink my scotch and listen to him talk, his face handsome and animated in the glow from the votive on the table, I try and imagine myself in that life. Tennis doubles. Driving a Volvo. Dinner with Ken and Rita every Friday night.

The men staying at the table to talk business while Rita and I head off to the kitchen to do the dishes and swap recipes.

Frankie is back and he's carrying a phone. Lots of people who eat and drink at Nick's need to be reachable at all times or give off that impression, so every table is equipped with a phone jack.

"I'm sorry to bother you, Miss Hoffman. But they said it was important." He places the phone on the table and plugs it in.

"Give me just a second," I say to Steve, and I pick up the receiver to hear Dan giggling in the background.

"Hey, how's it going?"

"Haven't you left the office yet?"

"Soon. We just were wondering how the date is going. Is he impressed by the phone thing?" I look over to Steve who does look pretty impressed.

"I appreciate your help with this project," I say, "but I'm not sure it's important that I have your input right now."

"Loser, huh?" I hear Dan yell out. "This one's not working out. Maybe we should go over to Nick's and rescue her."

Then I hear Harold. "Don't worry, Andrea. I'm dragging him to the train. Have a nice evening." To Dan he says, "Hang up the phone, Sir Galahad. I'm sure she has it covered."

"Wait, Andie, don't go yet," Dan says. "We're having an important discussion and we need your participation."

"Okay, I'll try and help." I roll my eyes at Steve and shrug my shoulders for good measure.

Steve gives me a little "don't worry about it" wave off.

"Why do you think," Dan asks, "that people can masturbate but they can't tickle themselves? I mean it should be the same thing, right?"

I can't help but snigger. Damn good question. "Hang on, Daniel." I look toward Steve. What the hell. I ask him the question.

He frowns. "You're kidding right?" he says. "I went to B-school. Not med school."

"Got nothing for you, Johnson," I say, and then before the conversation gets any weirder, I hang up the phone.

Steve is looking at me very strangely so I say, "Bio-tech offering. Just clearing up some details in the prospectus."

"What is it exactly that you do?"

"I make money," I say.

Frankie comes over to pick up the phone and Steve lavishly compliments him on the wine selection. We order new drinks and a more cheerful Frankie returns almost immediately with our fresh beverages and the tray of complimentary miniature steak sandwiches that Nick's is famous for. The chairs here are a lot more comfortable than in the old school cafeteria and it starts to feel like old times as we talk. I stop looking for reasons to be unhappy with him.

I excuse myself and go to the ladies room. I need to pee but I also need a coke bump to keep me sharp. When I'm paying attention to what he's saying, I recognize that Steve is more of an arrogant asshole than I remembered. But the other stuff keeps pushing those moments away. The pleasure of having shared memories with someone. My involuntary reaction when he touches my hand—how it causes my body to remember his skin, his touch, his rhythm, his sighs. I sigh. I want him to want me. I always have. I take a second small snort, inspect my nose while I reapply lipstick.

Steve stands and pulls out my chair when I return to him. "You are just so beautiful."

I feel beautiful.

When our third drink is delivered, he says, "I love this place. I can't believe I've been in Chicago so many times and I never came here." He raises his glass to toast wonderful Nick's Fishmarket. I leave my glass sit. I'm busy processing his words.

"Really," I say. "You've been coming to Chicago a lot?"

"Every couple of months for the last two years or so," he says. Such a proud look on his face. I should be so impressed that he travels so much.

"So why did you decide to call me now?" I ask quietly.

"Why did I call you now?" he repeats. His smile fades. His forehead wrinkles and his eyes squint like they always do when he is thinking. He looks around the room. Looks down at the table. Takes a little sip of his wine.

"Yes, now. And not the other eight times you were in town." Sometimes—blow or no blow—I can drink all night and not feel drunk and this is apparently one of those nights. My body may be conflicted but my mind is clear as the water in the lobster tank against the far wall. I know I'm being set up for something. My foot starts to jiggle under the table.

Steve looks into my eyes and says, "I've been wondering how I was going to tell you this. Since you were . . . are . . . so important to me, and this is so important to me. I decided I wanted to tell you in person." He pauses. He puts his hand on top of mine.

For a second I think—I hope—he is going to tell me he has some incurable disease. I brace myself for the news.

"I'm getting married next month and . . . "

I let out a snort. I put up my hand to stop him from saying anything further. "I get it. I really get it. Just spare me."

"Get what? I thought you deserved to hear the news from me personally."

"Right. We haven't seen each other for *six* years. You asked me for drinks because you wanted to make sure I didn't get fat. If I showed up and looked like a baby beluga, you had a 'business dinner' excuse in the bag. But I'm not fat and so we're still here. If I hadn't caught you, I doubt you would have told me you're getting married."

"Of course I would have. You didn't 'catch me' at

anything. Why else would I have called you for a drink?" Steve says righteously.

I keep my eyes on his face. Speak slowly. "To screw me."

His head snaps back. His eyes dart around to check the tables around us. "Whoa. Now who's being presumptuous? I just told you I'm getting married and you think I want to sleep with you? Yeah, you look good but . . . I have to say you're kind of full of yourself since you're a big shot Wall Street gal now."

Gal? The word rankles but still, a little uncertainty creeps over me. Maybe I did just lash out because of my own disappointment. I start a knee jerk apology. "I'm sorry. The guys I work with are such scumbags that I just assume that all guys are." I cannot admit that Steve getting married makes me feel like the loneliest person on earth. I look in his eyes. I don't see that he is insulted. I don't see righteous indignation. I see fear. And I'm not sorry any more. I'm angry. Because I know that I'm right. And worse, I don't want to be right. Every cell in my body is craving him and now I understand his game, I can't have him.

"I understand," he's saying. "This must have been a shock to you and I guess I should have handled it better. But no matter whatever else you were before, you were always nice and I guess I was taking advantage of that fact."

He's making it easier. "Yes, now you're talking. You were taking advantage of the fact that I was always nice."

Steve looks confused. He didn't catch the change in my expression. He thought he was in the clear just a second ago.

"You're getting married and you realize that you're going to sleep with the same woman for the rest of your life. Scary thought. You love your fiancée. You don't want to cheat on her but you *deserve* one last fling. So that's where I come in. I'm grandfathered right? I'm sure you learned about that escape clause at Harvard Business School. Actions that were legal before a law is passed to make them illegal are exempt from prosecution. Therefore, it's not cheating to sleep with someone you've slept with before. I'm the last fling. I'm the grandfathered fuck. Lucky me!"

The couple at the table next to us has stopped talking and is clearly listening in on my rant. I return their stares and say, "Well, which one of us do you think is right here?" They quickly look away.

"Jesus, Andrea. You've gone completely nuts."

"You know, when I was at school, I was incredibly stupid. I thought it was so great that you liked me. It was *enough* that you liked me. You cheated on me, you put me down, you didn't love me, but it was enough that you liked me. But I'm so much smarter now . . . not because I know about capital ratios and debt financing. No, now I know that people are nice to you for one hundred and one reasons and one hundred of them have to do with what *they* want and if you're lucky, one has to do with who you are. This business teaches you one thing. It's all about who you can trust. It's all about who has some fucking class."

Steve stands. "This was a bad idea. I didn't mean to make you mad. I just thought it would be fun . . . some laughs for old time's sake. You've changed. You're awfully cynical. You used to have a sense of humor."

"I haven't lost my sense of humor. I always thought my mother was so wrong not to like you. Shit. Now I have to call her and tell her she was right. How funny is that? You have a nice life, Steve. I wish you and your new bride much luck." I stand up.

"I have your coat check," he says. He fumbles in his pants pocket to pull out the plastic tag for my coat. What he lays down on the table is plastic and round but instead of my claim check number, it says "Trojan" on it.

"Nice touch," I say. "You can get the bill. I can manage to get my own goddamn coat."

"That isn't what you think it is," he says to me.

"It never was," I say. "Thanks for helping me figure that out."

I leave Steve at the table waiting for the check and I point out my Burberry to the coat check girl who hands it right over. I slip her a five dollar bill. As I ride up in the elevator, I make myself two promises. I'm buying myself a new watch. This Movado he gave me isn't keeping up with the times. And I'm finding a condo to buy. I'm not waiting for Steve to come back or a new guy to show up. I want what Charlene has. And I want it now.

Chapter 25

I wake up late because I haven't slept. The phone rang twice after I got home but I didn't answer it. It could have been Steve and it might have been my mother and if it was the former I would probably have gotten back into a cab, headed to his hotel, and stabbed him in the heart, and if it was the later, I'd probably have killed myself. So I smoked a joint, had a final glass of Dewar's, and took the phone off the hook. Then I played "who's a bigger asshole" with myself, trying to decide if it was him or me as I watched the clock flip from one to two to three, finally falling into a dead sleep about fifteen minutes before the alarm went off. I dash out of the house a blurry-eyed mess and arrive at my desk just as the call is starting. Harold's chair is empty. I didn't know he was going to be out today but I'm relieved I don't have to act professional. I'm pretty sure staring into space is going to be my major activity of the day. As soon as the call is over, we gather around the coffee pot.

Just Bob asks, "So, where's the boss?"

Dan says, "I rode the train with him last night and he didn't say anything about not being in today."

Johnny, who has the hearing of a bat, calls over, "I thought you had dinner with that oil analyst last night—that Castinelli guy."

"Blew me off for his fiancée. Can you believe it?"

"Yes, I've seen her. I believe it," says Bob.

"Big rack?" Johnny asks.

"Okay. I'm stopping this conversation right now." I say. "Charlene and I don't discuss dick dimensions at seven in the morning in front of you guys."

"Go right ahead," says Johnny.

"I think that would be hot," says Dan.

Charlene fixes a gaze on Dan that's the equivalent of a Mr. Freeze icicle blast.

"Can't blame a guy . . . " Dan starts while arranging his face into an innocent look I'm sure he practices in the mirror.

"Yes," says Charlene, "actually I can."

Dan shrugs and scoots away. He sits down at Harold's desk and picks up the phone leaning back in his chair, feet on the desk, Harold style.

"Ron, Harold Stackman of Kendall-Fitz here. I've got the perfect stock for your aggressive fund. You're busy now? Well then, I'll give you the short story. It'll just take a minute. B.S. Techno-crap. You've heard of it? You hate it? Just let me tell you three new facts that you may not be aware of. Hello? Hello?" Dan pantomimes redialing. "Ron, Harold Stackman of Kendall-Fitz. We got cut off. As I was saying . . . "

"He's relentless. I'll give him that," I say looking toward the door half expecting and hoping Harold will come in and catch Dan's act.

"He's a machine. Mr. Memorex. God, he tells the same story over and over again. He doesn't care if he is talking to someone who can use the stock or not. He sells the same way he did when he was a Fuller Brush man. The more doors you knock on, the more brushes you sell. I honestly think some people buy stock to get him off the phone."

"He speaks highly of you," I say, annoyed at Dan but thinking he has a point. Harold is classic old school.

"He's obsessive compulsive," Bob offers.

Mary Consuleo, Dan, and I glance at Bob's perfectly organized desk with his notebooks full of lists, calendars, outlines, and conversation summaries.

"You would know," notes Dan.

"Hey, I'm flexible. I'm responsive. I'm sensitive to the individual needs of my customers."

"You sound like a god damn condom advertisement," says Johnny.

"And I come in seven fiesta colors," Bob adds.

I think about the bright blue condom package lying on the shiny cocktail table at Nick's. The guys would love to hear that story and someday I'm going to be able to tell it, but I don't quite see the humor in it yet.

"Harold is never AWOL. We should start a pool. Ten bucks to get in. The reason why Harold is missing in action," Dan says. "I say he's interviewing."

Johnny pulls out two fives. "He's got a broad on the side. This kind of thing . . . it's always about a female."

"I can't believe that. Not Harold," I say. I really don't like to think of Harold as having sex. Ever. "I'm going with sick."

"Harold hasn't taken a sick day in the seven years I've known him," Bob says. "I'll say kidnapped by aliens. It's as likely as what you guys are coming up with."

Charlene is in: "Family problems."

Erin says it isn't nice to make fun of other people's trouble.

"We're not making fun," Dan says. "We're just trying to make a little money. Besides it's not necessarily a bad thing that happened to him. What do you think, Mary Consuelo?"

"You aren't getting ten bucks of my hard-earned money, but I think he won the Irish Sweepstakes."

"If he calls in, I sure as hell want to talk to him." Dan says.

When Harold's line finally does ring, it's not Consuelo or Dan that picks up. It's me that takes the call and it's not Harold. It's his wife, Blythe. And she's talking so quietly I can hardly hear her.

"Oh Andrea. Thank god you picked up." There's a catch in her voice.

My first thought is that Johnny's right. Harold is off with some other woman and Blythe is looking for him. Oh Lord. What do I say? I wish he'd left us a cover story.

"There's been an accident," she says, and then she emits a weird little laugh. "What am I saying? It wasn't an accident. It was a heart attack. This morning. While he was shaving. He came into the bedroom, picked up the phone, and called 911. Then he slumped to the floor."

I start to shiver like I'm standing at the lake front in the middle of January without a coat. "Oh gosh, Blythe" is all I can manage to say.

"When the ambulance arrived they asked him if he smoked and he said he gave it up. And they asked him when he gave up smoking and he said, 'about fifteen minutes ago when I realized I was having a heart attack.' Isn't that just like him?"

"Yes, just like him," I agree. I pause. Should I just ask? Or do I have to listen to more of her story before she gets to the punchline. I can't wait. I just can't. "Is Harold alright, Blythe?"

"Sorry," she says. "So sorry. I should have told you right away. I guess I'm not good at this. Harold takes care of all the calamities in the family."

I can control myself about ten more seconds before I start screaming at this poor women. Thankfully she says,

"He's okay for now. He's in Glenbrook hospital. They're running tests. Keeping him stable. They think they got him just in time."

I thank her for calling and ask if there is anything she needs. I tell her to tell Harold we are all rooting for him to get back here soon and for some reason, this causes her to start to sob and mumble thanks and it takes me a few seconds to register that she's hung up the phone.

I stare at the handset for a minute like I expect it to add commentary before I set it down. Then I stand up and shakily tell the guys what just happened.

Mary Consuelo crosses herself and although she tries hard to make us all believe she doesn't give two shits about any of us, clearly Harold is special to her if for no other reason than he gives her an exceptionally generous bonus every year. "He better get his old ass back here soon," she says. "I'm not answering his phone all day long." She stares at his phone as if she is daring it to ring and interrupt her magazine reading. When I look back at her a minute later she is still staring but she's biting her lower lip like just maybe she's trying not to cry.

Dan goes immediately to Harold's desk, pulls out his bottle of whisky and pours himself a drink. It's 10:00 in the morning. A new record for office imbibing. "Fifty-four years old," he says to no one in particular. "He's going to be fine. He played eighteen holes last weekend. How bad could it be?" He puts the bottle back without offering it to anyone else.

Bob picks up his phone and swivels away from his desk to face out the window. We all know this means he's calling his wife.

Johnny calls God. Charlene, who always know what to do in every situation, arranges for flowers to be sent to the hospital and a fruit basket to go to Harold's house.

It's Erin who points out I won the pool but I don't get up to take the bills off Johnny's desk. "Use it to replace his bottle of scotch before he comes back," I say.

The phones ring, the squawk box comes alive with traders looking for merchandise, and the ticker continues to flow with trades. The day goes on.

Just before noon, Mary Consuelo comes over and sits in Harold's chair. "I have a good deal for you," she says. "My cousin is investing in inventory. If you give me two thousand dollars today, I'll give you back four on Monday."

She looks at me casually like we are discussing ordering in lunch. I'm pretty shocked to hear her using words like "investing" and "inventory." I'm also trying to decide how you politely decline someone's offer to let you participate in a drug deal.

"I know you have the money," she says. Mary Consuelo takes my calls, distributes my check, and processes my health insurance forms. She probably knows a lot of things about me.

"I'm buying an apartment," I say. "I don't have extra money."

"You'll have it back in three days. If you're buying a place, you can use a little more dough. I help you. You help me. Good business, right? Think about it."

Clearly Consuelo has been picking up sales techniques while she has been answering our phones and filing her nails. I smile at her even though I'm pretty sure she just threatened me.

"Yeah, I'll think about it."

I walk over to Harold's desk and pick up the pink message slips she's been dropping on his desk all morning. I'll return some of these calls and see if I can help.

Then just after the close, a call from my oldest brother Jake.

"Hey, Rockefeller. I need some investing advice. My company is switching from our pension plan into something called a 401K? You know anything about that?"

I'm so shocked that he's asking me for advice and not a favor, I forget to answer him with a sarcastic remark. "I do," I say. And for the first time in our lives, my brother and I have an adult conversation. I hang up hoping I gave him useful advice, not because I don't want him blaming me later, but because I really want him to do the best thing possible with his money. Weird day, for fucking sure.

Chapter 26

I pass on going into business with Mary Consuelo and get the cold shoulder from her all week. But I might be imagining it. With Harold out, the entire office loses what little discipline we have. Even Johnny comes in a little later, leaves a little earlier, and yells less during the day. And without Harold sitting right next to me, I make fewer of the hard calls and spend more timing idly chatting on the phone with Allan and pretending it's business. What I need is some serious motivation and buying a condo and owing a shit ton of mortgage money is going to give me that. But until I pull the trigger on a place, I'm going to need some more of Mary Consuelo's product to keep me going. My first buy only lasted me a week.

I follow her into the bathroom. Four hundred dollars in an envelope in my hand. She shakes her head. "I don't think so. I'm only selling to investors these days."

"Really? You're really going to be that way?"

Her brown eyes are hard. She wags a finger at me. Her bright pink nail polish is chipped. "Yeah," she says quietly. "I'm gonna be that way. I can afford to be. Last week's buy was sold out. If you want to be on my customer list, I can fit you in to this week's deal as a favor. Come to my house with two thousand bucks cash after work today. I'll bring you four thousand on Monday and I'll throw in the blow you want now as a bonus."

She goes in the stall and pees while I stand in front of the sinks and evaluate my options. One hundred percent interest is a pretty good return for a three day loan. Which is very suspicious. It's like an Initial Public Offering for a new stock. The hot ones can double or triple the day they are listed, so giving customers an allocation of shares to buy through the offering is a gift. Let's face it. It's the firm's way of giving them a legal bribe for more business. If there's stock left over for my clients, I know it's a dog. Since Consuelo came to me with this offer and not Charlene, it doesn't pass the smell test. It's why I passed on it the first time. But clearly, now she's sweetened the deal. When I hear her flush, I've decided.

"Fine," I say when she emerges. "Write down your address. I'll be there by six."

Two minutes after the close Johnny yells over to me. "Andie, some shithead wants to talk to you on line thirty-two."

I pick it up at the empty desk next to Charlene.

"Hi. It's Patrick. How ya doing?"

Jesus. I look up to see if Johnny is looking at me but he's talking on another line and staring out the window.

"Hi, yourself. I'm . . . " I think of what I could say. I'm pissed you didn't call like you said you would. And now, I'm so happy to hear from you that I am disgusted with myself. . . .

"I'm fine," I say. "What's up?"

"Are you thirsty? It's been a long week. Sorry I didn't have time to call before now. I've been thinking about you every day. I'd like to see you. Tonight."

"Your weeks have more days in them than mine."

"It's been more like two weeks, huh."

"More like two and a half. But no. I got somewhere I have to be tonight." I look at the address Mary Consuelo gave me before she left.

"Not all night, though. Right? Tell you what. I'll stop at the East Bank Club and have a long workout. Maybe a steam. Then I'll be at Butch McGuire's. Stop by whenever. I have things I need to talk to you about. Given what's going on in your office."

"Maybe," I say. "I'll try." Curiosity nudging out my bruised pride and my suspicious mind.

When I hang up the phone, Johnny's looking at me funny, but he's had a long week too and no telling what's on his mind. According to Charlene, this is one of my problems. I assume people are always thinking about me and that their moods are always related to something I've said or done.

"People have whole lives—families, jobs, health problems—it's very egotistical of you to think you're so important to everybody." She's right, of course, but I don't think it's ego. It's more like paranoia.

"Andrea Hoffman."

Johnny's use of my whole name meant this was serious. "Yes?"

"We still know nothing about when he's coming back so don't talk about Harold's absence. Not even with your family and not with Patrick O'Neil."

"Yes, sir," I say, feeling about nine years old. Saying "Have a nice weekend" seems inappropriate, so I just nod my head at him and then hustle to the bank.

———

My cab driver's name is Flynn and when I give him the address he turns around to look at me. "You sure this is where you want to go, lady? This is not a good neighborhood."

"It's my secretary's place. It'll be fine. She's expecting me." And the huge wad of cash I have in my purse. "Are you okay with a South Side trip?"

He shrugs. "I can take care of myself."

I take note of the baseball bat he has in the front passenger seat and that there isn't also a baseball glove or ball.

We travel south on Lake Shore Drive, turn on W. Roosevelt Road and then into a neighborhood of small, rundown houses. Crappy cars parked at the curb. A corner bodega— all the signs in Spanish. Flynn is driving slow, his heading swinging left and right in the fading light.

"This is the street but goddamned if anyone puts a house number anywhere on their damn houses."

"She said it's a green house with a Madonna statue in the yard and there'll be lights strung up. They're having a party," I say.

The cabbie stops and points. "This one then."

A lime green house, three foot tall Madonna in a bathtub, Christmas lights and a banner across the front door that says "Bienvenido a casa." Latin dance music spilling out the open windows.

I pull out a twenty dollar bill for the fifteen dollar fare. Flynn eyes a couple of young men smoking on the porch steps. The smell of weed drifts over to the cab.

"You gonna be long? Cause I'm not getting a fare back from here. I might as well wait for you." He looks at me. "I got a daughter about your age."

I hand him the twenty. "Tell you what. I'll come out in a minute and let you know how long I'll be. Hang on to this in case." I get out of the car and give him a big brave smile as I walk to the house.

The smoking dudes move their legs so I can come up the steps. The guy closest to the door says, "Hey, you don't have to ring the bell, Linda, just go on in. Join the party."

I take a deep breath, hoping to inhale some of the weed smoke hanging in the air to calm me down, and open the screen door and step inside. Mary Consuelo is waiting for me. She's wearing skintight white pants, a low cut shiny black shirt, even more makeup than she wears in the office, and her hair is teased out to twice it's normal height. And unlike her usual office look, she's smiling. Her black eyes are dancing and she opens her arms to hug me. "Andrea, Andrea! So happy to see you, *mi Amiga*. Let me get you a drink. Come join the party."

"Wow! I'd love to but I have a cab waiting." I pat my purse. "You want to go somewhere I can give this to you?"

"The cab can go away. Somebody will drive you home later. No problem."

She shouts out the door. "Juan, *dile a ese taxista que puede ir.*"

And through the screen I see one of the young men stand up and head down the steps.

Two young women also dressed in ass-hugging jeans and boob-exposing blouses pass us in the hall and Mary Consuelo grabs one by the wrist. Yells over the music. "Don't be rude! Say hello. This is my boss lady." She leans in to me and says, "These bitches are my cousins. They do hair if you ever want to change your look."

The girls eye my chin length streaked hair. One of them raises a thin penciled eyebrow. "Come see us, pretty face boss lady. We'll fix your makeup too." Then giggling, they move on to the living room where I can see at least twenty people drinking, smoking, and dancing.

Mary Consuelo grabs my arm and pulls me in the other direction. We enter a small bedroom and she flicks on the light. Neatly made single bed. An oil painting of a seaside village on the wall behind it. She shuts the door. The party sounds fade. "You have the money?"

I pull out the thick envelope. She takes it and grins. "Nice doing business with you." She goes to the dresser and drops the money in the top drawer and then pulls out a small baggy for me. Then picks up a second one. "First time bonus."

I zip the coke into the side pocket of my purse. "Nice doing business with you too. *Gracias.*" I check her expression to see if she is insulted by my terrible pronunciation.

She rolls her eyes. "Come on, I want you to meet my cousin Richie. It's his welcome home party."

"Did he just get out of the service?" I ask.

Mary Consuelo throws her head back and laughs. "Shit no! Not the army. The joint. He's been downstate in Marion. Early release on a ten year sentence. Good behavior." She takes my arm *again* and pulls me toward the door. In all the time I've worked with her, I'm sure she never touched me before. Which was fine with me.

"Come on. You'll like him. He's a sweetheart." She opens the door and we're back in the noise, pushing our way through a small crowd and into the living room.

"Hey, Richie," she yells and a guy in jeans and a black t-shirt turns around.

I gasp. Mary Consuelo grins. "He's really cute, right?"

I know him. I know that face. I know what his voice sounds like. "Don't nobody fucking move." He's holding a beer and I clearly see the parrot tattoo on his hand. Holy fuck. It's Gun Guy. What if he recognizes me? Tells everyone I'm the one who identified him? I'm the one who sent him away.

He nods at his cousin, glances at me, and without showing the slightest interest in a yuppie white girl in a business suit and heels, turns back around. I exhale. But my legs are rubbery.

"You don't have to babysit me," I say to Mary Consuelo. "I'll go find myself a drink." Without waiting for her to answer, I walk slowly but purposefully toward the front door.

Over the music, I hear Ritchie call out. "Hey you, lady. Wait. I know you right? I know you."

I keep walking but I shake my head. He wouldn't know my name. The cop said he wouldn't have to tell him my name. I can just deny I'm who he thinks I am. It's true. I'm not that girl at Mariana's anymore. A man steps in front of me.

"I think Richie's talking to you." He points behind me. I turn. Richie is pushing through the dancers.

"I know you. *Eres la chica!*" His eyes are dark. His face contorted.

"I don't know you," I say. "You're wrong whoever you think I am. I've never seem you before. I . . . I just work with Mary Consuelo." I scan the room looking for her. The dancers have bunched together to watch Richie. I don't see her.

"You think I would forget you? A scared little face like that?" A cruel smile. "Same face right now. Scared."

The guy behind me moves closer, blocking me in more securely. Gun Guy takes a step toward me. "You made a mistake coming here, girl."

I hear shouting on the porch and the front door opens hard enough to slam against the wall and rattle the glass. Outside, I hear sirens coming closer. I turn and see my cabbie, bat in hand. "Let's go," he says. "Cops are on the way."

At the sound of those sirens, the crowd starts to push toward the door and I'm pushed out with them. Flynn, my savior, grabs my hand and half drags me to the cab and throws me in the back seat. As we drive away, I see two patrol cars heading up the street and partygoers running in all directions. I don't see Mary Consuelo. I don't see Gun Guy.

"I thought you would have left. Didn't someone come out and tell you I was staying?"

"I don't leave because some little Spic tells me to. Even from across the street, I could see nothing good was going on in there."

"Well, thanks. It . . . wasn't what I expected. Someone was there I wasn't expecting."

I flash back to the store and the sound of the gun shot and the broken glass and the sobbing customer. And just now, Mary Consuelo being so chummy with me. This was all a huge mistake. Will she tell him my name? Give him my address?

"Shit. Did you call the cops?" I ask.

"No. But when I heard the sirens I had a pretty good idea of where they were headed."

"Well, thanks for waiting," I say. I need a drink. I need some company. I don't want to go home and be alone. The thought of big shot Patrick O'Neil waiting for me is suddenly comforting. "Can you take me to Butch McGuire's?"

"Sure thing."

He drops the flag on the meter. I steal myself for more of a lecture but the driver turns on the radio and keeps his eyes on the road.

I stare out the window as we head north and blocks of houses disappear, replaced by warehouses and dark empty lots and then finally we join the river of traffic on the Drive and we roll by a calm Lake Michigan as my breath slows and my heart rate returns to normal.

Chapter 27

Butch McGuires is packed with yuppies elbow to elbow with the work boots and lunch box crowd. The smell of beer and burgers makes my stomach rumble. It's after seven o'clock and lunch was a long time ago. I walk the length of the bar, circumnavigate the back room, and push my way through the happy drinkers and back to the front room. No Patrick. Come and gone? Not here yet? How long can a workout and a steam take? Two hours. I'm not going to stand here like an idiot. I start for the door but as I pass, a group of guys vacate their bar stools. A tall man with unruly dark brown hair knocks into me. He turns and I recognize those green eyes. The pushy student from Wisconsin

"Sorry, sorry," he says. "I'm leaving. Do you want my . . ." Jack Keith finally looks at me and a smile spreads across his face. "Andrea Hoffman of Kendall-Fitz! Perfect. Join us." He gestured to the group of suits bunched around him. "We're headed to Pops! on Sheffield for some champagne. Celebrating. Closed a nice deal this week."

He fumbles in his suit pocket and hands me a business card. *Jack Keith. Vice President. Institutional Fixed Income. Goldman Sachs.*

Not a client. Not a competitor either.

"Congratulations," I say. "On the deal and on the job."

"So you'll come?"

I shake my head. "Meeting someone." I sit on his vacated stool. "But thanks for the chair and the invite."

Jack holds a finger up to his buddies to wait a minute. He looks down at me with a look of concern on his face. "Are you okay? You look kind of shell-shocked. Do you want me to stick around a bit?"

"I'm fine," I say. "Just been a long week. And a weird evening." I turn my head to the door. "Your friends are getting antsy. You better get going."

"They're just people I work with. They can wait a minute," he says. "How about I buy you a drink?" He signals the bartender. "What would you like?"

I don't need him to buy me a drink, but the bartender is looking right at me. "I'll have a scotch, please."

I turn to Jack. I'm still in shock from seeing Gun Guy. The robbery replaying in my mind for the first time in years. But the details are still sharp. "Did you ever hear a gun go off? I mean not in a movie or on television. I mean were you ever right there?"

Jack nods. "It's loud." He doesn't ask me why I'm asking.

I shudder. "Guns are scary." I take a take a gulp of my scotch.

"You might not want to hear this, but I own a gun," he says. "They're less scary when they're yours. I can teach you to shoot it. If you're interested."

The group by the door sends an emissary to hurry Jack up. "In a minute," he says calmly.

"Maybe," I say.

"You have an open mind," he says. "One of the things I like about you."

I've given him zero encouragement. Why would he like

anything about me? Unless he's psycho. A psycho with a gun. And yet. He doesn't look crazy. He just looks interested.

"I'll call you tomorrow. I want to hear more about your gun experience. Are you listed in the phone book?"

"I might not be home tomorrow," I say. I see Patrick at the door eying the crowd. I wave.

Jack glances in the direction I'm looking. "I'm still calling," he says and he goes. He gets to the door just as Patrick reaches me.

"Hey Jack," I hear his coworker say. "Sure you don't want to stick around so your friend can introduce you to her dad?"

If Patrick realizes this comment is directed toward him, he doesn't react. He's not *my* father's age but according to Dan he is someone's dad. I don't care. After the day I've had, I need a mature man. I can get some advice on how not to be such a dumbass sometimes. I'm happy he showed up.

"Wonderful that you're here. You're the best. I hope you weren't waiting long. Shitty about Harold, eh?" Patrick gestures to my drink. "Finish that up. The car's at the curb and dinner awaits."

I chug the last inch of scotch and stand up. Let my mood be buoyed by his tornado of words. "After you," I say.

He holds the door of the black town car open for me. I get in and slide over toward the far window. He gets in, leans back, and spreads his leg wide. Like when I met him in the Cohasset, I'm struck by the size of him. Not a fat man but he takes up a lot of room. I smell soap from the gym, and booze on his breath.

"Antonio's on Wells," he says to the driver.

Antonio's is not the Pump Room. It's a small neighborhood restaurant not far from my apartment.

He turns to me. "The Pump Room is a zoo on Friday nights. Too many tourists staying at the hotel clogging up the bar. Antonio's is quieter. You'll like it."

I would have *liked* the Pump Room. Antonio's is a one hundred basis point downtick. So much for Patrick trying to impress me. I suppress a sigh. And why should he be? He's doing me the favor. Educating me about options. Right?

"I love Italian food," I say.

"I can tell," he says. "I like girls with some meat on their bones." He puts a hand on my thigh. Gives it a squeeze for emphasis.

"Do you have a cigarette?" It's all I can think of to get his hand off my leg. He pulls a pack of Kents out of his suit jacket with his free hand. Leaves his left hand heavy on my thigh.

"Didn't know you smoked," he says.

"Sometimes. I've had a rough day. I needed to drop something off at my secretary's house and . . . "

"You should join the East Bank Club. So many important people have. I can never go there without being roped into a few cocktails after."

I take a cigarette. Patrick doesn't seem to notice that I don't have matches or that he interrupted me in the middle of a sentence.

"I'm not sure I can afford that place yet."

"We're going to make sure you can. I'd love to see you at the rooftop pool in a little bikini." He pats my leg and then shifts to rap on the window between us and the driver.

"Stop up here on the right. Park and wait for us."

The maître de greets Patrick like an old friend and leads us to a dark booth in the back and takes our drink order. A double for Patrick. Even though the place is full, a bus boy hustles over and fills our water glasses. Places a basket of warm bread on the table. Screw looking ladylike. I dig in for a large slice and butter it extravagantly.

"Starving," I say. "Facing death will do that to you."

Patrick doesn't bite. He gestures to the menu. "You look. I always have the same thing here. Terrific lasagna."

I leave my menu untouched. "Then I don't have to look. I'll have what you're having."

He signals for the waiter and orders for the both of us. When the waiter walks away, he turns to look at me. "I did hear you. By the way. In the car. When you said you had a rough day. But frankly, if I wanted to hear a woman complain about her day, I'd go home. You understand, right?" He swirls his single malt and then sips it. "Who the fuck cares if the washing machine is broke? It's not like she does the laundry anyway. You know what else she doesn't do?"

I shake my head. "Mow the lawn?" I offer.

"Suck my cock." He puts the drink down. "She's happy to spend my money but she's too much of a fucking princess to give me some head." He dips his index finger in his scotch and then pushes it against my lips.

Shocked, I open my mouth in surprise and he takes this as an invitation. Shoves the finger inside my mouth and pushes it in and out suggestively. Instinctively, my hand comes up and swats his hand away.

He smiles and puts the finger in his own mouth. What the fuck?

"You've got the right idea," he says. "You're going to have to open your mouth a lot wider though." He forms a circle with his fingers and thumb.

"I . . . " I take a breath. No other words come out.

The hand comes down on my thigh again. Higher up this time. His index finger pushes under my skirt. "Relax. I'm just joking with you. Johnny told me you had a great sense of humor. Typical Jew. Brainy and funny."

He's smiling at me, but that hungry look is in his eyes.

Typical Jew? I try and think of something brainy and funny to say about him being anti-Semitic but I got nothing.

"I'm going to go freshen up before our food comes," I say and try and smile. I pick up my purse and get out of the booth. Feel his eyes on my ass as I walk away.

I ignore the door that says signore and push through the swinging door into the kitchen. I spot the open door in the back and clutching my purse in front of me like a shield, rush past the surprised cooks and dishwasher and make my escape through the alley to the street. I turn and walk the opposite way so as not to pass the plate glass window in the front of the restaurant. I flag down a yellow cab and once inside, I picture Patrick sitting at the table awaiting my return and feel a moment of panic. Maybe I overreacted? What if he *was* only joking? He'll think I'm a fool. But I'm not a fool. There was nothing funny about the look on his face as he pushed his wet finger into my mouth. I shuddered. He was a big man. Alone with him I wouldn't had stood a chance. So not a fool but a coward? I could have told him I wasn't interested in him and left with some dignity. But probably not. I would have heard I was a cock tease and a user and a prude. Why give him the satisfaction? The cab pulls up in front of my building and after paying him, I bolt for my door. Desperate to be home. To be safe.

Gun Guy, aka. Mary Consuelo's cousin Richie, is not hiding in my lobby waiting to kill me. Relief about that but the sick feeling in my stomach doesn't go away. I ditched a Managing Director. Left him sitting in at the table—maybe literally—holding his dick. And I'm still fucking starving. Shit. I drop my purse and head toward the kitchen.

The answering machine light is blinking. It's Mary Consuelo. There's a lot of noise in the background. Music. People talking.

"I wanted to tell you. A bunch of the family is going to Iowa. I know, fucking Iowa, right? But they got jobs there and they need drug dealers." She snorts. "Chicago's not a good place for us right now. The cops are just going to keep hassling everyone that lives in the house." Something muffled and then, "Bad news though. I need to keep all your money. Sorry. Like really sorry. But good timing for me." Another snort. Someone is talking to her now. Telling her they need to get going and then Spanish I don't understand. "*Un minuto*," she says. That much Spanish I do understand. Back to me. ". . .and also I need to ask you a favor. At work, tell them I quit. Have them keep my last check in the office. I'll send someone to pick it up." She stops talking but I hear the background noise. She hasn't hung up. I hear her sigh. "It's crazy that Richie thought you were the person he robbed in that rich ladies' store. All you *gabacha*, you look alike. You looked so scared, when he was shouting at you. But, he's not a bad guy. Don't worry okay? Andrea . . . " Mary Consuelo continues after another short pause, "You should give up the coke. It's not really your scene." Another short silence and then so quietly I can barely hear her. " Tell Harold I said goodbye. And you know, thanks for putting up with me. Okay. Don't tell him . . . you know. Okay. Yeah. Goodbye." I hear the click.

I listen one more time and then I hit erase.

Chapter 28

Saturday, Jack did call. And again on Sunday. I didn't pick up. I listened to his messages but I didn't call back. He's a nice guy. I just don't think I can deal with a nice guy right now.

Monday morning at the coffee pot, I volunteer no details of my weekend. Except the one thing I have to do.

"Johnny," I say. "Can you call personnel? Mary Consuelo left a message on my answering machine at home Friday night to say she's not going to be in today . . . or ever again. She quit."

"Jesus Christ. We need people to stop disappearing in this fucking office," Johnny says. "Fucking disconcerting. Is she in jail?"

"Pretty sure if that was the case, she would've been hitting me up for bail. So, no. It wasn't a long message, but she said something about moving."

Charlene feigns surprise. But she already knew. Sunday, we had brunch. During the first Bloody Mary, she told me she met a man. A lawyer. And he was charming and generous and a good listener. Tall. Single. Drives a Jaguar. With a stick shift.

I'd immediately signaled the waiter for another round of drinks.

Since we'd become friendly enough to share this kind of information, Charlene always had a guy around but her previous men had always been reliably inappropriate. Men who were geographically undesirable (Ted that lived in Milwaukee) or possibly gay (Franco who knew all the best places to shop) or already encumbered (Sean who was still "sort of" married) and worse (Louis who was divorced but had shared custody of three children under the age of six.) I had gotten used to the idea that she liked it this way. Perfect companions were men who were lots of fun but who couldn't tie her down. And I'll admit I liked this too. She'd share marvelous stories with me but never cared enough about any one of these guys to let them interfere with our friendship. But now this. Lawrence the lawyer who was making her eyes shine like a commercial for diamond rings. Charlene had found her man and happy as I was for her—Jesus just look at her glowing face—it made me depressed and on top of that, I hated myself for feeling that way. Another round, *por favor*!

When our eggs benedicts came, she snapped out of her bliss long enough to notice I was less than effusive.

"I'm fine," I said.

"Fuck fine," she said. Even with minimal makeup and her hair pulled into a pony tail, Charlene was beautiful. Her friendship had always seemed to be a stroke of luck I didn't quite deserve. "Spill, little bitch."

So I told her the whole story. The robbery that brought me to Mosley, the disastrous trip to Mary Consuelo's house, the Butch McGuire's meet up with Jack and then Patrick. Him turning out to be an enormous shithead. By the time we had finished our food, I was telling her about the message from Mary Consuelo and getting inexplicably teary. Her solution? A round of shots. And then another.

We toasted Mary Consuelo—a truly awful secretary—and wished her happiness in her new life in Iowa. And we toasted Patrick. Hoping his extramarital adventures bring him herpes and an expensive divorce.

"You're going to have to open your mouth a lot wider than that," I repeated and that set us off, laughing so hard that we were rolling around on the benches of the booth gasping for air. My sanity saved. Thank God for Charlene and Sunday brunch.

Now Erin, who only ever drinks tea, walks over and joins us at the coffee pot. Her hair hangs limp. Her bangs are too short. She's wearing a shapeless brown dress. Where does she even find them?

Bob waves his cup in her direction. "Welcome stranger."

Erin, who hasn't changed out of her sneakers and into her low heeled pumps yet, shifts from one white Ked to the other and says, "I know something."

Everyone turns to stare at her. It would be only slightly less astonishing if the coffee pot itself started to speak.

"You don't need a formal invitation to tell us," Johnny says, but his tone is amused and not nasty.

Erin takes a breath and says, "My sister works at Glencoe? Glencoe Hospital? She was . . . uh . . . there when Harold came in?" She pauses for a second. "He's going to be discharged today."

"That's great," I say. "Thanks for telling us." It'll be a relief to have the office back to normal and maybe he'll want to lighten up his package and reshuffle some accounts.

Erin's still talking. "That's not all," she says. "While he was in the hospital? Okay, I'm sorry?" She stops. Takes a breath and then blurts out, "They found out Harold didn't just have a heart attack. He has lung cancer."

For a moment, there's complete silence.

"Well, that shits," Dan says.

Erin, her big news out, visibly deflates and then bursts into huge sobs and flees toward the bathroom. I start to follow her but Charlene shakes her head. "I got it, sweetie," she says, and then adds, "It'll be okay." It isn't a pat, but her hand rests gently for a fraction of a second on my shoulder. To my horror, this makes *my* eyes fill up with tears.

"Maybe we need to start dividing up his accounts," Dan says. "I want Minneapolis."

"It makes a lot more sense for me to cover Minneapolis because I already cover Milwaukee," Bob counters.

"What the fuck are you guys talking about?" Johnny booms. "Bunch of greedy animals. He's not dead yet."

"Of course not. Harold's stubborn as shit. He'll beat this and be back before we know it. Backup," says Dan. "We're just going to formalize the backup plan. During his recovery."

Johnny shakes his head and heads to his desk.

"Maybe *I* want the Minneapolis accounts," I say, practically whispering and less than half kidding.

Dan turns to me, stage whispers, "If I get—I mean—temporarily get Minneapolis, maybe you can—temporarily—handle some of my smaller accounts. Maybe even St. Louis."

I turn to Bob. "Any offers from you?"

"I'm not giving up Milwaukee, that's for damn sure. I love that town and they love me."

I smell a musky waft of Pheromone seconds before I notice Charlene has returned from the bathroom and is standing behind us.

"Hey, I'd like to make some money so I can support myself in the style to which I have become accustomed. I don't suppose any of you humps would like to make some phone calls today?" She gives Dan a gentle push toward his desk and walks over to Bob's desk, pulls out his chair for him, and gestures he should take a seat before she sits in her own chair and swivels her long legs around and picks up her phone.

"Hey, what about me?" I call out.

"You're self-motivated, sugar," she says.

I can't believe how much that tiny little compliment means to me.

The light on my phone is blinking and I pick it up. Kurt Winters, a portfolio manager at one of my bigger Indiana accounts.

"Hey, Kurt, how's it going?"

He sighs. "Did you hear that my wife is pregnant again? She's sick as a rabid dog." He tries to sound woeful but clearly he's pretty proud.

My immediate thought, *Jesus, what in the world do you want another kid for*, seems harsh so I just say, "That's great, Kurt. Not the sick part. The baby part."

"We're excited about another kid but they really mess up your life. Morgan Stanley has a block of tickets to the Rolling Stones concert in Chicago next week and they invited me up with Tracie. She's dying to go. The last fun thing before the new baby comes. But we'd be staying over-night and we don't have anyone to babysit Kurt Jr."

"Maybe Morgan will give you another ticket for him," I volunteer.

"He's three, Andie. His musical tastes run more along the lines of 'Itsy Bitsy Spider' than 'Satisfaction.'"

Fucking Morgan Stanley. Stones tickets and hotel rooms. This is costing them a fortune. If they invited Kurt, he must be doing a lot more business than I thought. I have a new stock offering coming and it would look really good if Kurt took a nice slug of it. It's not a total dog of a deal but it might encourage Kurt to commit to a nice chunk if thought he owed me a favor. "I live downtown. I could come to the hotel and babysit him," I say. "But . . . "

Kurt doesn't let me finish. "Done! Holy shit. There's dinner at 6:00 and we'd be back by midnight or 1:00 at the latest. He'll be asleep most of the time. Kurt, Jr. is a great little sleeper. I'm putting you on hold and calling Tracie."

While I'm on hold, I catch Bob's eye.

"Bob, what do you pay a babysitter these days?"

"Ours gets $4 an hour and all the chips and diet soda they can consume. Why do you need a babysitter? Is there something you haven't told us?"

"I don't need one. I just offered to be one. For Kurt Winters. I'm thinking it's worth 20,000 share of the New England Electric IPO."

Bob laughs. "What you won't do to make a buck."

"It's not so different from taking someone out to dinner," I say defensively.

Eye roll from Bob. Can't really blame him.

Kurt comes back on the line. "Tracie is thrilled with this plan. She remembers you from the softball game picnic last year. She gave you her potato salad recipe and she doesn't share that with just anybody."

"It was so delicious," I say, not remembering Tracie or the recipe exchange.

"I owe you big time."

"Don't be silly, Kurt," I say. "I'll love doing this. I never get to spend enough time with my nephews." Thank god! I have no baby lust. None. What I do know is that I'm calling Kurt the day after the concert to sell him some of this offering.

Thankfully, Dan's on the phone and hasn't heard any of my conversation with Bob. In fact, everyone in the office seems unusually busy. Even Erin, who apparently is having a worst day/best day, finally gets a decent sized buy order of Exxon from First Iowa Bank. Without Mary Consuelo, the phones ring until someone can grab them or whoever's calling gives up. It's just before noon when we realize that Harold's standing in the doorway.

He looks like crap. He's wearing his navy pinstripe suit with a blue striped shirt and a maroon and blue regiment tie, but without his usual attention to detail. He's missing a belt or suspenders. He's already lost enough weight to be sorely in need of one or the other. His breast pocket is without his customary handkerchief. He has matched brown socks with his blue suit. I can see his socks because Harold is not wearing his usual Tony Lama authentic cowboy boots or his spit-shined two-hundred-and-fifty-dollar black wing-tips—not even the cordovan tassel loafers. Today he's wearing Hush Puppies. Harold Stackman has shown up to work a week after a heart attack and a cancer diagnosis in brown suede Hush Puppies. With his navy pinstripe suit. Things are clearly worse than we thought.

When he realizes he's been spotted watching us like a shy kid at the playground, he puts a smile on his face and heads toward his desk with a pale approximation of his usual confident step.

"Anybody miss me?" he asks no one in particular. "And where's Mary Consuelo?"

I feel a stab of guilt. I could have called him over the weekend to give him her message, but why? I keep my phone conversation going and stare at my Quotron like the secrets of the universe are written there. If I stay occupied, somebody else will start the conversation with Harold. Someone else will tell him he has a small piece of toilet paper stuck to his face where presumably he has cut himself shaving.

Indeed, as soon as they finish their calls, Dan and Bob are at Harold's desk.

"Everything's fine," Harold insists.

"Harold, you don't have on a belt or suspenders and you're wearing ugly fucking Hush Puppies," Dan points out. "Everything is not fine."

I've seen Dan coming in to the office looking a lot worse plenty of times, but that's Dan and this is Harold.

Harold orders us all into the conference room. Dan, Bob, and I get up.

The four of us settle at the end of the table closest to the door and wait for Harold to say something. I hate silences so I wait about four seconds and then say, "So I think you look pretty good, boss."

"I feel pretty good too . . . for a guy with cancer."

None of us bother to look surprised.

"Tough fucking luck," says Dan.

"For eighty percent of my life, I smoked two packs of cigarettes a day and a dozen cigars a week so I guess—short of coal miners—I was at the head of the line."

We all laugh even though it isn't too funny.

"I'm going to be out of the office for a while so I came over here to tell you kids to play nicely together while I'm gone."

"What can we do to help?" I ask.

Dan puckers up and shoots me an "ass-kisser" look. "Yeah, boss, anything. You let us know. Like, I'd be happy to take the Northern Trust off your hands."

Harold laughs again. "You can just hold your horses there, pal. God said he'd work out coverage while I'm out. I assume you'll hear from him soon. I'll be back before opening day. I wouldn't want you to knock yourself out for nothing." He looks at his watch. "Blythe is waiting downstairs for me."

We wish him good luck and tell him we'll be over to visit him in a few days and similarly awkward stuff and then he leaves.

"You didn't say a word," I say to Bob.

"I didn't have anything to say."

"Harold's going to be ok," I say.

Bob places a hand on my head and ruffles my hair. "I know you think so, Andrea. You're our very own Little Mary Sunshine."

"Fuck you, Just Bob," I say.

Chapter 29

The taxi stops in front of a puddle and I awkwardly leap to the curb. It really isn't worth opening my umbrella for the six steps it takes me to enter the building so I just endure the cold April rain. My shoes are wet and the floor is slippery and I do a little slip-and-slide with a hula twist, but I manage to make it across the small and thankfully empty lobby without ending up on my ass. I get to the elevator just as the doors are closing. I jab my umbrella into the gap to trip the electric eye. The doors part to reveal Johnny Mac standing inside the car, a few rain drops falling from the brim of his Bears cap on to his wing tips.

"Hoffman."

The doors close.

"How's it going Johnny?"

"My kid got into Michigan," he says without much enthusiasm.

"That's great. Congratulations."

"My wife is devastated. She says Brandy is her best friend. Can't bear that she's leaving home." The elevators open and Johnny waits for me to exit first.

"Have you ever heard of such a thing? A forty-four-year-old woman having a seventeen-year-old as her best friend? And what does that make me? Odd man out."

I turn and look up at his classic Irish face—pale and sad eyed. "Not to worry. Girls always love their daddies, Johnny."

"The fuck you say, Hoffman." But he says it with a small smile.

I drop my coat, umbrella, briefcase, and purse at my desk and head to the coffee machine. Johnny goes directly to his desk and sits down. The rain is coming down in sheets behind him which makes the city look like it's melting.

Charlene arrives completely dry with every hair in place. Dan comes in a minute later with his enormous blue and white golf umbrella that says Kendall-Fitz. It's dripping but he's dry.

"Where can I get one of those, Dan?" I ask, running my fingers through my still damp hair. "My umbrella isn't worth shit."

"You're way too tiny to carry one of these. Hell, even a moderate wind would Mary Poppin you halfway to Michigan City."

It's been less than a month since Harold left. Dan's been dropping his coat on Harold's chair. Mail and research reports are piling up on his desk. Without much discussion, Bob started calling Minneapolis and Dan took on the major Chicago accounts. I fill in the gaps. God hasn't contacted us like Harold said he would and we sure as hell don't want to bother him. I survived the night of babysitting without serious damage to the hotel room, me or the kid. Kurt Winters came through with a nice order just the way I hoped. The market is up every day, business is being taken care of, and I went ahead and bought a condo.

It only took one weekend of driving around in a real estate agent's late model Mercedes and I found the perfect place. It's a newly renovated loft building in an up and coming neighborhood (still kind of commercial—not particularly dangerous) with an enormous Jacuzzi bathtub, access to a roof deck, and only one flight of stairs to climb. Even though I won't be moving in for another month, as soon as I signed that contract letter, turned over a deposit check for $3,200 and obligated myself for payments of $1,567.43 every single month of every single year until I turn fifty six years old, I turned motivated as hell. Each day after the morning call, I contact the analysts and pester them for more details. I stop waiting for customers to call me back and call them until I get through. I make sure I have a business lunch every day of the week. In short, with Harold gone, I've become Harold. It's not like I have anything else to do. Jack gave up calling me after the first weekend. Which is what I wanted. A few weeks after I ran into him in Butch's, I saw him on the street. Walking with his arm around a pretty girl. So good.

"Bob?" We have both arrived at the coffee pot for the first cup of the day. "If I wanted to take customers golfing here in Chicago, where would I do it?"

"Andrea, you don't golf." He runs a finger alongside his long Roman nose. "Do you?"

"I was thinking of taking lessons but there's no sense in me taking lessons if there isn't anywhere for me to take clients. Would I have to join a private club in the suburbs or something?"

Dan jumps in. "Not going to happen. Not if you take a trillion lessons and become the next Nancy Lopez. To get into a decent club, you're going to have to marry your way in . . . and convert to some form of Christianity." Dan looks over at Bob. "I'm right, aren't I buddy?"

Bob nods his head. "You're pretty right."

This is what I expected to hear, a little casual sexism and anti-Semitism so I don't take offense. "I think golf's stupid anyway. I was just wondering."

Dan flinches and says, "When you get married, Andie, those are four words that are going to make your husband really, really nervous. *I was just wondering.* Ha!"

The speaker crackles to life. Everybody grabs their coffee and sits down for the morning call.

Fifteen minutes into the meeting, a man—average height but strikingly thin with a pointy, pinched face and red hair carefully combed to disguise the bald spot on top—walks in to the office and, after looking around for a brief moment, chooses Harold's chair and sits down. He crosses his legs like a girl and languidly wags the dangling foot. Our investment strategist is revealing his new asset allocations and this is a lot more important than the stranger so after giving him a quick glance, we all go back to note taking.

Finally, the speaker falls silent and since I am the person closest to our new guest, I stick out my hand to introduce myself.

"Hi, I'm Andrea Hoffman."

"Yes, I know," he says. His thin lips press into a straight line and he reluctantly takes the ends of my fingers and presses them for a nanosecond.

My stomach turns. I hate those "ladies" handshakes and I notice his fingers look manicured.

The still unidentified speaker turns to Bob and Dan.

"Mr. Robert Parker and Mr. Daniel T. Johnson?"

Creepy Stranger looks at us expectantly. We all look back at him blankly.

"I'm B. Roger Tate," and he cracks a wide smile chock full of fake looking teeth the size of Chiclets.

"I'm sorry," I say. "Our office manager, Harold Stackman, has taken a leave of absence. Were you hoping to see him today? He didn't mention you'd be coming in."

"See him? No, I certainly didn't expect to see him." He

flings his arms out as if to claim the space he's in. "I'm here to replace him."

Dan's eyes narrow. He speaks slowly. "Like Andrea just said, Harold is on a leave of absence. I'm sure 'replace' is not the word you meant to use."

B. Roger Tate looks unperturbed. "Does this coat belong to one of you? You might want to move it so I don't wrinkle it."

"It's mine," Dan says. "And that's Harold's desk. You can take the empty desk on the end by the window."

It's the desk closest to Bob who shoots Dan a murderous look.

Tate opens his mouth to say something else, then stands, buttons and unbuttons his double breasted suit. He glances at the empty desk in front of the dark, rain splattered window. He looks at Bob's and Dan's unsmiling faces. He allows himself a last longing glance at Harold's desk.

"How's the coffee in this joint?"

"You get what you pay for, bud," says Bob as he picks up his phone.

B. Roger Tate turns toward the coffee machine and finds himself nose to chin with Johnny Mac. Johnny Mac doesn't move.

"And who the fuck are you?" Johnny asks.

Tate moves back slightly and holds out his hand.

"I'm B. Roger Tate. The new salesman."

"Don't we have enough fucking salesmen around here?"

"Apparently not." Tate flashes the toothy smile.

Johnny sighs. "What do we call you? B?"

"Oh no, just call me Roger. You must be Jonathan. It's nice to meet you."

Johnny turns away without a word.

My first call is to Allan. "Our strategist just made a bold call to reduce bond holdings by twenty percent and put all the money into tech stocks—specifically chip makers and software providers. I know you've been thinking about taking some profit in your Intel. We'll have buyers for you today."

"Thanks for the call. Anything else?"

"No research but news of the day. Harold's backup waltzed in this morning and I hate him on sight. A nice trade would cheer me up."

"Not sure I'm ready to pull the trigger on the Intel position yet but how about drinks at five? We can talk about you coming to work here."

"Drinks yes. Working for you? No. You can't afford me."

"There's more to life than money, Hoffman."

"Easy for you to say, Mosley!" and I hang up, laughing.

It's close to 11:00 a.m. when the call finally comes in from God. We gather around the speaker phone in the conference room. Roger stays at his new desk.

"Here's the deal," God says. "Tate's no random asshole. He's the right guy to handle all Harold's accounts while he's recuperating. He's had this package before."

"Where'd he come from?" Dan asks.

"He speaks fucking English, Johnson. Ask him."

Dan cracks his knuckles like he's getting ready to punch someone.

"Any other questions?" God only waits half a second. "I expect you all to help Tate get settled."

A sentence from God that didn't have a swear word in it. Odd. Short lived.

"And now how 'bout you get some goddamn business done today?"

PART THREE

Chapter 30

Three months of B. Roger Tate. Hearing his braying laugh. Watching him sit and pick at whatever gross shit is in his ear. At least he's still considered temporary. I hold out hope that Harold is coming back. So far this year, a man left the hospital with an artificial heart beating in his chest and scientists developed a blood test for Aids. Why not a cure for cancer?

B. Roger Tate slinks in late. His posture is unnaturally straight, as if he's carrying a tray of full martini glasses on his head. He sets each foot down carefully so as not to upset the delicate balance he's working very hard to maintain.

"Good morning, Roger," I say at full volume. I pick up my coffee, tip it in his direction and then give it a good long slurp.

He flinches like I zapped him with a stun gun and mumbles something that sounds like "easy for you to say" and which I translate to "just shut up, you little bitch."

The speaker crackles to life and the morning call begins with a technical overview of the market. I jot down a few notes and glance at what Tate is doing. He's holding a pen but his hand is trembling so violently, I doubt any of his scribbles are legible. I've never seen him so hung over. So enjoyable. For me. The oil service analyst takes over the squawk. His information—a discussion of the different qualities of mud pumps and drill bits—is a bit of a tough go even on a good day. I suspect that for Roger, the call may just as well have switched over to Yiddish.

"Yo, buddy. Are you with the program today or not?" Dan is grinning at Tate. "You used the Kendall-Fitz White Sox tickets last night. Those are some great seats."

"Doesn't everyone have great seats? To really entertain clients, you have to do more than put their fat butts in great seats."

Dan turns his head away from Tate and catches me observing their conversation. He silently mouths "asshole." I nod.

Tate goes on lecturing Dan about how to be a good salesman. "Limo'd to Morton's for dinner. Hot dogs at the ball park are so disgusting. We missed the first three innings of the game but that was no big deal."

"Yeah, the only White Sox runs came in the second inning but scoring is a very overrated part of sports," Dan says.

Roger doesn't have a very good sarcasm detector when he's sober. In his present condition, Dan's comment soars over his head like a red-tailed hawk.

"And after the game we piled back into the limo and motored down to Rush Street."

Dan says, "Anyone get lucky?"

B. Roger Tate says, "Ha ha."

This sounds nothing like laughing.

"I wouldn't know. I made it an early evening. Around midnight, I had the limo take me home."

"Sounds fun," I say. More missed sarcasm.

"I don't do it for fun," says B. Roger. "Do you really think I would choose to spend my free time watching grown men try to swat at a little ball in the company of a bunch of yahoos from the Midwest, who went to no-name colleges and have fascinating discussions about lawn fertilization techniques?"

I look at Dan, a huge baseball fan, a native of Illinois, and the go-to guy in the office when the conversation turns to the merits of various seeds and weed killers to see if he is finally going to give Tate the beating he has coming to him. Instead, he just asks, "Where'd you go to college?"

"Out east," Roger says with a wave in the general direction of Lake Michigan.

"Did they have a good football team?" Dan asks, clearly trying to pin Roger down to a specific school somewhere between Indiana and Maine.

Roger doesn't answer. He's totally occupied with trying to light a cigarette. He glares at his phone and checks his Rolex. Could that be a knockoff?

I start calling the oil analysts at my accounts. It's difficult making information about oil reserves and weather patterns sound interesting but as Harold had been fond of saying, "that is why you're paid the big bucks."

I look up and watch Tate sipping his coffee with his eyes closed. I can almost see the caffeine zoom upward, like little Tour de France bicycle racers lapping each other in the frantic climb to his small, empty, booze soaked brain.

"Shit! SHIT!" Johnny screams and he yanks the plug on the handset of his phone and sends it whizzing through the air. It flies behind Roger's head and cracks against the wall landing on his desk.

Roger's eyes fly open and he shakily sets down his paper coffee cup. "Jesus, Jonathan! You almost hit me with that thing."

I end my phone call. I notice Bob and Dan end their calls as well.

"Fucking . . . faggot . . . .asshole." Johnny jumps out of his chair. Roger sits perfectly still as Johnny's face reddens and seems to grow larger as he gets closer and closer to

Tate. "Stupid . . . stupid . . . son of a bitch . . . fuck up."

"Did you have a nice time last night?" Johnny's shouting into Roger's upturned face.

"Marvelous. I was just about to call Peters—the port-folio manager—for some indications for you." He gestures toward the phone but doesn't pick it up. He looks confused but considerably more alert than before. A monstrous shot of adrenalin beats coffee any day, and nobody delivers that shot better than Johnny.

"I've been in this town longer than you. I fucking know who Peters is. The question is, did you enjoy the ride home, pea-brain?"

"Oh, that's what this is about." Roger looks relieved. "I just thought the driver was going in my direction anyway. It probably worked out to be the same amount of money as letting the driver go early and then expensing a cab." Johnny doesn't look at all satisfied with this explanation, so Roger keeps talking. "I'll take care of the limo charges. Not a problem."

"How drunk could you have been to not say goodnight to your clients? Or are you just an idiot?"

"I . . . I . . . couldn't find them. I went to the bathroom and I stopped at the bar to clean up the tab and I looked around and I didn't see them and I thought they'd left and so I just left . . ." his voice peters out and he rubs his hand across his face as if removing cobwebs that had attached themselves to the details of the evening.

"If you had looked a little harder and said goodnight to your guests," Johnny continues in a soft voice that was scarier than the yelling, "they would have told you that their suit coats were still in the car and that at least one of them had keys in their jacket pockets and that none of them appreciated taking cabs home at one in the fucking morning without their fucking coats and Peters in particular did not like waking up his entire goddamn household just to get into his own fucking front door."

Johnny is almost nose to nose with Tate by the time he finishes his speech. I'm not sure whether the expression on his face indicated that B. Roger's breath smelled or that he just loathed him in general. "They taped the key," he says flatly.

Tate just stares at him.

"That means we're cut off. Totally. We won't see a dime from them. They won't even pick up the wire."

"For how long?" Roger croaks.

Johnny just says, "Get on the phone to the limo company and find their jackets and deliver them by noon on your hands and knees if possible. I hope to Christ you didn't puke on them."

I see Roger flip through his Rolodex and pick up his phone. He shuffles out of the office two minutes later.

The room seems unnaturally quiet after all that drama. It's the quiet you hear after a waiter drops a full tray and the restaurant buzz ceases for a moment as everybody stops to look at the mess.

Dan, Bob, and I are all looking at B. Roger Tate's empty chair. "Should we call Harold and tell him he better hurry with his recovery or he won't have any clients to come back to?" I ask.

"Don't you humps have any calls to make?" Johnny booms out. "And Tate's a huge dickhead, but he works here. This story doesn't go outside this office."

Damn! But even as Dan, Bob, and I roll our eyes at one another, I understand what Johnny means. It's that "there is no I in team" crap. Tate is a moron but he's *our* moron. I pick up my phone and call the next oil analyst on my list.

Chapter 31

By Thursday, everybody is ready for this week to be over. B. Roger Tate showed up the afternoon of the "limo" incident and acted like nothing happened. The next day the account resumed business with the firm, although I expect that had more to do with their respect for Johnny than anything Tate did to make things right.

At the close, Charlene swivels in her chair. "We're going to the Cohassett. Join us, Andrea?"

"Pass. Dad's still working weekdays down in Springfield and so I'm being a good daughter and having dinner with Mom."

"Your mom can come too," Johnny says.

"I'll think about it," I say. The guys probably would love my mom. She tells a well-timed joke and she's very good at listening to other people's problems. All my friends love my mom. Why not? She isn't their mother. But I wasn't bringing her. Seeing Mom mixing it up with the traders would be way too confusing for me. It would be bad if they didn't like her and worse if they liked her too much. I wonder if this is why no one ever brought their spouses along.

"I'll be at Twin Anchors eating dinner later," Charlene says. "It's time for you to meet Lawrence."

Lawrence, the Mr. Wonderful lawyer that Charlene can't stop talking about. If she wants me to meet him, their relationship has totally moved to the next level.

"Am I supposed to act surprised to see you there or are you telling him I'm coming?"

"Let's surprise him."

Mom and I have dinner at the Berghoff—not an obvious choice for two women. The waiters are gruff and all the food is fattening. But it's close by, and I adore the salad dressing which is primarily a big dollop of sour cream with tons of garlic mixed in. Yes, even the salad is fattening.

After we order, Mom starts right in. The conversation is a recap of everything my brothers are doing right (like I care) and everything my father and her coworkers are doing wrong. I'm happy she's not grilling me about my life but I do have news and by the time I get a chance to tell her about my new condo, we've finished the piece of apple strudel we split and Mom's trying to catch the waiter's eye to get the check. When he finally saunters over with the bill, I pull out my Amex and pay. Like I always do. Outside, she almost gets run over by a delivery truck in her rush to flag down a cab to the train station. A quick peck on the cheek and a "good to see you, sweetie" and she's gone. I should be relieved the dinner is over but I'm a little . . . insulted? Were we both thinking we were doing each other a favor? Mom telling her friends, "I had dinner with Andrea the other night. She works so hard and I worry she doesn't have any social life. Sad."

I check my watch. The Cohasset crew will be long gone so I grab a cab to Twin Anchors to meet Charlene.

Twin Anchors is one of the oldest restaurants in Chicago, famous for its tavern atmosphere, barbeque ribs and the fact that Frank Sinatra used to hang out there. It's also around the corner from my apartment.

A quick look around confirms that Charlene is not here. I stand by the bar and the bartender waves me over. "Are you Andrea?"

I confirm my identity. He consults a note written on an order pad.

"A lady named Charlene called and said sorry, she had to meet Lawrence at a dinner thing he couldn't get out of."

This is so unlike Charlene. She's blown me off for clients a thousand times but never for a guy. It's upsetting to think that things between Charlene and me can change, that my mother has a life beyond being my mother, that Harold could be replaced. What's permanent in my life? A huge mortgage. I picture the stack of $1,567.43 payments flying one by one by one out an open window.

The bartender disturbs my thoughts. "So your friend's not coming. You want a drink anyway?"

"Maybe just one." I sit.

The bartender's wearing dark jeans, a plaid shirt, a skinny black tie. He's good looking in that wide-eyed down-state farm boy sort of way. He's even got a smattering of adorable freckles. I briefly wonder what time his shift is over. I order a Dewars on the rocks and in my mind, I, perhaps unfairly, name him Barney. He nods at my briefcase.

"So what kind of work do you do?"

Sometimes I lie and say I design lingerie for Victoria Secret or I work in the coal mine at the Science and Industry museum. I'm not in the mood. "I'm kind of a stockbroker," I say. "But I only work with professional money managers."

He grins. "That's so cool. I'm a day trader myself."

"Really." I shouldn't be surprised. Everybody from my mother's dentist to my Uncle Martin thinks they can beat the market and make a fortune these days. "How's that working for you?" I don't know why I am asking. I don't really care.

"Barney" looks around to see if anyone is listening to our conversation. They're not. It's dead at the bar. Not much busier at the tables. He leans over and I can smell his spearmint gum. "I can't lose. The Bible is my chart. God shows me the way."

"That's very interesting," I say. I say "interesting" but my tone implies "totally ridiculous."

Unfortunately, he interprets my comment to mean that I want to hear more. "For example," he says, "In Ecclesiastes, God tells us 'Give portions to seven, yes to eight, for you do not know what disaster may come upon the land . . .'" He looks at me triumphantly. I just stare back at him.

"Buy diversified food companies," he says. "It's so clear. God is so generous with his wisdom."

He's passionate about investing. I can relate to that. And really, is looking for investment strategies in a 3000 year old book crazier than looking at Fibonacci sequences or forecasting unknowable growth rates? I think it is but what do I know? I've had enough stock talk for today and good looking though he is, I don't fancy a threesome with "Barney" and Mr. Dow Jones.

I get up from my bar stool and fish in my suit pocket for some money.

I'm already at the door when he asks, "What do you think about drug stocks at these prices?"

"Good things come to those who wait," I say. Sounds vaguely biblical.

"Barney" the bartender gives me a thumbs up and I exit wondering if I am totally a snobby asshole if he thinks I was being sincere.

On the street, a drunken sailor in his white dress uniform on leave from the Great Lake Naval Base tries to block my way on the sidewalk. "Hey baby, smile. Let me see your pretty smile." I throw him a head fake and dodge him as he lurches clumsily in the wrong direction. I heard his buddies hoot and holler.

"Faked you out of your socks, man."

"Bested by a little girl!"

"Come back! I think I love you! Let's get married!"

I did the sailor thing. Once. Years ago. I keep walking. They don't follow and four uneventful minutes later I am walking up the five stone steps that lead to my front door. I fish out my keys and turn the lock and after a quick look around for muggers and more drunken sailors or drunken accountants, I enter the vestibule and join a couple leaning against the inner door wrapped in a passionate embrace. I need them to move so I can get to the stairs. I say "Excuse me." They separate and I am shocked to see Daniel T. Johnson grinning at me.

"Hey, Andie. You came home!"

"What the hell are you doing in my lobby? How do you even know where I live?"

"You should get that lock fixed. I was in the neighborhood with my friend," he grins at the woman hanging on to his arm. "And I knew you lived here because the limo dropped you off here after the Blackhawks game. 'Member?"

I remembered. Dan was taking clients to see Wayne Gretzky skate against the Blackhawks and five minutes before he left the office, someone called to say they couldn't come. God knows why, but when he hung up he offered me the extra ticket. I took it. Gretzky and the chance to meet some new clients. I surprised myself by having a lot of fun. We all had a lot of fun. "Next time I won't be here," I say. "I'm moving soon."

"Duly noted." The girl nudges him in the ribs. "Ah, Andie, could we borrow a joint?" Dan says. The girl nods and giggles. She is very young and multiple cocktails seem to have removed most of the bones from her body. She sways like a tulip on a breezy day.

I shrug and point up the stairs and push through the door to lead the way. It's only one flight up but Dan and his "date" only make it halfway before they have to take a break as Dan is having trouble holding on to his briefcase, the banister, and the ass of his new best friend. I go inside and leave the door slightly open. I'm in the bathroom when I hear a loud thud that I assume is his briefcase, and then the door slams. I make a half-hearted swipe at the toothpaste in the sink and pull the towel off the side of the bathtub and hang it on the rack.

I come back into the hall just in time to hear Dan say, "Jesus, Andie. You are a total slob. Not that I didn't expect it but . . . "

"That's not nice, Tommy," the girl says. Whether she is too drunk to remember his name or he has been sober enough not to give her his real name, I couldn't guess.

"Not nice, *Tommy*," I say. "But I'll go roll you a joint anyway. Make yourself at home." I go into the kitchen and get my bag of dope out of the freezer. I open the fridge and pull out a can of Tab. I sit down at the kitchen table and roll a perfect, not too generous joint with my nifty joint roller machine. Just as I am walking into the living room, the girl whose name I still don't know and probably Dan doesn't remember comes up to me and takes the joint out of my hand.

"Thanks so much and sorry about this." I think she means barging in on me.

"Don't worry about it," I say. "Let me just get matches from the kitchen." I go back into the kitchen and I hear my front door open and close. "Bathroom is the other way," I call out. The door doesn't open again, so I pick up the matches and open the door and look down the stairs. The girl and my joint are gone.

"Danny," I call out. "I hate to tell you, but you just lost your date." No response.

Dan isn't in my living room. The door to the bathroom is slightly open and I knock on it and then stick my head in hoping that her apology wasn't vomit-related, but no, the bathroom is as empty and as clean as it ever is. Birth control pills sitting out on the sink. Nair hair remover on the side of the tub.

That leaves the bedroom.

I flick the light switch. My bed's a rumpled mess but then it always is. I have never understood why people make their beds. I do understand sheet changing and mine are going to be done tomorrow because right now Daniel T. Johnson is curled up in the fetal position passed out in the tangle of sheets and blankets, drooling all over my pillow. I look down and see his shoes and suit jacket on the floor but he appears to be wearing the rest of his clothes, including his tie. "Sorry about this" starts to take on meaning. I creep closer to Dan and shake his shoulder to revive him. He mumbles and rolls over onto his back but doesn't respond.

"Daniel!" I try slapping him, not with a big back swing, but just hard enough to rouse him. "Fire! Dan! Wake up! Your wife's here! Dan! I love you! Wake up and have sex with me!" When the last plea doesn't work, I'm pretty sure he's going to go on sleeping for hours. Jesus. What an asshole! I stare down at him. An asshole with fabulous eyelashes. They rest on his cheeks as black and thick as crow feathers.

I go in the kitchen and transfer my Tab into a glass with ice and then pull my bottle of rum out from the cabinet and pour in a healthy shot. Not a cocktail Harold would approve of. I take the drink into the living room and sit down on the couch. I glance at my watch. It's nine forty-five.

A couple of things are bugging me. First, I wonder if Dan will choke to death sleeping in his tie. Second, I worry that if he drunk wets the bed, he will have no pants to wear to work tomorrow. Finally, I realize that I have no idea where his wife thinks he is or if she's expecting him home. If she thinks he's out of town and I call her, he'll be busted. But if she's waiting for him, well, I don't know what that feels like but I suspect it feels shitty.

I pick up the phone and call Charlene. The answering machines picks up. Still out with Lawrence or back home but busy. I don't leave a message. Harold would know how to handle this but since I haven't called even once to see how he's doing, it's too awkward. Calling Mom for advice? I laugh, finish my drink and head back into my bedroom.

"Dan?" I push his shoulder and he straightens out his legs. I yank the covers off him. "Dan?" He mumbles but his eyes don't open. Common sense. I'll just use my common sense. I pull off his tie so he doesn't choke himself and then I reach down, unbutton his pants and gingerly pull the zipper down. I move to the foot of the bed and start to tug. The pants begin to come off but his boxers are sliding down as well, exposing a patch of soft hair that is darker than the hair on his head. I immediately stop the tugging and stare at the bare patch of skin. I could keep tugging. But do I want to see? I have to be sure because this isn't going to be something I can easily forget. I move back up to the side of the bed. I slip my fingers into the waistband of the boxers, feeling skin that is cool and surprisingly soft. I pull the boxers back up far enough to give him a wedgie. No reaction. I need to get the pants over his ass before I can tug them off. I hitch my skirt up, straddle his legs and then shove my hands under his thighs and grab the material that covers his butt. I pull slowly this time and the pants slide over his hips. I notice a thick six-inch scar on the outside of each knee. I want to touch the shiny skin, but I don't. I'm glad I haven't pulled his boxers down because when I look up, Dan's bloodshot blue eyes are wide open.

"Hi Andie," he says softly. He reaches out and pushes the hair out of my eyes. He doesn't seem particularly surprised that I am kneeling on top of him. "I'm really thirsty."

"If I get you a drink of water, will you get up and go home?"

He shakes his head. "I can't go home. Janine thinks I'm in Milwaukee."

"Milwaukee is only a couple of hours from your house. You could tell her you got the stomach flu or your hotel caught on fire."

"I don't want to go home," he says. "Everyone there thinks I am terrific. Janine thinks I'm perfect. The kids think I'm Superman. It makes me feel so guilty."

"If you went home you wouldn't have anything to feel guilty about."

"Are you kidding me? I'm Catholic. I feel guilty about everything."

"Okay, then. I'm going to get you some water. Maybe that will make you feel better."

I take a while letting the water get cold and halfway out of the kitchen, I turn around and get a couple of Tylenols too. Dan's sitting up with both my pillows propped behind his back. He's finished taking his pants off and has taken his shirt off too—both thrown over the chair with his other clothes. In high school, I had secretly dreamed of a handsome football player lover. The dream did not include that he was married with three young kids, two bum knees, and a desk next to mine in the office.

I hand him the water and the pills.

He throws his head back to swallow the pills. Like a kid. Like I do.

"Thanks. I feel like shit."

"Maybe you're allergic to that jailbait's bubble gum."

"She looked old enough to me."

"So you're staying, huh?" I ask.

"Obviously. Are you coming to bed, now?"

"Actually, I think I might take the couch."

"Don't be silly. I won't touch you," he says with just a little too much certainty. "Am I on your side? I can switch over." He grabs the top pillow, throws it on the far side of the bed and scooches over. He pats the spot where he had been. "Here you go."

"Don't you find this even the least bit weird, Johnson?" I ask.

"Do I think it's weird because you don't like me but you're too nice to kick me out? That's pretty much what I was counting on."

"I don't *not* like you," I say.

"Too drunk to figure out what that means, Andrea," he says. His eyes are closed again. "Man, it must be late. I'm so tired. Come to bed."

"Have you met Charlene's new boyfriend?" I ask as I rummage through my drawers until I find the floor length, long sleeve, high neck Lanz flannel nightgown that my mother gave me as a Hanukkah present years ago. It seemed like my dinner with Mom had been months and not hours ago.

"I thought Charlene had something going on with Johnny," Dan says.

"Oh for god's sake. Not like that. Johnny and Charlene are, you know, like a team. Tina and Ike." I change in the bathroom and come back to the bedroom. Hesitate in my own doorway. "But that's not a good example. Since Tina and Ike were actually married and Johnny's married but not to Charlene."

"Of course, Johnny is married. Everybody is married. Except you and that pathetic Ellen."

It takes me a minute to realize he means Erin on the trading desk but I don't bother to correct him.

"Well, she does. Charlene. Have a boyfriend."

"That's nice," Dan says. "I'm happy for her. You should stop fucking around and get a boyfriend too. Then you wouldn't be tempted to have dinner with old assholes like Patrick O'Neil."

"And you know this how?"

"Johnny might have said something about him calling you on the desk."

"No fucking privacy at all in that office."

"None needed. We're all family, right?"

"I suspect you and Patrick don't get along."

"Did he say something?"

"No. At the Coh it was kind of obvious. Anyway, dinner was supposed to be a business thing. I wanted to learn more about derivatives. Not exactly how it turned out. You're right about the asshole assessment."

"Wow! We agree on something. Let's celebrate. Can we smoke that joint?"

"The bimbo took the joint," I say. "I'll get another one." I pad into the kitchen to repeat the whole joint-rolling procedure and bring the joint and an ashtray into the bedroom. Dan is sitting up again and absentmindedly rubbing his beautifully muscled chest. My fingers twitch. Like a statue in a museum, I want to touch him and know I shouldn't. I turn off the light as I enter the room but the glow from the street lamp outside my window keeps the room from being truly dark.

I sit down on the bed, keep my bare feet on the floor and, with my back to Dan, light the joint. Outside a truck rumbles by.

"I like city street sounds," Dan says. "I hate the suburbs. Fucking birds tweeting at the top of their fucking little lungs at 5:30 in the fucking morning." He reaches for the joint. Our hands touch. "Is it good?" He takes a deep drag. "Being single?"

I avoid looking at him. "I like living alone. I like feeling independent. I've never lived with anyone so . . . I don't know."

"I'm jealous of you. I was never single. I met Janine in college. We moved in together when I went to law school. We got married when I graduated."

My head snaps around to look at him now. "Wait, back up. You went to law school? I've known you all this time and I didn't know this. Why didn't I know this?"

"Surprise. I went to Northwestern law school. There's lots of stuff about me you don't know. Like I do needlepoint."

"No, really?" He finally returns the joint to me.

"Andie, no. I'm just screwing with you. I don't do needlepoint. I work. I watch sports. I drink too much. I'm frequently a jerk. I like to have more sex than I get at home."

"You left out chauvinist pig."

"Am not!"

"You are too. You're always telling me I'm taking a job away from someone with nuts."

"Jesus, Andie, don't you even mellow out when you *smoke*?" He grabs my shoulders and pulls me closer to him, holding me inches from his face with the strength of his arms. "I was trained as a trial lawyer. I like to argue with people. I like to argue with you. You look cute when you're mad. Like now." He pushes me back into an upright position. "Look, here's what I really believe. You're into all that supply and demand crap. Well, I believe in the division of labor. I work. My wife stays home and takes care of the kids. If she worked, some stranger would be teaching my daughters 'Ring around the Rosie' in Polish or Spanish. I don't want that. But I don't really believe that other crap. You want me to stop teasing you, I'll stop."

Even through the thick flannel, I feel the spot where his hands held my shoulders. My mind is foggy from the dope but crystal clear about the signals my body is sending it. "Don't bother. You're too late. Just Bob already has the nice guy role locked up in the office. You have to keep being the creep."

"Okay. Then I'll tell you that's a really ugly nightgown." He looks thoughtful. "You should take it off."

"Can't. Sorry. Too awkward." I put out the joint. "Go to sleep, Dan."

"Your ugly nightgown is keeping me awake."

I arrange my pillow, lie on my back and listen to him breathe. I can feel the bed rise and fall. "Your parents must be very disappointed you're not practicing law."

Dan snorts. "I don't have that kind of parents. They had a lot of kids and the only expectation they have for all of us is that we stay out of jail."

"Still, they must be proud of you. You're doing so well."

"Proud of me? No, I don't hear too much of that. What I do hear is that I don't give them enough money. I don't go to Mass often enough. I never should have moved out of the neighborhood and a host of other depressing things."

I want to tell him my parents aren't proud of me either but I'm starting to wonder if that's true. While they refuse to understand my choice of a job, they do understand the money and I think they might be sort of proud of the fact that I'm making so much. Of course, they don't know I do things like this.

"Can I tell you something else?"

"No! Just shut the fuck up, Dan." I wait and then giggle. "Kidding you. What?"

"I'm going to run for city council. It's kind of a joke because councilmen are unpaid and they only meet a dozen times a year so it's no big deal, but I have to start somewhere.

I want to get out of this business and I think I want to go into politics. How does Governor Johnson sound?"

I think of a bunch of sarcastic things I could say but I change my mind. "It sounds crazy but I'd probably vote for you. But I thought you loved being a salesman. You're so good at it."

He rolls back over to face me again. "Hmmm. I assumed you thought I was a shitty salesman. We both have secrets." He wiggles his eyebrows at me and I giggle again. The weed. How the hell did this night end with me having a slumber party with Daniel Johnson?

He's more serious now. "No such thing as a free lunch, dandy Andie. This business isn't always going be like this. Bull markets end. People catch on. Kemper is putting in an automated phone system. If you are one of the top ten brokers, you can use a password and leave a message. Everybody else is screwed."

"That doesn't make any sense. You'd think they'd want to talk to the top ten brokers and it's all the rest of the slobs who should just have to leave a message."

"That's one of the reasons you have trouble, Andrea. You're too logical and you believe in being fair. This business is neither logical nor fair and the party won't last forever."

"Great. You are talking to someone who just bought a condo."

"Have a backup plan. Find a husband."

"That's a great idea, but I'm pretty sure all the good guys have been taken."

I roll over on my side with my back to him. Perhaps I should stick to the original plan and go sleep on the couch but that seems egotistical. In a minute, I hear deep breathing and assume my very temporary roommate is asleep.

It could be ten minutes or three hours later. I'm awake just enough to realize there are warm hands trying to find a way under my nightgown. Lips are kissing the back of my neck. It's dark, it's late, and it feels damn good. Thirty seconds later, my nightgown is off, Dan is turning me toward him, his hands exploring. My hands reach out as well— discovering hard muscles, soft skin. He moves on top of me. Slides inside me. Thrusting insistently. His hands tight on my ass. "This feels so amazing," he whispers. "I want to do this all night long." I moan in agreement. We move as one. For maybe fifteen seconds. Then he cries out "My sweet Jesus!" lies still for a fraction of a heartbeat and then pulls out and he's done. "Great ride," he says and he rolls over flat on his back with a heavy arm across my chest and instantly falls back to sleep.

I say "Jesus" too but in a different tone of voice and push his arm off me. Two years of feeling guilty about my fantasies about the sexy Daniel T. Johnson. Two years of jealousy hearing him brag about conquests. Two years of watching him flirt with Charlene wondering what it would be like to have his attention turned my way and now I find out the reality of having him in my bed is not wonderful and not awful, it's just kind of boring.

I wake up to the alarm and an empty bed. I find my crumpled nightgown tangled up in the sheets and put it back on and tour the apartment. Empty as well. I head into the shower. Both my toothbrush and razor have been used.

Dan's in the office when I come in looking presentable. "Andie. Thanks for letting me crash at your place last night," he says loud enough for everyone to hear.

"No problem," I say.

He turns to Johnny. "She's not much of a housekeeper."

"Didn't expect her to be," Johnny says.

I'm thinking *and you're not much of a lay*, but I think the smart thing to do is pretend the sex never happened.

Chapter 32

*M*y parents are late and I am standing, keys in hand, on the sidewalk in front of my new place. I'm pretty sure they're going to hate it and I've already run upstairs and done two short lines of coke.

I see the tan Dodge Dart slowly roll down the street toward me. My mother is peering intently at a piece of paper and my father has a bewildered look on his face. Who would live on such a block, above a linen store and next to a check cashing business and across the street from an antiques dealer? At least my old neighborhood had a small strip of grass alongside the sidewalks and there were trees. There's just parking meters here. Which is precisely why I love the place. From the outside, nothing; it's special on the inside.

My mother finally sees me waving to her, and I see her pointing and gesturing to my dad. He slows down even more and signals and then pulls carefully into the spot directly in front of where I'm standing. The driver behind him makes a rude gesture as he zooms past. "Mishugina," my father mutters as he gets out of the car. They hug me and my mother dives into the back seat and retrieves packages.

"Mom? I haven't moved in yet. The moving truck comes tomorrow after the closing."

"I just brought you bread and salt. It's traditional. You should never be hungry in your new home."

I take the plastic bags from her. There's more in there than just bread and salt. "That's nice, Mom. Thanks."

"Do I need to feed the meter?"

"Not today, Dad."

"Good parking in this area. I like that. Will the car still be here when we come back?"

"I don't know, Dad. Who'd want it?"

"It runs," Dad says.

I usher them into the building and we pause at the top of the stairs so everybody can catch their breath and I can add a little drama to the moment. Then I open the door and wave them in. The sun streams in through the huge plate glass windows in the front of the building. I had placed a vase of bright orange Gerber daisies on the kitchen counter right under the skylight. The loft looks stunning.

"You're going to have to spend a fortune on curtains," my dad says.

I look over to Mom who's saying nothing but more shocking, isn't shushing my dad. Her eyes are huge.

"It's gorgeous, darling. Are you sure you can afford this?"

"Hey, I'm the finance professional. I worked the numbers out pretty carefully."

"I'm sure you did. I'm just being your mother. I love it. I really do." She is looking everywhere . . . in the stove, in the refrigerator. "Such a great kitchen. We could cook up a storm in here."

"I hope we do, Mom. Passover here this year?"

"And next year in Israel." She doesn't mean it literally. It's a traditional prayer.

"I'm going to check out the rest of the place," she says, and disappears into the powder room. I hear the bathroom door close and lock. Who does she think is going to barge in on her? She has such annoying habits.

I'm on the terrace with my father when she comes out.

"Do you think," she says, "you'll do this job much longer?"

"Well, since I just signed this mortgage, I definitely do. Why?"

She's looking south to the downtown skyline. "We talked about you maybe going to law school."

"No, *you* talked about it. I don't know why you are so obsessed with me being a lawyer." My father has retreated and is busy inspecting the neighbor's grill.

"Lawyers help people," my mom continues. "I want to think I created a person who's making the world a better place."

I wave to my father that I am going back. I have no idea why my mother is on this kick right now. She follows me into the bedroom.

"You don't think I am contributing anything to make the world a better place?" I say.

"Not through work, you aren't."

"That isn't true. I help people create wealth and thus security for themselves and their families. They can educate their kids, give to charity, buy goods and services. All that creates jobs. I help companies obtain financing to grow and create jobs. I invest the money I make and that creates jobs or opportunities for someone else. How does all that not make the world a better place?"

"You're fooling yourself, Dee. Those people you help? They would do okay without you. Those people always do. It's the other people in this world that need a hand. It's like a very expensive restaurant saying they feed the hungry.

The people that eat there might *be* hungry but they aren't *the* hungry."

"I'm sorry to be such a disappointment to this family. Some people think my job is incredibly cool."

"Fine, it's cool but I'm your mother. You think I care about the limos and the theater tickets and the dinners at Le Francais? You think this job is making you a grownup but you're just a big kid."

"I own a home now. Is that childish?" Why am I surprised we are having this conversation? I knew they wouldn't be happy for me.

"So you're a kid with better toys than the other kids," Mom says.

"Do you mean better toys than *your* other kids? I'm sure it bugs you that I'm doing better than the boys." My parents wanted us all to do well so they set us up against one another as competitors. I guess to the outside world, that looks like a pretty successful strategy but I would have preferred having siblings that support me rather than sabotage me. I would certainly have preferred not to have this conversation with my mother today.

My father has been examining the plumbing in the bathroom and testing all the hardware on the windows and opening and closing the closet doors. I imagine he would be going around and checking all the electrical outlets if he could—anything to avoid the conversation my mother and I are having.

"Very nice quality, this place. Some good craftsmen built it. Guys that cared about their work."

"Thanks, Dad." I try to smile.

"So now you're mad at me," my mother says. "I should just keep my mouth shut and tell you everything is great. I'm not entitled to my opinion?"

"I don't know why nothing I do satisfies you."

"So, okay. Mazel Tov! You have a lovely apartment and a big fat mortgage. I am impressed. If that's want you want, then I'm impressed."

"Jesus, Mom. When you walked in here I thought you liked the place. What is bugging you?"

She opens her hand and places my little brown bottle of cocaine down on the kitchen counter.

"This is bugging me. This. You're so happy you've got to do drugs? This is what it means to be a Wall Street hot shot? You snort cocaine?"

"Mom, where in the world did you get that?"

"It was on the floor in the bathroom. Behind the wastepaper basket."

I almost smile thinking about Mom inspecting the bathroom so thoroughly, but this is serious and requires a forceful response. "So you really think that's cocaine? It could be anything. Anyway, it's not mine. I can't believe you think that's mine. A thousand people must have been in the apartment. All the workmen, people looking to buy it, realtors, appraisers. Anyone could have dropped that. Maybe it's magic plumber's powder."

In any lie, there is the liar and the one who chooses to accept the lie. My mother looks at me and turns the small bottle over and over in her hand. She shakes the contents and watches it settle like sand in a tiny hour glass. She doesn't look at my father who is staring at the grout between the kitchen tiles. Finally, she capitulates.

"I'm sorry. I don't know how I could think my baby would do such a thing. I'm a crazy old lady. I was just so worried. You read so much in the paper about the wild goings on. The drugs. The sex."

I hold out my hand to take the bottle but she shakes her head, "I don't even want you to touch this filthy thing.

There is a storm drain right out front. I almost caught my heel in it on my way in. I'll drop it down on our way out."

"Good idea," I say. I try to calculate how much coke was left in the bottle. Maybe half. About two hundred worth of blow, literally going down the drain.

"Let's go to lunch," I say. "I'm totally starving. Or do you want to look in the closet for some marijuana?"

"Are you sure you're not too high to walk?" Dad jokes.

"Funny. Make jokes you two!" my mother says. "I love my daughter. I worry about her." She pulls me to her in a tight hug. "I don't know what I was thinking. If you were using cocaine, you'd be much thinner."

I'm not at all hungry because I did those lines just a half hour ago but now I am going to have to wolf down a cheeseburger and fries just to make a point. I usher my parents out and turn to lock the door behind me and find that my hand is shaking just enough to make it difficult to slip the key in the lock.

Some people say that being in love is the best feeling in the world. Some people say it's winning a big game or a coveted prize. But for me, the best feeling in the world is that whoosh of relief when you think that you fucked up and then you find out you didn't. All the time that would've been spent worrying and then fixing the problem is given back to you like a gift. Life is suddenly perfect and bountiful. Like right now.

I had convinced them the coke wasn't mine. I wasn't in trouble. And why should I be? I wasn't a coke addict. Every now and then I used a little to get me through a boring patch of the day or to give me a little extra energy when I have to be up late. My parents guzzle coffee for the same reason and like a cocktail or three whenever they socialize. My life is tame compared to a lot of what I see. My mother is right about that. Not to mention that with Mary Consuelo gone, this was likely the last coke I'll ever buy.

"Are we moving the car?" my father hollers up from the bottom of the stairs.

"No, we'll stay in the neighborhood," I say.

I lock the door and head down the single flight of stairs to the street.

My mother looks up at me sharply. "That took you a long time. Is everything okay?"

"I'm just getting used to the new lock," I say cheerfully, but my feeling of euphoria fades. Nothing else is going to be said but I can tell from my mom's face that she didn't buy my bullshit after all. And we're both going to pretend she did.

"Did you dump the bottle?" I ask.

She looks to my father who is checking out the bargains in the antique store window and then hands it to me. "I don't think the drain is a good idea. You take care of it later."

I nod and drop it in my purse.

Chapter 33

We're all gathered by the coffee pot Monday morning when Dan says, "I bought the wife a new car this weekend."

Bob immediately says, "What do you feel guilty about?

"Nah, this wasn't an apology purchase. That's got to be expensive jewelry. We just really needed a new car."

I had spent some of the weekend wondering about Dan. He seemed a little distracted Friday. Whenever I looked his way he seemed very, very busy. I wondered for half a millisecond if maybe there was a misunderstanding about what happened in my apartment, but stewing was not his style. I figured if he were confused, he'd just come right out and ask, "So, did I ball you or not?"

"A white Dodge Caravan," Dan is saying. "I live in the suburbs and I own a fucking minivan. What's next?"

"'Baby on Board' window decal?"

"Got that," he says.

"You'll go bald," Bob says.

"I'll kill myself first."

"No comments from you?" Dan is looking at me. "You always have something to say. Are you feeling okay?"

"Just thinking," I say. "If you kill yourself, I'd get St. Louis."

I get busy making calls since I have to leave in an hour to attend the closing and then meet the movers over at the loft. I'm mid-dial when my phone rings. I look over at the third temp the agency sent over. We really need to find a Mary Consuelo replacement. This one's staring at the phone like it's electrified. I pick it up myself.

"Andrea, this is Reggie Flynn from R. H. Peterson. I've heard some very nice things about you. I'm in Chicago today and wonder if you're free for a drink later this afternoon."

My real estate closing shouldn't take long and I have next to nothing to move into the new apartment so that won't take long either. A meeting with this Flynn guy could lead to a fresh start and a two year guarantee.

"I'd like that," I say. "Where should I meet you?"

When I hang up, I call Allan.

"Did you recommend me for a job at R.H. Peterson?"

"Why the hell would I have done that? I've been trying to get you to come here."

"Fair enough. Do you know Reggie Flynn? Their head of sales?"

"He's self-conscious about being short. Makes dumb self-deprecating jokes."

"Is he a midget?"

"Nah, he's like five-six. Compared to you he'll seem tall."

"Did you ever have cocktails with him? Do you remember what he drinks?"

"I did have a drink with him and I do remember because he drinks Knob Creek. It's an expensive bourbon that was created during the Civil War to paralyze wounded soldiers so they could be operated on without anesthetic."

"That's really interesting."

"And also completely untrue. But that is the name of the stuff he drinks."

"Thanks, Allan. Keep your fingers crossed for me."

"I won't. You're supposed to work here."

———

Reggie Flynn, wearing a purple tie, is easy to spot at the Nick's Fishmarket bar. He hops down from his bar stool as I approach and I can tell he is pleased to be looking at the top of my head. I tilt my face up to say hello.

"Let's take drinks over to a table. What can I get you?" he asks.

"I'll take a Maker's Mark," I say. Asking for Knob's Creek would have been too much of a coincidence but this is another decent bourbon.

"A bourbon drinker! Bless you, my child. You don't find many women who drink bourbon. Good choice. Have you ever tried Knob's Creek?"

"Never. But I love a new experience. Do you think they have it here?"

"I know they do," he says.

He signals the bartender, points at his glass, and raises two fingers. Then he leads me to a nearby table. "Let's just sit and have a chat about you coming to work for me."

Before we get to our second drink, Reggie has asked me to fly to New York for more interviews on Friday. I tell him I'd be happy to do so and ask him one last question.

"I'm curious how I showed up on your radar."

"We interviewed your colleague, Dan Johnson. He wasn't interested but he did a very nice sales job on you."

That's freaking weird, I think. "I think highly of him too," I say.

Chapter 34

I finish making my plane reservations when I see my other line light up. Today's replacement temp pounces on it.

"Your brother," she hollers. Better than the timid girl but still . . .

I put up my finger so she can tell him I'll be right there. This can't be good. None of my brothers randomly call me. They only call if they need me to do them a favor, like buy Mom and Dad's anniversary gift and say it's from all of us. I take a breath and pick up the phone.

"Hey." It's my brother Pete. The "real" doctor. Then I hear Mark and Jake on the line and they tell me it's a conference call

"Jesus. All three of you. Is something wrong with Mom or Dad?"

"Well actually, Mom called us and she was very upset. She thinks something's wrong with you. She thinks you're doing drugs."

I have to close my eyes for a second and take a breath. I hiss into the phone, "Are you fucking kidding me! You guys are calling me at work during market hours to have this discussion?"

"Well, with Mark in California and Pete always at the hospital, it was hard to get a time for all of us to do this," Jake breaks in.

"What is it you thought you were going to do? Get me to admit I'm a crackhead and check myself into Betty Ford?"

"It's kind of hard to hear you, Dee," Pete says. "Can you talk a little louder?"

"No, I can't talk a little louder. I'm at my fucking job. That means I am sitting in an open room with seven other people around me. Maybe if all of you weren't so wrapped up in your own lives, you'd know something about how I spend my days."

"Sorry," Pete says. "That a little uncalled for, though. Mom's really worried about you."

"Oh, my God. Why didn't you just tell her I was fine and she was being ridiculous? Mark, that summer when you were between sophomore and junior years and you were high out of your mind every single day, who covered for you? I told Mom you were working out while she was at work and that was why you ate all the food in the house. And Jake, how about that bad LSD trip when you came home and filled the bathtub with cold water and then got in with all your clothes on? Who cleaned up that mess? Pete? You still carry a flask of Bacardi with you everywhere you go?"

"You're getting kind of loud now, Dee. I thought you said everybody could hear you," Pete says.

"Yeah, well you know what? Even if they hear, they aren't judgmental assholes like my own brothers. I'm fine. I don't have a problem except that I have a family that thinks I'm an idiot. Go back to saving the world. If you want to help me, tell Mom that she's wrong. I don't have a problem with drugs. I just make money which apparently is some kind of sin. I guess they feel guilty I'm helping them out."

"You're being straight with us? You don't have a problem?" I hear the relief in Mark's voice. I sigh. It's possible they are truly worried about me. Who wants a sister in rehab?

"Guys, it's not like I don't appreciate the big brother act. But I'm not your little sister anymore. I'm a grownup. I do grownup stuff. I handle things in a grownup way. If I need your help, I'll be a grownup and ask for it. I gotta go. I have a client on the other line."

"Okay. We get your point. You know Mom. She can be pretty persuasive." It's Mark again, the peacemaker.

"Just know that we're watching out for you," Jake says. As the oldest, he has to have the last word.

I hang up the phone and then rip the top sheet off my yellow pad where I'd been scribbling CRAP CRAP CRAP, crumble it up and throw it away.

Chapter 35

*M*y carefully crafted cover story is that I'm going to Long Island for my cousin's Bat Mitzvah. Nobody cares. I work until the close so I hit rush hour traffic on the Kennedy Expressway and I'm running down the terminal corridor at O'Hare late for my flight to LaGuardia. The gate agent sees me waving my ticket at her. She points to the jet way and I stupidly say "bad traffic" like she cares why I'm late. I hear them close the door behind me as I step on the plane, panting like an overheated dog. The stewardess smiles and says "Did you think we'd go without you?" She looks at my ticket. "You have 15C but we're not crowded. Just flop into the first seat you see. We're ready to push back."

I speed through the near empty first class cabin and fall into a window seat in an empty row and watch through the round thick glass as we head down the runway and into the sky. The bell announces the fasten seat belt light has been turned off and the captain comes on the intercom to tell us we are free to move about the cabin. I step into the aisle to remove my suit jacket and feel a helping hand at the back of my neck. I turn expecting to see the stewardess and instead find Jack Keith, my Wisconsin student turned Goldman Sachs VP, in jeans and a black Polo shirt, holding my jacket and grinning at me. I forgot he was this good looking. The messy hair now tamed with whatever guys use to do that. But the eyes still . . . . The plane lurches. He reaches out to steady me.

"Jack. Where the hell did you come from?"

"A few rows in front of you. You were in a blind rush and didn't spot me waving."

"Couldn't miss me though. Sweaty crazed passenger who just made the flight."

"Well, I've seen you look better . . . "

"I appreciate the honesty."

". . . but I've been trying to get some time with you for months now and so when I saw you barge on to this plane with that harried look on your face, I was thinking it was a little miracle. Mind if I sit with you?"

Weirdly, I don't. I might even be a little happy to see him. "Window or aisle?"

"You take the window," he says and as I sit, he folds my jacket and puts it into the overhead bin.

When he settles I say, "I'm sorry I didn't pick up your calls. Or call you back."

"And ran away from me whenever I saw you on the street or in a bar."

"In my defense, the last time I saw you, you were with another girl."

He waves his hand and shakes his head. "She was nobody." He looks down at my left hand. "How about you? You got a somebody?"

I shake my head. "Not even a goldfish." I'd usually say how this is how I like it but I don't. Instead I ask, "So New York? Business trip?"

"Nope. Family thing. You?"

I tell him that I'm interviewing and explain about Harold's absence and about the arrival of B. Roger Tate.

"It's like Tate's always watching and listening. I don't feel like I can just be myself. He hates what he calls 'broads' in the business. The other men in the office, sure they make jokes but it's different . . . somehow. They consider me one of the guys."

"Doubt it."

"What?"

"Never mind. Does this Tate really matter? It's not like he's your boss."

"No, you're right. It's just that the office used to seem comfortable and now it seems . . . complicated." I want to drop this topic. Unless I talk about having late night sixty second sex with Dan, buying drugs from Mary Consuelo, and getting hit on by Patrick, I can't fully explain my dissatisfaction and I'm not getting to all that tonight. So I say, "Tell me what it's like being a bond guy."

"Admit it. You think bonds are boring."

"Aren't they?"

"Government bonds, yes. Corporate bonds, not at all. The suspense of a call option, the looming threat of a default. Oh yes. The exciting stories I could tell you."

I look more than a little skeptical. Exaggerate a yawn.

"Funny. You're an equity snob. But I could make you fall in love with debt. I could."

He reaches over and takes my hand. His green eyes gaze deep into mine. I feel color rise in my face. I return his stare. "Andrea," he says, "Will you diversify your assets with me?"

I laugh. This guy is a strange combination of silly and smart in a totally appealing package. And the confidence it must take to be so ridiculous. It's out-and-out sexy.

"You are a very peculiar man, Jack Keith. But I happen to like financial humor so we have that going for us."

The overhead lights in the plane are turned off so people can sleep. We get drinks from the stewardess, lean our seats back and talk on in low voices.

He brings up our short conversation in Butch's and asks me what he didn't ask me then. Why was I asking him about guns?

I tell him about the robbery.

"And the night I saw you? Was it the anniversary or something?"

"No. I saw him," I say. "My gun guy."

"Did he threaten you?" Jack's hands clench.

This isn't the conversation I want to have right now. Too pathetic. "Sort of? But everything turned out fine. Is fine now."

"Well, good." Jack runs his tongue over his lips. A tell. "Uh, I don't actually own a gun. I just wanted to see you and I thought that might work."

"Well, shit. Not a cowboy?"

"But I'll take you to a shooting range if you want. Shooting range, archery targets, Kung Fu class."

This is the conversation I want to have. Someone telling me they want to do whatever would make me happy.

"I'll pass on the self-defense lessons. I don't plan on being in any more dangerous situations," I say. My infatuation with Bolivian Marching Powder has dissipated. I love that popping feeling. The zip of it. The power of knowing a little rocket fuel is tucked in my bag ready if I need a boost. Even though I still have the bottle Mom found, I haven't been using it. My sneaky Mom. She gave the vessel back to me but somehow, she took the magic out of it. I freely confess I already miss it. But, Mary Consuelo was right. It's really not my scene.

"Maybe we could go bowling and get Chinese food," I suggest.

When the plane lands, Jack pulls my bag down from the overhead bin and hands it to me. Doesn't try to carry it for me. I like that.

"Share a cab?" he asks as we hit the warm nighttime air outside the terminal. The taxi line is constantly moving but we are shuffling slowly enough for me to notice that something in the sidewalk cement makes it twinkle like diamonds.

"Sure. I'm staying at the Waldorf. You?"

"I'm staying at my Aunt Norma's. The bed's not too comfortable but the breakfast is awesome. I'll drop you off first."

I love New York City and I spend most of the cab ride looking out the window waiting for the minute when the industrial ugliness of Queens switches over to the magic of Manhattan. Every once in a while, the cab sways and our knees or shoulders or hands or hips touch. It's pleasant. I'd like to find out how much more pleasant it could be. I wait for some kind of move to show me that he's thinking along the same lines.

When we stop in front of the Waldorf, I turn and with what I hope is a subtle but sexy smile, ask Jack if he would like to come in for a drink.

"I'm really sorry. I'd like to come in, but I won't," he says. "I'm expected at my aunt's and calls to the police and hospitals in all five boroughs will be made if I don't show up there soon. I'll take a rain check though."

"Sure," I say. "The very next time I'm going to be staying at the Waldorf, I'll let you know." I busy myself finding my wallet in my briefcase so he can't see how disappointed I am. And confused. I thought this was where all our conversation was leading. To my bed at the Waldorf. Maybe this is his revenge for all those times I turned him down.

"Let me pay for the taxi," I say.

"No, you get it next time."

I don't want to prolong this so I just thank him.

Jack leans over and gives me a kiss. It's on the lips, but it's brief and feels dry and polite. The uniformed doorman opens the cab door and I slide out. He speaks to Jack briefly. Jack pulls a bill from his pocket and hands it to him. The doorman smiles and then closes the cab door and turns to pick up my small overnight bag he has retrieved from the trunk.

"I've got it," I say to him.

He hangs on to it. "Your boyfriend asked me to take care of you."

"Not my boyfriend," I say.

"You sure? The address your taxi buddy just gave the driver was in Queens about ten minutes from the airport. Dropping you off was way out of his way."

It takes me a moment to process the meaning of what the doorman has just said. I regret my lack of effort in returning his kiss. I look up the street and raise my hand in a little wave in case he is looking out the taxi window. When the traffic swallows him up, I push through the revolving door and with my heels clicking, I cross the mosaic tile floor of the ornate lobby to check in.

———

The offices of R.H. Peterson are just a few blocks west of Rockefeller Plaza. Most of the Wall Street firms are downtown but working at an office that is closer to Saks Fifth Avenue than the Statue of Liberty works just fine for me. The taxi drops me on the edge of the large plaza in front of the correct address. A push cart selling coffee and buttered hard rolls is doing a brisk business, as is the newspaper stand on the opposite corner. The random chaos of the sidewalk crowd becomes a tight group of workers forming a single mass as they get closer to the building. The throng looks like it's being pulled through the massive front doors by strong suction. An Art Deco clock on the outside of the building tells me I have four minutes to get up to the office. I'm swept into the lobby along with the crowd and find the bank of elevators to go to the twenty-fifth floor. The car with open doors is packed tight and I can only watch as the bodies shuffle backward and collectively inhale to allow the doors to close. As soon as I see the "up" light above the car that's next to open, I follow an elderly, bald man toward its door. I still have a shot at being exactly on time.

A uniformed guard standing behind a wooden stand is watching the elevators and he says, "The gentleman rides alone."

I glance at his face. Is he saying this to me? He is looking over my head so I think it's more of a general announce-ment so I continue moving forward. Now the guard steps out from behind his stand and blocks my way. The mass of people behind me have already moved to the next elevator about to open. I'll be shut out of that one too.

"The gentleman rides alone," he repeats. I look into the elevator and notice the old gentleman standing in the direct center of the car with his black umbrella holding the door open. He speaks. "What floor, young lady?"

"Twenty-five . . . "

"It's alright, Franklin," he says. The guard steps aside, and with a "humph" and a head jerk, he indicates that I can enter the elevator.

The elevator is as quiet as a tomb. No happy elevator music. I turn to my companion and thank him for letting me ride.

"I'm from Chicago. I wasn't prepared for New York City elevators to have a rush hour just like the subway. Thank you so much."

"It's my pleasure." He shifts his weight and I am con-scious of the fact that he is quite close to me now. He extends

his hand. "Mr. Ralph Peterson. Nice to meet you Miss . . .?
Do you work for me?"

I shake Mr. Peterson's hand. R.H. Peterson? Holy shit!
His grip is firm and he holds on to my hand as I say, "Andrea
Hoffman. And I'm here to interview today. So I guess my
answer is that I hope I'll work here soon."

"Good luck to you, Miss Hoffman." Smiling, he drops
my hand.

I smile back. My legs feel like jelly but the ride is so
smooth the only way I know that the elevator is moving is
that the floor lights are changing. A bell chimes when we
reach the twenty-fifth floor.

"Ladies first," he says. He sweeps his arm toward the door
and then brings it up under my skirt to grab a handful of
my ass. I almost laugh because it is such a bozo move, more
pimply high school boy than boss who rides a private elevator.

I step out without looking at my randy new friend. The
receptionist sees me coming toward her, but her eyes focus
on the man coming out of the elevator behind me. Her
mouth opens like a fish as her eyes dart from me to Mr.
Peterson and back.

"Thanks for the ride," I say to Mr. Peterson.

"The pleasure was all mine, Miss Hoffman," he says.

The receptionist stands and gives the old man a glossy
smile. "Good morning, Mr. Peterson," she says. "The meeting is just starting in the blue room."

He doesn't acknowledge her. He just strides off down
the hall his big black umbrella swinging at his side.

She turns the smile off the second he turns away, but her
eyes follow him a moment longer. From the bitter expression in her eyes, I'm pretty sure she had an "elevator ride"
or two.

"Can I help you?" she says. She puts the accent on *you*
and not *help*. It takes a massive amount of willpower to

refrain from pointing out that I am certain she *can* help me if she wants to. She doesn't really look like she wants to.

"I have an appointment with Reggie Flynn," I say. "Please tell him it's Andrea Hoffman."

She picks up her phone. "Tell him the girl is here," she says.

I let her "girl" comment go. She thinks she's tough but Mary Consuelo would have had her on the mat without breaking a sweat. "What's your name?" I ask.

"Shellie." She's not giving me her last name.

"Well, thanks for your help, Shellie," I say with a smile. I lean in closer, bare my teeth and wiggle my forefinger in front of my mouth. "You have lipstick on your teeth."

She grabs a tissue and starts rubbing her teeth.

There wasn't any lipstick. I just hate working with women. Too many games. If I were a strange guy who walked out of the elevator with Mr. Peterson, she'd be all smiles, using her elbows to push up her cleavage and I'd have a hot cup of coffee in a china cup by now.

I turn my back on her and sit on the couch, pick up the latest Peterson investment strategy piece from the pile of pamphlets on the coffee table in front of me. Reggie appears within a minute. I stand and drop the report on the table but Reggie says, "Keep it. It's great stuff."

I slide it into my briefcase and we walk down the hall. Even though Reggie does not have long legs, he keeps a rapid pace and I have to throw in a little hop every few steps to keep up with him.

"I hear," he calls back over his shoulder as we slow to round a corner, "that you rode up with Mr. Peterson today. That took some balls."

I say nothing. I don't know if Flynn thinks barging in on Mr. Peterson was a tactical coup on my part or just that it took guts to be alone with him in such a confined space.

We stop rather abruptly at an unmanned desk in front of large open doors. I peek in and see a large office with an oversized red couch in the middle of the room and a grouping of red, green, yellow, and blue chairs around a glass table. The desk by the windows is glass as well. Where does all of your essential junk go when you have no desk drawers? The desk top is clean, save for a Quotron, a phone, and a single picture in a silver frame turned the other way. I see an enormous painting on the far wall that looks familiar.

"Is that a Jackson Pollock?" I ask.

"You wouldn't believe what Peterson paid for that years ago when nobody had ever heard of the guy. Now it's worth a bloody fortune even though my twelve-year-old could make a dozen of them in an hour. Good thing I'm never in my office. If I had to look at that all day I'd puke."

He plucks a folder off his secretary's desk. "Here's your schedule. I have you set up in meetings with a bunch of the analysts and then you'll have lunch with a couple of the sales guys and you can spend some time on the trading desk. I'll send somebody to come get you later and we'll talk at the end of the day."

"That sounds great, Reggie," I say taking the folder from him.

"You know you're the only one I brought out here to New York from all the people I interviewed in Chicago. You have the kind of attitude we need around here. Shake up some of those older, lazier guys."

Great! I really don't see myself playing that role. I just want to make a lot more money than I do now and get far away from B. Roger Tate. "This is known as a top-notch firm. I'm happy to think that I might be able to contribute."

A tall brunette with huge hair is heading our way.

"Donna! Where the fuck have you been? I'm gone fifteen seconds and you disappear. This is Andrea Hoffman. Make sure she gets down to the research department. See if she wants coffee. I'm going over to the desk to kick some ass." Having successfully passed me off, Reggie Flynn strides away without a word or gesture in my direction.

I meet five analysts, one after the next. Serial déjà vu. I learn that the guy whose job I was interviewing for had played a lot of golf and never made any calls. I wonder if it was B. Roger Tate. How ironic would *that* be? But subsequent conversations inform me the guy was named Frederick who chose to go by Fred and not Rick so I instantly form an opinion of him. Loser. And this is good news. It is much harder to take over accounts from someone who was doing a great job.

Analyst number six is the last one on my schedule and he makes me wait for ten minutes. I can see him on the phone through his open door. He's a pacer. In motion to speak, stopping to listen and look at the view or his Quotron. It's an entertaining performance. He's my age, undeniably handsome and completely full of himself judging by the way he gestures and mugs even when alone.

He finally hangs up and beckons for me to enter. He shakes my hand and leans back in his huge leather chair until he is almost horizontal. "I have found, Andrea, that some salesmen sell ideas to their accounts and some salesmen merely feed them maintenance research. Which kind of salesman are you?"

It's surprising to me that a man who spends his day looking at hundreds of different parameters to decide whether a stock is correctly valued can devalue my job in such a way. I talk slowly because it drives these fast-talking New Yorkers crazy. "The reality is that some accounts want new ideas and some of them want hand-holding. I've even had some accounts that just want to be entertained. But most of them want all three. Thus, I'm the kind of salesman who gets to really know an account, finds out not just what they say they want but more importantly, what they pay for. And I give them that."

Wonder Boy Analyst starts to nod so vigorously that his whole body rocks and I worry he will end up tipping his chair over.

I'm not done yet: "But, bringing in commissions isn't my only job. Let's face facts. Some of my accounts are pretty small potatoes in terms of total dollars but they also have votes and I would be wrong if I didn't put getting institutional investors votes as one of my top priorities."

He's sold. "I like you," he says. "I'm actually surprised that dumbass Flynn was smart enough to find you."

I change my tune the minute I sit down for lunch at a comfortable table in the back of a clubby steakhouse with four of the salesmen. "All I want to know," I say, "is if you guys think your analysts are any good. Do they give you action-oriented calls or just a bunch of maintenance dribble?"

I get the responses I expect. Salesmen always have lots of complaints. The analysts aren't doing original work, investment banking wants them to push crappy deals, management is getting stingy on the entertainment dollars, and they're trying to haircut their pay outs. Thank God the market's going up. We drink to that. They're okay guys. They don't seem to have a big problem with me. I'll be off in the Chicago office. What do they care?

My last stop is the trading desk. I'm seated between two block traders named Frankie and Sean who couldn't be less thrilled to see me. They nod at the introduction but they keep their eyes on their screens and their phones.

After an awkward minute, Sean says, "You're the chick who rode up with Peterson."

"Oh my God! Everybody knows. I guess that's going to be on my tombstone. I was hoping it would be something else but I guess 'Peterson grabbed her ass' is my claim to fame from now on."

A few of the guys around us laugh. I only see two women on the desk.

Frank lights a cigarette and because guys like him were raised with good manners, offers me one. Grudgingly, he asks me where I'm from.

I decline the cigarette and I tell them I work at Kendall-Fitz in Chicago.

"You work with that piece of shit Johnny Mac?"

"I most certainly do."

Now they're looking right at me. All smiles. "What a great fucking guy he is," Sean says.

"Yeah," I say, "he's a great fucking guy. The first day I walked into the office he stood up and took one look at me and hollered to my boss, 'Jesus Harold, you hired another bitch without tits!'"

Frank and Sean explode in laughter.

"That's quite a mouth you got on you for a little girl," Frank says.

"Quoting Johnny! It's what salesmen do. We repeat shit."

They nod in agreement and tell me a story about Johnny Mac at a trading convention that involved dismantling and removing a bed from the hotel room of some giant dick from an unnamed firm. It's a good story. We're all having a good time. I love it here. I love interviewing. It is a hell of a lot more fun than working. The market is trading higher on some pretty nice volume and Frankie and Sean get busy, but I am happy just to listen to them and watch the tape.

Suddenly Sean is waving his phone in my direction and pointing at a blinking light on the console in front of me. "Pick up line thirty-six."

I'm a little surprised that they've had time to set up a little joke on me. No one knows I'm here, so it has to be a typical traders' prank. I'm flattered they are taking the time to tease me and curious to see what they've come up with.

"Andrea Hoffman," I say.

"I need you to come over to the office at the end of the day. Not now. When you're finished talking with Flynn." My hand starts to shake. This is no practical joke. This is God. I don't need to wonder how he knows I am here. Of course he knows.

I say, "Yes, sir," and the phone goes dead.

Frankie looks at me and just says "Whoa!" He too knows who that was.

I've always wanted to meet God and now I get my wish. I imagine it'll be a short meeting. He'll say "You're fired" and I'll leave. I'm not sure what I could have done differently here. I haven't been disloyal. When asked direct questions about things at Kendall–Fitz, I've been very neutral. "Things are good there," I've told the analysts, "I'm just looking for a better opportunity." None of the other guys have been fired for interviewing, but then again, what applies to the guys doesn't necessarily apply to me. I've found that out often enough.

At the end of the trading day, Donna finally comes and escorts me back to Reggie Flynn's office. He points to the round glass table. He takes the red chair and I sit in the blue one.

"Everybody loves you as much as I do, Andrea. Not that I am surprised. I want to offer you what we think is an extremely attractive package. You'll cover all of Chicago, St. Louis, and Kansas City. We'll bring you in as a vice president, naturally. You'll start with a one year guarantee of $200,000. And you'll have a moving allowance of five thousand dollars." He hands me a folder with what I assume are the details of the offer. Much more formal then when a handshake with Harold cemented my move to Kendall-Fitz.

And a lot more money. $200,000 is probably $25,000 less than they would offer a man but it's still a lot of money. I could be deliriously happy with that kind of money. But I'm stuck on the second figure he mentioned. "A moving allowance?" I repeat.

"Naturally. We want you here in New York."

I'm shaking my head. "It never occurred to me. I just assumed you wanted a presence in Chicago. Like I'd work out of your retail office there."

"You can have a desk there for when you're in town—certainly we want you out there entertaining and showing the flag—but I want you here. It'll be good for you and good for us."

For some reason, the receptionist's sour face pops into my mind. That'll be the first thing I see each and every morning. What a way to start the day. Then I remember that I am headed over to Kendall-Fitz to be fired and I'm going to need this job.

"Well, I love New York," I say, "and I was very impressed with everyone I met here. Of course, I'd want to hash out the particulars of your offer beyond the generous salary you mentioned. Can I give you my firm answer by the end of next week?"

"Of course." He smiles. "I'm pretty confident you'll be giving me a start date then." We shake hands and Flynn personally escorts me to the elevator. He'd be a good boss. He's a straightforward guy. Maybe I *can* fit in here. But instead of being elated that I got this job, I'm terrified. The whole interview thing seemed like a fun game. I never expected the outcome to be a major life change.

I flag a cab and settle back in my seat for the ride downtown. I lean my head back and close my eyes which makes the smell of the driver's curry lunch all the more noticeable. This'll be an everyday occurrence for me when I live here—cabs that smell like Indian restaurants, street corners that smell like souvlaki and roasting chestnuts, subways that smell like outhouses. I need to find somewhere to live. I need to sell the condo . . . or maybe I'll wait and rent it out for a while. Sometimes things don't work out. Or maybe I'll be so valuable at Peterson that they'll have to indulge me and move me back to Chicago.

"Lady, we're here. Eight bucks."

I must've dozed off. I give him a ten and tell him to keep the change and stand a minute on the sidewalk breathing in the thick summer air. I force myself to put one foot in front of the other and enter World Trade Tower Two, pushing against the tide. People are streaming out into the plaza to head home. In the cab, I worried about running into someone I knew in the office, but I imagine they'll have already left. And really, what difference does that make now? The elevator doors open and a mass of human beings flow out. I trudge in. The doors close. This afternoon, I ride alone.

An older woman in a dark pant suit is sitting at the reception desk when I walk in. She smiles when she sees me. "Andrea?"

I nod.

"Let me take you into the conference room. Can I get you coffee or water or anything?"

I shake my head. I've lost my ability to speak. In all my fantasies about leaving Kendall-Fitz, I never envisioned getting sacked in a conference room. I've been staging my resignation ever since Reggie Flynn invited me to interview in New York. In scenario one, I bring blueberry muffins to the office and graciously resign at the coffee pot. In scenario two, I confront B. Roger Tate, tell him he is a misogynist douche bag, and then quit. Now they'll pack my desk and send its contents to me by UPS. I'll never see the office again.

As we enter the conference room and sit she says, "I'm Rosa Bloom. I'm Ned's—that is, God's—secretary. Have been for thirty two years. So I know what it's like to be very close to someone you work with."

Is this about Dan? Are they firing me because they found out I slept with Dan and not because I am interviewing? What about *him*? I don't suppose they'll fire him. He's got all those kids. I feel the fear in my gut being edged out by anger. "Is God coming in soon?" I ask.

"God's not here. He leaves early on Fridays to spend time with his little brother. He's very active in the Big Brother/Little Brother program."

This really stinks. I came all the way downtown to be fired by God's secretary? Hell, she doesn't even bother to call herself his assistant. I'm so important to this company that after three years they don't even have Charlie Finnegan, the new sales manager, fire me. I'm glad I'm going to Peterson. They'll treat me with respect there. I look at my watch. "I have a flight back to Chicago in two hours," I say. Let's get this show on the road.

"Oh, good. That's one of the things we wanted to know. We didn't know if you were planning on staying in New York for the weekend and we didn't want to ask in your office for obvious reasons. Protect your privacy."

"I don't see why that matters now," I say.

A look of understanding flickers across Rosa's face. Then she looks sad.

"I've done this all wrong," she says. "I'm sure you're confused as to what you're doing here." She takes in a breath and looks directly at me. "Harold died this morning, Andrea. I'm very sorry. God didn't want you to get the news where you were, and he wanted to help you get back home in case some of your plans had to change."

I drop my head into my hands. Draw in a very shaky

breath. Relief floods through me. I'm not being fired. Then in the silence, Rosa's words hit me. Harold has died. I'm here because Harold's dead. My relief turns to shame. What kind of fucked up person am I? I was so happy I wasn't being fired from a job I don't even want that I didn't react to Harold's death.

"How did he die?" I ask and then add, "Stupid question. My brain doesn't seem to be working. I know he had lung cancer. But I thought he was getting better. I didn't realize he was in imminent danger. Nobody said anything." I sound a little defensive but Rosa just answers me calmly.

"Blood clot. It was very quick and painless and," she adds, "unexpected."

There is a box of Kleenex on the table and I pluck a tissue and wad it up in my fist. To be doing something. I know what I should be doing is crying. Harold's dead and I'm sitting here like a lox. What must this woman think?

"The funeral will be on Monday morning. Your office will be closed except for a temp answering the sales phones and we're sending out a New York trader to run the desk for the day. I have a car voucher for you. I'll call right now and it'll arrive in fifteen minutes. Why don't you just wait in here? You can use that phone if you need to."

She stands up and pulls the voucher from her pocket.

"I hope I see you again, my dear. Under happier circumstances. I know you are well thought of around here by many people. Ned told me to tell you he was sorry he couldn't be here himself and he's sorry for your loss. Is there anything else you need?"

What could I need? I'm starting to feel cold. I could use a scotch or more accurately—an entire bottle of scotch. "No, thank you. You've been so kind." I try to think of this woman's name. I know she told it to me. Do I really not know her name?

"Please thank God for arranging the car service and for not telling my office where I was and everything else. I hope to see you again too." I manage a small smile. So this is how it is. How people keep it together when they are falling apart. You just say the things you know you should say and do the things you know you should do. No thinking involved. In fact, I can see how not thinking is the most important thing. I stand up and shake Rosa's hand. Rosa. Of course I know her name. When she leaves the room, I fall back into my chair and I picture another conference room.

This one is filled with cigar smoke and I see Harold handing me his card. "You're going to help me make money." And what he didn't say but I understand now. "And in return, I'm going to change your whole life." I shake the vision from my mind. I blink the tears out of my eyes. And swallow the lump out of my throat. I feel empty. Weightless. Untethered to anyone anywhere. If I put down my briefcase, take off my expensive suit, heavy watch and thick gold bracelet, I'll just float away. I need to make a phone call. And get into a town car. On to a plane. Then I can fall apart.

Chapter 36

The plane lands smoothly and a handful of inexperienced passengers clap. I look around to make sure I'm not leaving anything behind and head for the exit feeling like it's after midnight even though it's only eight. I step out of the gangway into the terminal and see a man and a woman sitting in an empty waiting area. She's engrossed in a book. He's reading the *New York Times*. Odd. These two look exactly like my parents. Except that my parents don't buy the *Times*. But of course it is Mom and Dad sitting in the blue plastic chairs at good old gate two terminal one.

"Mom?"

She looks up from her book and shrugs.

"You didn't sound so good on the phone. I thought you might like a ride home."

I don't even ask how my mother knew what flight I would be on. My mother could find out where Jimmy Hoffa was buried if she cared about him.

Dad looks happy. "Somebody left today's *Times* behind," he says. For my dad, it was worth a thirty-five minute drive from home, a four dollar parking charge, a half an hour drive into the city to drop me off, and a forty minute trip back to Downers Grove just to get a free, slightly used newspaper.

"Well, you guessed right. I'd love a ride home."

"See, Stan, I told you she'd like a ride. It was a tough trip. She's tired. You look tired, darling." She looks at me. "You should wear a little makeup when you travel."

She reaches up and pushes my hair out of my face. My father takes my bag off my shoulder.

"Finally, you take it," she says to my dad. She takes my hand like I am four years old as we walk down the long terminal corridor.

"We're sorry to hear about your Harold, darling."

"You never even met him," I say.

"We're sorry about that too, but it doesn't mean we didn't know him."

I nod but I don't say anything. Can't.

The car smells like an Italian restaurant. "Did you guys have a pizza on the way to the airport?"

"I brought you a little spaghetti and meatballs. In case you didn't eat on the plane. Or you can eat it tomorrow."

"Thanks Mom. The bag's huge. There's only one of me."

"Well, there is a little salad and a few slices of garlic bread and a half of a sour cream chocolate cake. Sad people eat."

"Sad *Jewish* people eat. Gentiles just waste away." My stomach rumbles. I'm not hungry but it apparently is. "Thanks, Mom. It smells great and you're right, I didn't eat on the plane." I bought a scotch on the plane, and I looked around for Jack. But family things are usually weekend type things.

I know mentioning Jack to my mother is asking a doctor about a rash. I'm going to get a lot of nosy questions. But . . . "I talked with a nice guy on the plane ride to New York." I hope I sound nonchalant. "I'd met him before—through work. What a coincidence. That he was on the plane. We sat together and we ended up talking and we shared a taxi."

My mother turns around in her seat to look at me. "Does he have a name, this nice guy?"

"His name is Jack Keith and before you ask, I'll just tell you that he has an Aunt Norma in Queens so I'm going to go out on a limb here and say he's probably at least partly Jewish."

My mother smiles and says, "You never know . . . " and turns around.

I'd expected her a dozen questions and all she says is "You never know."

I settle back in the seat and smile at the back of her head. "Nah, I guess you never do."

As we speed down the expressway in the dark, I tell them about my interview and the job offer. When I tell them it involves a move to New York, I brace for their objections.

"Maybe we'll sell the house and move into your fancy loft if you're not going to need it," my dad says.

"I think you should live in Greenwich Village. I always wanted to do that when I was young," Mom says.

"I can't believe you two," I say. "No lecture. No suggestion that while I'm in New York I might check out Columbia Law School?"

"We just want what's best for you," my mom says. "Because we're so proud of you and think you deserve the best."

I don't answer her. I don't breathe. I want the words to hang in the air as long as I can hold them there.

Chapter 37

'm up early on the morning of Harold's funeral. I didn't sleep much anyway. All night long I was talking to Harold. *Thank you for hiring me. Thank you for not firing me when I messed up in the beginning. You were a good role model. I'm sorry if I was a disappointment to you or an embarrassment. I'm sorry I didn't ask you more questions. I'm sorry I didn't listen to your answers. I'm sorry I didn't take your advice as seriously as I should have. I'm sorry I didn't visit you. I'm sorry I didn't call you. I'm sorry that I made fun of you when the other guys did.* My sorry tally would have filled an entire page but Harold wouldn't have been interested in these apologies.

"Save them for Yom Kippur," he would have said.

Knowing he didn't want to hear it doesn't stop the tape from playing in my head. I make some coffee and turn on the local news. A three alarm factory fire, a sports report, a gang shooting, then the weather. They don't mention Harold's death. How could they not?

I shower and blow-dry my hair until it's smooth. I choose my outfit carefully. Black gabardine suit, silk blouse, Ferragamo pumps, small gold hoops. For some reason I pull out the old Movado watch. *I know how to dress myself now, Harold*. I load up my handbag with Kleenex. I grab my sunglasses.

I hear a car horn and it's the black limo that Charlene, Bob, and I are taking out to Lake Forest. I lock my door and head downstairs. It's a beautiful September day. I'm glad the sun is shining but Harold would say that such a day was for sneaking in nine holes of golf and not for staying inside listening to bullshit.

Charlene is already in the car—also hiding her eyes behind dark sunglasses.

"Should we smoke a joint before we pick up Bob?" she asks.

"I don't . . . "

"Honey, I'm kidding. You look nice." I'm glad I'm wearing the sunglasses because my eyes fill with tears.

At Bob's house, I am surprised to see Judy come out with him and get into the car with us. Bob, wearing a blue tie covered in bright green shamrocks, pats her leg and leaves his hand on her thigh.

"Not a black tie?" I say.

"Harold liked this one."

"I brought some bagels," Judy says, and puts a paper bag on the seat next to her. "And some orange juice." She points to Bob who is carrying a Thermos. "Coffee."

Who thinks about packing a picnic on the way to a funeral? I start to shake my head but Charlene says, "Thanks, Judy. I couldn't eat anything when I got up this morning but Harold would be annoyed if one of us fainted dead away in front of the casket. Maybe Andrea will split one with me . . . "

"Sure. Thanks." I'm starving. Have been all weekend. "I'd love some coffee too."

"When my dad died," Bob says, "I was ravenous all the time and felt so guilty. I loved my dad. Wasn't grief supposed to take away your appetite? People were coming to the house with lasagna and meatballs and cake. I ate it all and gained thirty pounds."

"I'm continually amazed at how much Jews and Italians are alike. Maybe you guys are the lost tribe. Should we have brought something today?" I ask.

"It's taken care of. God sent flowers to the funeral home and a fruit basket to the house," Charlene says. "Johnny told me the firm paid all of Harold's medical bills and cut him a six-month bonus check based on his commission totals just like if he had been here."

"Nice," I say. "Wall Street's not totally cold-hearted capitalists."

We're silent as the car moves through the morning traffic. The people we pass try to see through the tinted glass of our car. It seemed like such a long time ago I'd been excited about my first limo ride.

"So, Bobby tells me you do babysitting," Judy says. "Want to sit for Robbie and Sarah sometime?" She has a slightly evil smile on her face which makes me think that perhaps Bob hasn't told us everything about Judy.

"You couldn't afford me," I say. "But honestly, I don't see why everyone thinks it's so funny. Bob takes clients to Wrigley. And it gets him business. I babysat to get business."

"I don't think it's funny. I think it's very clever. Manipulating female stereotypes to achieve non-sexual goals. I used you as an example in one of my classes the other week."

"I didn't know you were taking classes," I say.

Judy shoots Bob a look and I know I just got him into trouble.

"The class is one I'm *teaching*, not taking. I'm getting my doctorate in clinical psychology. I'm planning on a private practice specializing in kids with depression."

"That's great," Charlene says. "Bob, maybe you should

shut up about your wonderful kids sometime and tell us a story about Judy now and then."

Or maybe a different kind of story, I think and take a quick glance at Judy's hands to see if she's still going to Viva nails.

We turn off at the Lake Forest exit. The town looks like a movie set. The streets are wide. There are no trash cans at the curbs, no trikes on the lawns. The houses are enormous and freshly painted. The hedges are clipped and the flower beds weeded. No wonder Harold liked it so much. Everything's in its place here.

We turn a corner and the driver tells us the funeral home is up ahead. The sidewalks are full of people walking in the direction of the service. Bob's wife and Charlene both start rummaging through their purses and come up with lipsticks and small mirrors.

Judy looks at me over the top of her compact. "Are you all right, Andrea?"

I'm not close to all right. I'm not even in the same time zone as all right. I don't have a lipstick. And Harold died. Harold died before I had a chance to visit him so Harold died thinking I was a spoiled, ungrateful, selfish brat. I have no idea why I never picked up the phone to call him. I was so busy making and spending money and now I am flattened under the weight of my regret.

Judy is staring at me with an intense look on her face, and I expect her to put her hand on my forehead to see if I have a fever. Bob's looking at Judy. Charlene is holding a cigarette and looking in the bottom of her bag for her lighter. I'm not going to tell these people what I'm thinking but I can tell them something different that's still true.

"I've never been to a funeral. I was too young to go when my grandmother died. When my grandfather died I was at college and it was finals week." I do not add that my mother had a meeting at work and so my dad went alone to his own father's funeral. My dad has a wife and four children and none of us went with him. This makes me very, very sad and my eyes fill up with tears for the second time today.

Charlene hands me a tissue. "This day is going to be the pits. Let's get it over with." The limo driver comes around and opens the door for us. Charlene swings her legs out and stands up just like you see the movie stars do. Judy follows. Bob puts his hand on my well-padded shoulder. "He thought the world of you, you know. He was so happy when you came back to Kendall-Fitz."

Fucking Bob. I dissolve in tears. He shakes his head. "Okay, that wasn't what I wanted to do." I wave him out of the car like I'm shooing a dog. Judy sticks her head back in.

"Take a minute. We'll save you a seat."

The driver closes the door and leans against the car. What am I supposed to do in a minute? Go back in time? Communicate with a ghost? I look out the tinted window and see people pouring into the funeral home. I recognize portfolio managers, analysts and traders from accounts all over town. The driver's left the car running. It's quiet inside except for my sniffling and the hum of the engine. I remember something that Harold always said to me: "You're only as good as your last trade." Well, Harold made his last trade a long time ago and yet here were all these people coming to pay their respects.

"What do you know, Harold? You were wrong," I say out loud.

I imagine what his answer would be: "What are you doing in the goddamn limo? Get out there. Have some class. Show some dignity. Blow your nose."

I see B. Roger Tate standing at the door of the funeral home greeting people like he's at a golf outing. As far as I know, he never even met Harold. It feels good to feel angry.

It takes me a minute to find Judy, Bob, and Charlene. They are about halfway up the aisle and for a minute I wonder if they are on the correct side. Then I remember that's for weddings. Everybody here just fits into the "friends of the deceased" category.

The first day of seventh grade, I was sitting in homeroom and the teacher was looking through the information cards we had just filled out.

"Tony Clarkson?" she called out. Tony was a sullen greaser I was half in love with. "Tony, what does this say your father's occupation is?"

From two rows behind me, Tony mumbled, "My father's deceased."

"I'm sorry—I didn't hear you," she said.

Tony spoke up. "My father is deceased." All the kids heard him perfectly well and we held our breath as old Mrs. Hilliard said, "Tony, you'll have to speak up in this class."

"My father's *dead*, okay?!?" he yelled. I didn't turn around to look at his face.

Mrs. Hilliard looked down at the card she held in her hand. "Oh. That's not spelled correctly," she said.

Like it was yesterday I remember the moment. I'm glad Harold's sons are well out of school. One's at a bank in Minneapolis. The other one's a lawyer here in Chicago. I see them sitting on either side of Blythe in the front row with their heads facing straight ahead.

I thank god for making me short because I can't see Harold's body in the open casket.

The service starts with a hymn. Dan's sitting directly behind me with his wife. He sings loudly but not particularly well. His wife's fatter than I remember but still pretty in a girl-next-door way. Johnny's alone and he looks grim. Erin with red puffy eyes in a high-necked black dress in a material that looks itchy sits in the same row as Johnny. Two empty chairs between them. After the singing, Harold's minister starts speaking about death and everlasting life and living on in memory and being with Christ but I'm not really listening. I'm looking at the casket with Harold Stackman lying in it and I'm thinking about the first time I saw him. I never could have imagined that I might be at his funeral one day. Too naïve to think I'd ever be at *anyone's* funeral. Ever.

Blythe stands and walk toward the lectern. A rustle of whispers sweeps through the crowd. She's a beautiful woman. She looks a lot like Harold—tall with the same pure white hair and blue eyes. She holds onto the lectern but otherwise looks composed. I notice that I've been holding my breath. I consciously breathe.

"Harold," she says in a voice I know so well from years of phone calls, "would be amazed to see you all here on a day that the markets are open for trading." A little nervous chuckling erupts around the room. "The boys and I are not surprised but we are very grateful that you have come."

I reach in my bag and pull out a fistful of Kleenex to keep at the ready.

"Harold was a terrific husband and father and member of this community but I suspect that those of you who worked with him knew a different Harold than those of us who did not. He loved his job and I think it brought out the best in him. You . . . brought out the best in him. He thought, pretty much until the very end, that he was going back to work. He didn't make it there but I am glad to see that you have come to him." She turns her head slightly and looks directly at Dan. "You're pretty smooth, but I saw you slip that Macanudo into the casket as you filed by." There is another ripple of soft laughter.

Johnny stage whispers, "Class move, dipshit."

"Thank you. Harold would certainly appreciate the gesture. I guess that's all I wanted to say. Thanks to all of you who recognized what a terrific guy my husband was. It was . . . " She stops and smiles the saddest smile I have ever seen. Tears are pouring down my face and I'm trying not to make that braying noise as I struggle to keep breathing. I hear sniffling and nose-blowing all over the room. Blythe turns and places her hand on Harold's casket and her sons come up and walk her back to her seat.

Blythe was wrong. Harold wasn't all about work. Work was all about her and the boys. I can see that now. The late nights and the relentless phone calls—it wasn't about the money or the ego boost. It was about doing the right thing and doing the right thing for the right reason. For his family. He had told me. I hadn't heard him.

There's another hymn and the casket is closed. We file out and I feel a hand on my shoulder. It's Dan.

"Okay?" he says.

"Okay." I reach up and pat his hand.

It's a shock to see the sun when we get outside. Dan mimes a golf swing as we gather on the carpet-like lawn. "Remember when Harold took Fred Olsen from IDS golfing and it was so windy that Fred's toupee blew off and they had to chase it over to the sixth hole?"

Our laughter's a little hysterical but we keep it under control.

"Did you see Charlie Finnegan?" Johnny Mac asks "He's coming into the office tomorrow."

"The day after Harold's funeral?" I say.

"The head of institutional sales is a busy guy. He doesn't want to waste a trip to Chicago. Knowing him he would've liked to have a dinner meeting tonight and get it over with. God just wouldn't let him," Johnny says.

I feel a tap on my shoulder and turn around to see Allan standing behind me. We hug.

"If it isn't the mail guy," I say.

Allan just shakes his head. "I want to talk to you."

"We talk almost every day, Allan." I say.

"Not work. Something else." he says. "It can wait. But not for too long, okay?" He squeezes my arm and turns to go. "I'm sorry about Harold. He was a good man," he says as he disappears into the crowd.

Dan's wife suggests we all go to a local place for lunch. I look closely at her now that she's standing. She's not fat. She's pregnant again. Dan sees me looking. He looks at me and bites his bottom lip. I roll my eyes at him but force myself to smile and he nods proudly and puts his arm on her shoulder. She smiles at him. A fourth kid! Jesus.

All of us head out to eat and toss back a drink and some of us have quite a few more. Then I smoke a cigar. Feel Harold with us. Feel his absence more.

There's a message from Jack on my answering machine when I get home. He heard about Harold. Condolences. Could he take me out to dinner Thursday night? I replay the message. He sounds sincere. Concerned. I play the message a third time. He sounds . . . hopeful. I can't think of any reason to say no. The fourth time I play the message, I write down his phone number. I call him back.

Chapter 38

When I walk into the office on Tuesday morning, something seems off. I look up at the ceiling lights to see if a bulb or two is burned out. But no. The only thing different is that Harold isn't coming back. I stop at his desk. Look in his desk drawer. All the Macanudo cigars are gone.

"I took them Friday when we got the call," Dan says coming in behind me.

I jump. "Jesus, Dan! You scared the shit out of me. Since when have you developed little cat feet?"

"Since when have you gone deaf?"

Bob says, "Why didn't you tell us you knocked up your wife again?"

I pile on. "Have you lost your mind?"

Dan must have known she was pregnant the night he was at my house. I should be angrier but I'm not. No harm no foul.

"Jesus, you assholes, I think the appropriate thing to do is congratulate me!"

"I hope it's twin girls," I say.

Charlene comes in and stops to kiss Dan on the cheek. "Congratulations Stud."

Dan turns to me. "Now that's what I'm talking about."

"Congratulations for what?" B. Roger Tate asks as he slithers in.

"My kid's football team won this weekend," Dan says and sits down at his desk.

Roger couldn't give a rat's ass about that and he sits without further comment.

A few minutes later, Charlene comes into the bathroom as I'm putting in my contacts.

"Lock and load. Your new boss just showed up. Put on some war paint."

"Thanks for the warning," I say, and I apply some mascara and blush before I head back to the office.

Charles Finnegan, head of all Kendall-Fitz sales, is sitting next to Johnny. He sees me come in and walks over to meet me at the coffee machine.

The first thing I notice is his close-cut salt and pepper hair. Despite the grey, he's clearly a young man. Early forties I'd guess. Under his bespoke suit, I sense the wiry body of a runner. I understand why Charlene had warned me to spiff up. This guy's like a shiny new penny. His shirt's heavily starched and snowy white. His pants are creased as sharp as razor blades. The shine on his shoes is dazzling. His body seems to pulse with energy. I expect him to drop to the floor and do fifty pushups just to keep all that vigor from exploding. He sticks his hand out and I clasp it.

"Nice to meet you, sir. I'm Andrea Hoffman."

I hold my breath waiting for some indication that Patrick O'Neil mentioned me to him, but he just gives me a penetrating but not unfriendly stare and says. "Call me Charlie." Rhymes with Holly. Pure Boston. "I gave up the sir stuff when I left the Marines."

I pour myself a coffee and ask, "What did you do in the Marines . . . Charlie?"

"Whatever they told me to do."

I laugh. Look at my boss. He's dead serious.

"My dad was in the army," I say. Like he would give a shit.

"So you know then," he says. Although clearly I know nothing at all.

Dan and Bob walk over to the coffee pot. They all shake hands and Charlie slaps Dan on the back. Clearly, Dan had met Charlie before. Like law school, a pregnant wife, and recommending me for the Peterson job, something else he's failed to mention.

"Charlie, my man!" Tate yells from the doorway. He waves a white bag. "Brought you a donut. Help you get down the swill they call coffee here."

I doubt Finnegan has eaten a donut in the last decade. Egg whites. Dry toast.

As soon as the call is over, Charlie disappears into the conference room and as the morning goes by, I almost forget he's here until he makes a reappearance at eleven. He's ditched his suit coat and as he passes my desk, I notice his athletic body again. His shoulders are broad but his hips are smaller than mine and he's got a nice round ass. I look away. I'm not supposed to be having these kinds of thoughts about my boss.

Charlie refills his coffee cup and when Bob finishes a call he says something to him and the two of them leave the room. About a half an hour later, Bob comes back. He gives me a thumbs-up when I raise my eyebrows and heads to his desk, spins his chair to the windows, and gets right on his phone. I finish my call and when I look up again, Bob is heading out the door. Soon after, Charlie comes back into the room and is sitting at the trading desk talking to Johnny. Maybe the rest of us will have private meetings after lunch.

Lunch is in the small private room at the Italian Village. I sit down across from Dan, which puts me next to Roger.

At least I don't have to look at him while I eat. Charlie starts buttering a roll. He holds the roll halfway to his mouth and says, "I fired Bob this morning." Then he takes a big bite and chews with a satisfied smile.

No! My stomach lurches. I thought Bob had left the office early to do an errand on the way to the restaurant. Now I notice there isn't a place setting for him. What if I take the Peterson job? If I had resigned this morning, would that have saved him?

"Did he do something?" I say.

"Nothing like that. Fired was a harsh word. He's a good man. He'll be taken care of but Bob's just not the kind of salesman we're going to need going forward." Charlie scans our faces. Dan is looking down at his plate. Tate is smiling broadly.

I want to ask what kind of salesman we're going to need going forward, but Charlie is moving on.

"I've ordered the lunch. Let's get down to business."

I force myself to listen.

"Everybody in New York says that this is the best regional office Kendall-Fitz has." I feel the tiniest bit of recovery from the Bob body slam. "But," Charlie continues, "I don't think any of you guys are all that great."

Pow! I look around the table. The other guys didn't expect that either.

"You're all good enough," he continues. "You're just not *great*. I'm going to make you better."

Okay. True enough. Tate's a complete asshole. Dan spends too much time drinking and golfing. I myself avoid making some of my calls, and could try harder to get into the accounts that don't like me. Yes, we could all do better.

Step one in the Chicago Office Improvement Plan is to rearrange some of the account coverage. Charlie hands us each a piece of paper. Dan picks up Madison and Milwaukee from Bob. Tate gets the best of Bob's Chicago accounts. Tate dumps on me a few of the smaller Harold accounts that are a waste of his time and I get Bob's Iowa accounts. More Iowa? I'm trying to get *out* of the boonies. My account package is a bit better than before but not nearly as good as it would be if I took the Peterson job. Some accounts seem to be missing. If Bob's gone, there should be more to spread around.

"You might notice that Kansas City and St. Louis are gone. They're going to be covered out of the Dallas office from now on." Finnegan takes a break to eat some of his salad. I turn the leaves of lettuce over on my plate as if I am looking for caterpillars. I can't imagine chewing and swallowing.

"This business is changing," Finnegan resumes, "you might not be seeing it out here, but in New York, the competition is mobilizing for a full frontal attack. The huge Japanese firms are moving in—Nomura and Nikko. They do things differently and we're going to have to adopt some of their methods. Primarily, they demand accountability and clear lines of communication. So from now on, all salesmen are going to be filling out daily contact sheets. You'll list every call you make and detail what you talk about. These'll be distributed to the trading desks and the analysts so that they can follow up on your efforts. This isn't a numbers game. We aren't looking for sheer volume of calls. We want quality information we can make trades on."

I sneak a peek at Dan who is intently studying the mural of an Italian vineyard behind Charlie's head. Roger is looking directly at Charlie, a look on his face that can only be called glee. Fucker.

"Will we get sheets in return from the traders and analysts?" I ask.

"There are no plans for that at this time. Of course, they should already be communicating with you if they know something that is relevant." He looks at me intently. "Are you having a problem with information flow?"

"No, sir. I'm not. I am just curious as to how the Japanese are doing it."

Charlie waves his fork at me and the penne he has impaled drops to his plate.

"Fair enough. We've got to keep up with the enemy's tactics. Can't let them eat our lunch." He's about to take another bite when he spies his empty fork and grins. Roger gives a big fake laugh, spies the waiter in the doorway, and holds up his glass to get a refill on his cocktail. Dan has half his beer remaining and Charlie and I aren't drinking.

"The Japanese are actually doing all sorts of interesting things with cost controls/risk reduction. That's going to be our phase two. Commissions will now be paid out twice a year instead of quarterly and we'll be putting a portion of your money in a pool that will be held over until the next payout period. The distribution of this money can be adjusted in case of sudden market downturn or an unfortunate drop-off in your productivity. But for most of you, you can expect all that money will be paid out."

"So what you're basically saying," Dan says in a factual tone of voice, "is that we'll be expected to do more work for less money. I understand how that would be management's goal, but I don't see the connection between that and the foreign competition stuff. My clients are not going to respond favorably to a foreign brokerage firm. While they can be ball-busters, my clients are loyal to those of us who have been here and paid our dues."

"Thanks for your input," Charlie says, voice flat. "Anyone want coffee or dessert?"

I haven't eaten more than three bites of my lunch but no one seems to notice. The full plate of pasta is whisked away and coffee is poured.

"One more thing I want to tell you," Charlie says as he pours cream into his cup. "Roger is going to assume the office manager duties. In fact, I want those duties to be more than administrative. I want all the accounts in the region to know him and feel that if they have a problem or suggestion, they can have access to a problem solver. I hope you'll all be on board with this." He takes a second to look at Dan. "This office has been lacking a chain of command. Johnny is a fine trader but he's not the head of this office. If you have a problem, you go to Tate. If he has a problem, he'll come to me. If I have a problem, I go to God. But," this time he looks at B. Roger, "I don't expect to have any problems."

I want to put my hands to my face and scream like the Munch painting. But I just stare at the tablecloth. Wrong, wrong, wrong. He's a lousy salesman, so he gets to be boss? I can't live with this. I don't have to.

I clear my throat and say, "Charlie, I've got to confess that I'm *not* on board with your decision."

Dan's looking at me with real concern. I could have told him about the Peterson offer.

Tate's smirking as usual. I take a breath and continue. "Making Tate the office manager is a horrible idea. He's a lazy, incompetent salesman and a bigoted, despicable human being. And he's a drunk." Tate glances over at Charlie, puts down the glass he's about to drain.

"You should be ashamed of yourself," I say to Charlie, "firing a good man like Bob Parker and promoting a douche like this. I can put up with the changed account assignments, but for the record, I'm not an idiot. I see that you gave me shit. And I can deal with the commission haircut. Everybody in this firm thinks salesmen make too much money so I guess I expected that eventually. And I can play your silly games and fill out forms until the office is buried in a blizzard of white paper." I'm standing up now. Not shouting but pretty darn loud. "But this business only works to the extent that people respect each other. We don't sign contracts with our customers. We don't charge them by the hour. The whole damn thing hangs together on the principle of respect and cooperation. There's loyalty. Maybe if you're cynical you call it mutual self-interest. You want this lying jerk to represent the Chicago Kendall-Fitz office? He'll put us out of business faster than Nomura will."

Charlie is sitting up ramrod straight. He says, "The customers do like you, Andrea, but I've heard internally you're not a true team player. No regret at leaving a colleague hanging."

So, there it is. Patrick O'Neil did talk.

"And maybe your perspective on this is colored by your personal feelings toward Roger. He's well respected by everyone I've talked to."

"No, he's not. That's what's wrong with this system." Why stop now. "We all cover each other's ass and instead of it being good for the team, it just protects the lazy and the weak. You don't hear the truth. You probably don't even know about the key taping incident. I don't blame you. I blame us. We got what we deserved."

I know I'm reinforcing every stereotype that these men have about emotional women who don't know how to play the game, but I don't care. I crumple the piece of paper with the new account assignments on it and I chuck it at Tate. "Here's your first job as office manager. You're going to have to redo the account assignments." I can't look at Dan. I keep my eyes trained on Charlie and say slowly and succinctly, "I am not working for that asshole. I quit." I pick up my purse and turn to leave the room. Dan says nothing but he looks epically pissed.

"I'm sorry you feel this way," Charlie says. "You do what you have to do, Andrea."

I finally look at B. Roger Tate and he grins at me and then he raises his hands and slowly claps them together once, twice, three times. Heat flashes through my face. I ball my fists. I'd love to hit him but then I see both Charlie and Dan staring him down. Dan clearly has a look of disgust on his face, and Charlie? I think it might be the beginning of doubt. I force myself to smile. "Good luck," I say and I stride out.

———

I'd love to find a place to sit down for a minute until the roaring noise in my ears goes away and I can establish better control over my uncontrollable shaking, but I know I have to hurry back to the office. I need to use the phone to call Reggie Flynn and accept the Peterson job, get my stuff out of my desk, and say goodbye to everybody before the guys get back. I concentrate on forcing one foot in front of the other. I try to think *left-right left-right* instead of *what the hell did I just do? Now I have to move to New York!*

I'm exhausted by the time I walk the four blocks back to the office. When I walk in the door without the rest of the group, no one looks surprised.

"They're dropping like flies," Erin says.

I look over to Bob's empty desk.

"Finnegan told you? I say.

"It was on the tape," Erin says.

"Bob getting fired was on the tape?" I say.

"What the fuck are you talking about?" Johnny asks.

"Finnegan fired Bob, made Tate office manager, and I quit!" I turn to Erin. "What are you talking about?"

"More mergers," she says, the quaver back in her voice. "Merrill Lynch bought Peterson today."

"Peterson? That's not possible," I say. I pull the empty chair out from the trading desk and sit down. "How could that have happened?"

"Fuck Peterson," Charlene says. "What do we give a shit? Just Bob didn't say a word. And what do you mean you quit? Why the hell would you do that?"

"I just told you that Tate is the new office manager. I'm not working for him. A person has to have some scruples."

Charlene runs a hand through her hair. "What did Dan say?"

"He stood up to Charlie when he announced the commission cuts but he didn't say anything about Tate. I guess he figures he can just ignore him. I can't."

"Johnny, can't you do something? We can't lose all our salesmen." Charlene says. She turns to me. "Andrea, you can't leave. Please. Johnny. Call God."

"I'm not calling God. Shit happens in this business. If you can't handle it, Charlene, have some balls like Hoffman here and take a powder."

"Eat shit, Johnny," Charlene flings back at him.

I say, "I have to get my stuff and get out of here."

"Get out of here and go where?" Charlene asks.

"Well, here's the funny part," I say. The impact of what I'm about to say hits me hard. "It didn't take the big balls that Johnny has just endowed me with to quit. I had another job offer in my pocket. I thought I was quitting here and going to New York to work for Peterson but since as of today, they're history, I expect I'm just going home."

Chapter 39

I tell Jack that Thursday night dinner no longer works for me as I'm having a mental breakdown over my job situation and I wouldn't be good company. But he insists that he's coming over to my place at six-thirty with takeout whether I want him to or not. I don't have the strength to argue. And I do want him to come.

The loud knock on my door at exactly six-thirty startles me even though I have been pacing the apartment waiting for what seems like hours. I open the door and Jack leans down and gathers me into a tight hug. I smell Barbasol shaving crème and feel the warm air as he breathes against my neck. "Come on in," I say as I step back into the apartment. It's amazing that someone I've been in the same room with only three other times could seem so familiar to me.

"Hold the door. I have some stuff to bring in," he says as he disappears into the hall.

Then he's back with a brown shopping bag in one hand and a large cardboard box with a handle on top in the other. The box swings in his hand and I hear meowing when he sets it down.

"Is that what I think it is?"

"What do you think it is?"

"I think it is a box with a cat in it."

"Wow, that's amazing, but you're wrong."

"Thank god!" I say. "The last thing I need is a cat."

"Of course you don't. So I didn't bring you a cat. I brought you two kittens."

I stand like a statue as he opens the box and places the tiny cats on my living room rug. They remain huddled together—one black and white and one calico. I refuse to yield even though they are impossibly cute.

"How do you know I'm not allergic?"

"Are you?"

"No, but I can't have cats. How will I take care of them? What if I move to New York? I just . . . "

"Sorry. I didn't really explain. I'm not a complete lunatic. Owning a living thing is a big commitment. I would never force something like that on you. These are loaner kittens. My Mom works at the SPCA and sometimes she takes cats home to socialize them for adoption. Sort of like a foster situation. They're just to keep you company for a few weeks. You're not used to being home by yourself all day."

"That's a relief. Only a few weeks. Still, I need some stuff, don't I?"

Jack points to the bag. "Litter box, litter, litter scoop. Food bowls, food. That's pretty much it." He empties the stuff on the floor.

I'm still standing watching as the kittens sniff their paraphernalia and then disappear into the empty bag. I shake my head but I can't help smiling. "You jerk! I can't believe you brought me *kittens*."

"I brought you Chinese food, too. It's in the car. I'll go get it if you promise you'll let me back in."

"Yes! Go. I'm starving." And I am, even though I haven't been hungry since the Italian Village lunch debacle two days ago. All that's visible of the little beasts right now is one swishing black tail sticking out of the bag. "I'll leave the door unlocked. And hurry or I might start on the cat food."

When I hear his footsteps heading down the stairs, I sit on the rug and reach into the bag and extract cat number one. The black and white fur ball just looks at me calmly with large green eyes. I rub under its chin with one finger and it closes its eyes and starts to purr. Cat number two sticks a pink nose out of the bag to see what is going on with cat number one. It's a calico with yellow eyes. I drop black and white in my lap and reach for calico. I can feel its tiny heart beating against my palm. I cup my hand under its dangling legs and rub my face against the soft fur of its back. I hear the door handle start to turn and I drop the cat before Jack comes in. Still, he catches me sitting on the rug.

"Did you name them yet?" he asks.

"You mean I can't just call them One and Two?"

"Lazy but acceptable. They're both girls by the way. You said you have brothers and you work with mostly guys. I thought a little sisterhood might be nice."

One pounces on Two who retaliates by ineffectively batting her across the head. Little bitches. They both jump up and run off in opposite directions.

"I'm going to admit to a certain level of entertainment value here."

I look at Jack who's scooped up tiny Two in his hand and is using a long finger to gently stroke her spine. My spine tingles.

Jack sets up the litter box in the guest bathroom while I set out the food. Then he sits down at the table near the huge front window where I have put out the food. "Do you have a couple of beers?"

I get the beers out of the fridge and sit down. Dish myself a generous plate of food.

"Do you feel sorry for them?" he asks.

"For who?"

"Your friends who are left in the office."

"Sort of. Their choice to stay though. Bob, the guy they fired, walked out of Kendall-Fitz and was immediately hired by a small regional firm. He'll do fine and I'm so glad."

I set down my chopsticks and help myself to more beef with green beans. "It's been two days and I already miss working. I went to the grocery store yesterday and I couldn't believe so many people were in there. Everybody's not on the job from 9 to 5? I felt out of place. I have a mortgage and . . . " I look down as cat two tries to climb up my jeans, ". . . and now I have two cats to feed. I shouldn't be in a store in the middle of the afternoon."

"Really?" He deftly rolls up some moo shu pork in a wrapper, spreads it with hoisin sauce and hands it to me. "I bet you have at least a year's worth of savings."

"A year probably but not a *lifetime*'s worth of savings. I need to get back to work."

"Andrea, you're a victim of 'velocitization.'"

Seeing as I have a large mouth full of fried rice, I just raise my eyebrows and wait for him to say more.

"When you have been driving for a long time at seventy miles an hour, you get used to that speed. It seems normal to you and when you have to slow down to fifty-five, it seems like you're just poking along. You've been moving so fast that normal seems too slow for you."

"What's your point?"

"I don't have a point. I was making an observation. I don't think I know you well enough yet to be telling you how to live your life."

I should agree with him. No one tells me how to live my

life. But I'm getting tired of going it alone. Jack seems to have a fair amount of common sense and a decent sense of humor. "Well, I'm not saying I wouldn't be open to hearing a suggestion or two," I say.

He pulls a fortune cookie from the bag and tosses it to me. I open the cellophane bag and pop half of the cookie into my mouth before I read the little slip of paper. *The path is seldom straight.* "Not helpful," I say. "And the cookie's stale."

The phone rings while we are cleaning up the dishes. I think about letting it ring because it is probably my mother, but I don't want Jack to hear the embarrassing message she's sure to leave on the answering machine. It's better to answer it and blow her off.

"Andrea? Allan."

"Hey, Allan. Jeez . . . calling me at home. Is everything okay?"

"Well, that's kind of what I called to ask you."

"I'm okay," I say, and am somewhat surprised to mean it.

"Can we have a drink tomorrow after work?"

"You'll have to be a little more specific on the timing, Allan. Since I don't have work, 'after work' is a pretty vague concept for me."

"Oh, for God's sake. Five o'clock at The Billy Goat Tavern."

"Is this a pity drink?"

"No, it's a 'I'm trying to take advantage of your crisis' drink.

"Are you going to offer me a job?"

"Just show up and you'll find out," he says and hangs up the phone before I can tell him I'm not interested.

Jack is absorbed with the cats which I assume is his way of trying not to appear too curious about the call.

"Client," I say when I come back to the table. "But also a friend. I've know him since I started working at Mosley. In fact, he is a Mosley. You'll like him."

Jack gets up and moves to the couch. "I'd like to meet him. And Charlene. And your family. All the people you told me about on the plane."

I sit down next to him and he pulls me onto his lap. "I plan on spending lots of time with you." He takes my chin in his hand and kisses me slowly and thoroughly. "Is that okay with you?"

I like the damn kittens. He did a good job of choosing Chinese food. In fact, the list is long of the things that are likeable about this man. But an inconsequential list compared to the heat I'm feeling. I want to melt onto him. And into him. Feel every inch of his body touching mine. Match my breath to the rhythm of his breath. Let my heart beat to the beat of his heart. I want. I want. I want. For the first time in such a long time, I know, with no ambiguity, what I want. His hands travel under my shirt. Deftly undoes my bra one handed. He pulls away just enough make me want to push toward him. Looks me in the eye. Not smiling. His face questioning. Beckoning. Repeats his question. "Is that okay with you?"

I could think of a dozen clever answers. I say, "Yes," and I take his free hand and, hopping out of my jeans as I go, kittens tumbling after, pull him into my bedroom.

Chapter 40

Even though I'm not enthusiastic about hearing what Allan has to say, I'm still early to our meeting. What else did I have to do? In the morning I had called a few of my favorite clients to tell them I was leaving. Already gone, actually. I kept the calls short because I was paying for the long-distance charges myself and because I didn't want to get into the truth of why I left. Even if Charlie Finnegan didn't think I was a team player, I didn't want to say anything about Kendall Fitz that would end up hurting Johnny, Charlene, Erin, or Dan. But it was tricky. If I implied I had a new job that I wasn't ready to reveal, I'd squash the possibility they may have a good lead for me. But if I admitted I left without a job, it would look like I was fired. The other possibility, that these people didn't really care as long as someone from Kendal Fitz called with the earnings updates, was painful to contemplate, so I picked my calls carefully. So far, Roger hadn't called any of them which was what I was really trying to find out. Charlene told me Charlie Finnegan had stopped by the trading desk on his way out and promised them he'd unfuck this situation and have a new guy to replace Bob and me ASAP.

In the afternoon, I'd gone to the public library. They have a room with typewriters for public use and I tried to create a professional looking resume. I have the one I created with the least typos in my purse right now to show Allan who arrives in jeans, sneakers, and a Grateful Dead t-shirt. We sit at the bar.

"This is what you wore to work?" I say as a greeting. "No important meetings today?"

"I dress like this every day. I keep a suit, shirt, and tie in my closet in case I need to put on the costume, but I can't think of the last time that happened. We have over $500 million under management now. People have to take me seriously even if I am wearing a clown nose."

He signals the bartender and orders his usual shot of bourbon with a beer back. Old school establishments like the Billy Goat Tavern don't have "two-fer" happy hours, so Allan tells the guy to bring him two to start and keep them coming. I order a bourbon without the beer.

"Isn't that Mike Royko over there?" I point to a middle-aged man with large glasses and a thin-lipped smile.

Allan looks, gives the man a nod. The man nods back and lifts his glass in salute.

I'm impressed. "It's good to be you, Allan Mosley. Buddies with Chicago's most famous writer."

"I don't know him from that. I know him from softball. Mosley had a team that played in the same league as the Sun-Times. Anyway, I think Studs Terkel might be more famous."

"Royko's column *How to Cure a Hangover* is the funniest thing I've ever read. I'm picking him over Terkel."

"He's a better softball player than Studs too."

And then silence. Allan finishes his drink and signals he's ready for round three.

I sit and wait for Allan to start talking again. It's been a long time since I felt the need to fill the space between us with chatter.

"Want a cheeseburger?" Allan asks after he's knocked back his third shot.

I shake my head.

"Want to come over and be the Director of Research at the Mosely Foundation?" he asks in the same casual tone he used to ask me about the burger.

"Aren't I kind of young to be a Director of Research?"

"Actually, no. You're what, twenty-nine? Almost thirty? Your days of being a financial child prodigy are over."

"Fuck you, Allan."

"I called you a grownup and you swear at me."

I take a long drink to stop the flutter in my chest. I look in the mirror behind the bar for the girl I think I am. See a grown ass woman.

"About the job?" Allan presses.

"I don't think so."

"But you don't *know* so." He turns on his bar stool to face me. "You said it yourself when I was first given the position. It's a great job to be paid to invest money and then give it away. *You* told me I'll make people happy. And I do. You could too."

"The fund is doing great, Allan. I don't understand what you need *me* for."

"The asset growth is good but I don't want to just continue to do things the way they've always been done. I want Mosley to be a new model for foundations. You know what's wrong with this business. Here's your chance to put your knowledge to work and come up with some better ideas."

"So this isn't just a mercy hire?"

"Shit, Andrea. Be serious here. I have a responsibility. To my board. To the people we help. This isn't a personal whim."

"Okay. Sorry. Do you have something in mind? A specific reason you think I'm right for the job?"

"I want to add at least four more analysts to the research department in the next six months. Over the years I've heard you bitch and bitch that there aren't enough women in the business. Fix that. Hire all women."

I sit and let that soak in. I'd be a female boss with a majority female department. Instantly I start to formulate plans. "And if that meant taking women from industry and teaching them how to be analysts instead of finding women already doing financial work?"

"Sure. Whatever you think works best. When can you start?"

"Hang on there. Let's not get ahead of ourselves."

"Oh, right. How much money do you want?"

"I want two hundred thousand. It's what I'd get for another sales job. And I want the company to pay for an MBA. I'll go to the University of Chicago executive program. Nights and weekends. I'll need that for my credibility."

"Done."

"You said that really fast. Could I have asked for more?"

He shrugs. Signals the bartender to bring me another drink. "There's a year-end bonus. If you and your new team of Supergirls make the Foundation money, we can find more for everybody. Okay? Just say yes already. You're so annoying sometimes but . . . " He hesitates. Runs a hand through his hair. An old gesture of frustration. "I need you to do this. You're the perfect person. You're smart, you think differently and, not insignificantly, we get along. I'm not the easiest person to get along with. Or so I've been told."

I think back to a time when what I wanted from Allan was a proposal of a much different kind. Is there any part of me that is taking this job because I'm still delusionally attracted to Allan in that way?

"Could we explore the 'get along' bit?" I scan the immediate area to see if anyone is listening to our conversation.

Allan again runs a nervous hand through his hair and eyes his empty glass.

"If you think we need to," he says.

"When we first met, I thought maybe we had the potential for . . . " My turn for nerves. My leg starts to beat uncontrollably. I put a hand on my knee to stop it and continue. "You know, like, maybe a more physical and romantic relationship? But of course, that never happened and I think before we start working together you should know that I'm totally over you. I won't be having any of those thoughts any more. I've accepted that you aren't interested in me that way." I finish abruptly.

Allan shakes his head. "Have you been mad at me for the last five years because I haven't wanted to sleep with you?"

"Mad's a bit extreme." I shred the bar napkin while I talk. "Occasionally annoyed. You've never mentioned you were dating anyone else, so also insulted that I wasn't even better than nothing. I mean the few times things got started, they didn't get finished. So I was confused." I finally force myself to look directly at him. "The correct statement is that I've been confused."

"Andrea, I think you're beautiful." Allan's blue eyes are just starting to develop some attractive worry lines. He leans closer. His arm on the bar. His hand so close to my hand. "And I think you're one of the smartest people I know. Funniest. Nicest."

I give him an eye roll, but he continues. "And sexy. I see the way other guys look at you. But I'm never going to look at you that way because . . . "

"You respect me too much?" I say.

"No, you idiot." He lowers his voice to a whisper. "Because I'm gay. Can't believe you didn't figure it out yourself." He leans back now and takes a drink from an empty glass.

Gay? I stare at him, trying to rearrange my perceptions of both Allan and what a gay man looks like. Acts like. I'm a fucking idiot. "You might have told me sooner," I say. "Saved me from acting like a fool. It's not like I care. Well, I do care. But . . . " Shit. AIDS. It's not possible to hear gay and not think of AIDS. I can see on Allen's face that he knows what I am thinking.

"I'm a very careful person. You know that. I'll be fine."

"I know you will be. I want you to be happy. And thanks for telling me. It's every girl's dream to think that the only reason a guy isn't attracted to her is that he's gay."

"This is between us. Has to be. Finance isn't the fashion industry."

"Got it." I love him so much for telling me this. "Do you want me to tell you something secret about myself now?"

"No. Please, no."

I pull my resume and a pen out of my purse. We push our empty glasses aside and turn the paper over to the blank side and start scribbling notes. Planning the future of the Mosley Foundation. My future. A future that I didn't know I wanted but now it seems so amazingly obvious that everything that happened since the gun went off in Mariana's has led me to the best job in the world. The laws and effects of money truly as beautiful as roses.

Chapter 41

JANUARY 28, 1986

Six months have flown by. I've hired four amazing women. My research department of an even dozen analysts has produced some great ideas and the fund's investment performance has beaten the averages—amazing given that 1985 was a stellar year for the market with lower interest rates, low inflation, and crazy takeover fever.

"The Mosley Foundation, Andrea Hoffman speaking." Good phone manners are still important.

Dan, still at Kendall Fitz and now less of an idiot to me as I'm an important client, is screaming. "Turn on your fucking TV. Now! The Challenger just blew to fucking smithereens. With the teacher on board. We say sell all the suppliers. That includes your Morton Thiokol. Sell it right fucking now." The phone slams down in my ear. I punch in the symbol for Morton Thiokol. No time to call the portfolio manager or my trader. I pick up the phone myself and call Charlene.

"It's Andrea. Sell 10,000 shares of Thiokol at ½ or better."

I don't have to wait for her to say anything. I know she's got it. I jump up from my desk and run down the hall to the small conference room, yelling for Allan to come watch with me. He's already there.

"What happened? I heard explosion." I say. The TV screen is showing only a beautiful blue sky and a fluffy plume of pure white smoke that looks eerily like a caterpillar.

We hear someone from NASA on the TV. "Flight controllers are looking very carefully at the situation. Obviously a major malfunction."

"No shit, Sherlock. Pretty damn obvious." Allan says.

"Are they dead?"

"All dead." Allan says.

I can't take my eyes off the screen. It's beautiful in a horrifying way. "Dan called with a sell on Morton Thiokol. Our only exposure to this. I sold half the position. It seemed the prudent thing to do."

Allan nods his head but his eyes are still glued to the screen. Two parallel lines of smoke race each other down to the sea like rain drops on a windshield.

The phone on the sideboard rings and I pick it up.

"Hey, it's Sheila from Merrill. The Challenger has exploded. All astronauts are assumed dead. They've halted trading in Thiokol. I'll call you later when our analyst makes a comment."

"Thanks. Please do."

I fill Allan in. "The new girl at Merrill. Have you noticed we now have two female salespeople?"

"Can't believe that shithead Dan called it," Allan says.

The phone again. Charlene. "I sold it at 5/8, sweetie. They've halted trading now."

"You're the best."

"I know that," she says. "Drinks next week?"

"For sure."

———

When lunch is delivered, Allan brings his sandwich into my office and sits down. Takes off the tortoise shell glasses he's just started wearing. A good look for him.

"You did good selling this morning," he says.

"Well, now we probably owe Dan something. We're going to have to take some piece of a crappy new issue or something worse."

"What's worse?"

"We're going to have to go to one of his boring political fundraisers."

"That's on you. I'm going to be busy that night."

"Yes, boss."

"You know I hate it when you call me that."

"Yes, I do know that. But you *are* my boss, boss."

The phone rings. Its Allan's line. He stands, smiling. "Hoping for that call. Will you answer and put him on hold. I'll pick it up in my office."

I go back to the TV in the conference room. Most of the staff is there. They're replaying the launch from the beginning. The shots of the astronauts waving and grinning as they enter the capsule. The rockets firing. The countdown and then the space craft lifting strongly and cleanly off the launch pad. It cuts through the blue sky. The booster rockets fire. And then the massive explosion. The camera pans to the viewing stands where dignitaries and the families and friends are all looking skyward. They move closer together, confusion on their faces. I think of all the classrooms tuned in to see the first school teacher go off into space and my stomach tightens. I think of the astronauts, their parents watching. What a sad mess. The hopeful faces on the screen continue to scan the empty sky.

I leave the quiet bunch and head back to my desk because even though the launch of the space shuttle Challenger, a shining symbol of everything we do right in this country, has turned into a fiery shitstorm of scrap metal, technological failure, and human tragedy, the market trades on.

My phone rings. "Andrea Hoffman."

It's our Solomon Brothers salesman. "Do you know why all of the vending machines at NASA serve Sprite?"

"I have no idea."

"Because they can't get seven up!" He laughs.

"Way too soon. Those poor astronauts and all the kids watching. I can't . . . "

"There's more."

"Not interested." I interrupt, "Call me when you have something to say that will make me some money." I hang up.

I look out my window. I can see a slice of the Chicago River through the buildings. I go to the small but well stocked break room to make another pot of coffee. I've got to stay sharp. This market is moving and I have some decisions to make about stocks I want to lighten up on. I need to talk to our drug analyst. Have her call a few New York analysts for some additional information.

When I get back to my desk, there are three messages on my answering machine. Two are from salesmen. The third is from Jack. The kittens went to permanent homes after two weeks. Jack stayed.

"Hey, beautiful. Such sad news." His voice so warm on the tape, I can't help but smile. "Let me know if you want company tonight."

I don't even have to think about it. I love my job, but I finally understand that it'll never love me back. But I think I've found someone who does. The sales calls can wait. The number crunching can wait. While I listen to the message one more time, I scribble on my ever present yellow legal pad. *Yes Yes Yes Yes Yes,* and then I pick up my phone and return Jack's call first.

THE END

ACKNOWLEDGMENTS

One of the biggest shocks of my life was when I learned (spoiler alert) that books are not written by one person. My plot twists, characters, phrases—many of them came from suggestions from editors, discussions in classes and workshops, conversations with fellow authors, family, friends, and sometimes I "borrowed" a line I heard from a total stranger in the supermarket. My name may be listed as the author of this book, but it has taken me decades to write and publish this novel and there are many, many people who helped me that I want to thank!

First of all, I want to thank Brooke Warner, publisher at She Writes Press, and my project manager Lauren Wise. Shout out to Cait Levin for her attention to detail. Their professionalism and support were invaluable to me in getting this story out to the world. I am honored to be a She Writes author.

I am eternally grateful to Julie Metz, a brilliant cover designer, for the cover she created for my book. A picture is truly worth 89,000 words!

To the wonderful publicity team at BookSparks: Crystal Patriache, CEO, and Tabitha Bailey, Senior Publicist. Thank you for walking a complete novice out into this world.

This book would be so much crappier without the editing I received from Bill Roorbach. Bill was fabulous to work with and I am eternally grateful that a writer as talented and accomplished as Bill helped me turn my thoughts and words into a story. He inspires everyone who has the lucky opportunity to meet him to love writing, reading, nature and life well lived.

Long before this manuscript was done, I had wonderful writing teachers. Jimin Han and Patricia Dunn at The Writing Institute at Sarah Lawrence are simply the best. Sandy Shelton who writes as Maddy Dawson ran an amazing workshop. And maybe the best thing about taking workshops and classes are the writing friends you make. Donnaldson Brown, Kristen Sherman, Ken Olsen, Jen McInerney, Barbara Smith, Margaret Burton, Ginger McKnight Chavers, Linda Zohman Avellar. Thank you for reading my early drafts and making them better. And thanks to everybody at Women's Fiction Writing Association. The programs they offer and the support of their members are invaluable.

Barbara Josselsohn, and Karen Fortunati—a special thank you for being great writing pals and even better friends. You are such talented writers and have generously offered me so much of your wisdom. It is wonderful to take this journey with you laughing all the way.

In addition to all these helpful humans, I must mention public libraries. I spent much of my life in the library—reading, studying, writing. They are truly one of the great American institutions and they deserve your support. Thank a librarian today.

Finally (almost), this novel would not exist without the love of my siblings. Carol Sue Caswell, Barbara Polinsky, and Larry K. Cohen. The siblings in the novel are in no way based on these wonderful three people who made my childhood a joy and as an adult, have been my best example of how to live meaningful, generous, and successful lives.

And last (really) but certainly not least, to my kids—Nathan, Molly, and Samantha—and my husband Rich, you are special to me beyond my ability to express. I am continually inspired by your efforts and proud of all your accomplishments. Most of all, I am forever grateful for your love and support.

ABOUT THE AUTHOR

*D*iane Cohen Schneider grew up in Illinois but spent most of her adult life in Stamford, CT, with her husband and their three children. Her career as a finance sales executive during the 1980s inspired her debut novel, Andrea Hoffman Goes All In. After leaving Wall Street, she continued her love of finance. Believing everyone should have basic financial literacy skills, she has taught courses and workshops, and because she feels money management is not only necessary but fun, she has an Instagram account called @Moneylikeuhmother. Seeking to expand their horizons, Diane and her husband recently moved to Santa Fe, NM.

Connect with Diane at www.dianecohenschneider.com

Author photo © Gabriella Marks

SELECTED TITLES FROM SHE WRITES PRESS

She Writes Press is an independent publishing
company founded to serve women writers everywhere.
Visit us at www.shewritespress.com.

Unreasonable Doubts by Reyna Marder Gentin. $16.95, 978-1-63152-413-4. Approaching thirty and questioning both her career path and her future with her long-time boyfriend, jaded New York City Public Defender Liana Cohen gets a new client—magnetic, articulate, earnest Danny Shea. When she finds herself slipping beyond the professional with him, she is forced to confront fundamental questions about truth, faith, and love.

Beautiful Garbage by Jill DiDonato. $16.95, 978-1-938314-01-8. Talented but troubled young artist Jodi Plum leaves suburbia for the excitement of the city—and is soon swept up in the sexual politics and downtown art scene of 1980s New York.

A Better Next by Maren Cooper. $16.95, 978-1-63152-493-6. At the top of her career, twenty plus years married, and with one child left to launch, Jess Lawson is blindsided by her husband's decision to move across the country without her—news that shakes her personal and professional life and forces her to make surprising new choices moving forward.

Royal Entertainment by Marni Fechter. $16.95, 978-1-93831-452-0. After being fired from her job for blowing the whistle on her boss, social worker Melody Frank has to adapt to her new life as the assistant to an elite New York party planner.

The Tolling of Mercedes Bell by Jennifer Dwight. $18.95, 978-1-63152-070-9. When she meets a magnetic lawyer at her work, recently widowed Mercedes Bell unwittingly drinks a noxious cocktail of grief, legal intrigue, desire, and deception—but when she realizes that her life and her daughter's safety hang in the balance, she is jolted into action.